One Summer in Crete

Nadia Marks (née Kitromilides, which in Greek means 'bitter lemons') was born in Cyprus, but grew up in London. An ex-creative director and associate editor on a number of leading British women's magazines, she is now a novelist and works as a freelance writer for several national and international publications. She has two sons and lives in North London with her partner Mike.

By Nadia Marks

Among the Lemon Trees
Secrets Under the Sun
Between the Orange Groves
One Summer in Crete

Nadia Marks

One Summer in Crete

PAN BOOKS

First published 2020 by Pan Books
an imprint of Pan Macmillan
The Smithson, 6 Briset Street, London EC1M 5NR
Associated companies throughout the world
www.panmacmillan.com

ISBN 978-1-5098-8974-7

1 3 5 7 9 8 6 4 2

A CIP catalogue record for this book is available from the British Library.

Typeset by Palimpsest Book Production Ltd, Falkirk, Stirlingshire
Printed and bound by CPI Group (UK) Ltd, Croydon, CR0 4YY

Visit **www.panmacmillan.com** to read more about all our books
and to buy them. You will also find features, author interviews and
news of any author events, and you can sign up for e-newsletters
so that you're always first to hear about our new releases.

For my cousin Christina

Part One

1

The music was blasting out from the CD player, filling the room with its catchy rhythm. Calli far preferred to listen to her favourite tracks on her old sound system, rather than on her mobile. She cherished her collection of CDs amassed over the years and couldn't bring herself to throw them out, much to James's irritation.

'You're cluttering up the place with last century's technology,' he would complain; James liked to do things his own way, but when it came to music she didn't care. She had them all categorized and in alphabetical order, allowing her to wallow in nostalgia whenever she had the chance to play them; when they were together it was usually his choice.

That morning she had been sitting in front of her state-of-the-art computer for the past few hours, editing a batch of photographs for her latest commission and singing along to old favourite hits as she worked. Her voice, loud and clear, merged with the girl singer of Ace of Base. She liked their music – it was played often in her parents' house when she was growing up. This part of her work was very much to her liking: sifting through the images and choosing which ones to use. Writing was a different matter, demanding far more concentration and no distractions. She was a good writer, but she always struggled with her spelling and had to focus all her attention on the storyline and how best to put it across, so her rule was strictly no music during that stage of a project. As a photojournalist she saw everything in images. Taking pictures was instinctive – the words always followed later, after time to reflect.

The story she was working on that day, which had influenced her choice of music, was for a Sunday newspaper supplement. The theme was teen parenthood, focusing on young fathers. She had spent a couple of days interviewing and photographing six lads aged between sixteen and nineteen who had unexpectedly found that their girlfriends were in the family way. With the exception of just one boy, all had embraced fatherhood with relative ease and apparently without regrets. The experience had been a revelation for Calli. She marvelled at these young men and their commitment to parenthood and sense of responsibility. She herself, at a similar age during her first year at university, had feared she might be pregnant and remembered the panic that had set in, followed by relief after the discovery that it was a false alarm for her and her then boyfriend. Under no circumstances would she or the boy have wanted a baby, unlike the song she was now singing along to. In fact, Calli mused, she had spent all her adult life panicking at the thought of pregnancy and the restrictions that it would bring into her busy life. James, her partner and the man she loved and had lived with for the past ten years, felt as she did; a baby had no place in their London metropolitan life.

'When will you two be getting married?' one of her Greek aunts had asked them while they were visiting family in Crete one year soon after Calli and James had moved into a flat together. 'It's time to start thinking about having some babies soon, no?' the aunt carried on.

'We've only been together for a few months,' Calli had protested, horrified at the prospect of children.

'That's plenty of time,' the aunt replied. 'Besides, you're twenty-five or six now, no? You're not so young anymore!'

'For goodness' sake, Auntie, you make me sound ancient.' Calli threw her arms in the air with mock despair. Her own mother never pressurized her, but her Greek aunties were always quizzing her.

'You might not feel ancient, *koritsi mou*, my girl,' the aunt continued, 'but your eggs soon will be. You are only born with so many of them and if you don't start using them soon they will go off and be no good anymore!' All Calli could do was laugh at her aunt's gloomy prophecy.

'I'll take a chance on it,' she replied, still laughing. But James had considered the aunt's questioning inappropriate and rude. 'None of her business,' he had said grumpily later. Calli, being half Greek herself, knew her aunt's comments were not unusual. In their community, when people made a commitment to one another, marriage and babies inevitably would soon follow. 'It's cultural, you see,' she told James. 'She wasn't trying to cause offence, she was just being her typically blunt Greek self!'

But that was then, and this was now, and Calli was no longer twenty-something but thirty-five, and for the past few months she had often found herself thinking about her aunt's words and wondering how those eggs of hers were holding up. Everyone around her seemed to be having babies; several of her friends had embarked on their second pregnancies and whereas a year or two ago she had never entertained such an idea for herself, she now found it had begun to preoccupy her. Perhaps, she thought, it was time to have a conversation with James: see how he felt about the subject instead of brooding over it on her own.

'I am not going to say that you *should* have a baby,' Eleni, Calli's mother, had said to her a few years earlier when the subject of having a family came up. 'It's up to you to decide and something you do because you want to, not because you have to, or because anyone else pushes you into it. It's your decision, Calli *mou*, but I won't say that a grandchild wouldn't be wonderful!'

'How do you know that you want to, or that the time is right, Mum?' Calli asked, looking at her mother for answers.

'I don't know, you just do!' Eleni replied. 'For some people the time is never right – there's always something to get in the way. Maybe you are one of those women, with your career and busy life. But if you discovered yourself pregnant and you felt happy about it, then I would say that's when you know that you want to *and* that the time is right for you . . . I certainly did when you came along without my planning it.'

'The thought terrifies me,' the young woman had replied.

But of late Calli's feelings had become confused. There was a shift, not only in the way she felt, but in her body too. In the past she'd given her friends' babies a wide berth, making the appropriate noises of approval but keeping her distance. Recently she had felt a softening in her heart whenever someone handed her a baby to hold. Could it be, she wondered, that the overused cliché, *her biological clock was starting to tick*, applied to her too now, as it had for so many of her friends? She began to observe herself with interest. She became aware that this assignment for the Sunday magazine was having a significant effect on her and had brought to the surface some uneasy feelings.

While sitting in front of her computer reviewing pictures of those young fathers and listening to the interviews she had recorded of them, she began to consider her own life: in comparison, it felt rather empty. She and James, she realized, had been living a life of convenience, a life of indulgence with no adversities or great responsibilities. In contrast to what those teenage boys and their girls were having to deal with, the two of them could be described by some as narcissistic and superficial. It was quite a harsh discovery, but for the first time in years she was finding herself questioning her choice of lifestyle for the future. She hadn't really given it too much thought; she went along with a lot of what James wanted. She knew she was something of a people-pleaser, and James needed a lot of pleasing, but she didn't really mind – they got on pretty well most of the time.

That evening she stopped working earlier than usual and decided to make dinner. She didn't always bother to cook. If she was working until James came home, then more often than not they would go out to eat. There were so many cool places where they lived or they'd order in – why not? They could afford it and they were free to do as they pleased. Tonight, she wanted to be at home, she wanted them to be able to talk. She decided the time had come for a serious conversation. She needed James's full attention and she wanted him to be in a super good mood. She would cook something simple like baked fish and salad which was quick and easy to prepare but she would spend longer making his favourite dessert, the one Susan, his mum, made for him that always brought a smile to his face. She was going to make a crème caramel following her mother-in-law's recipe, which Calli had to admit was pretty good.

'Always best to make your crème caramel the day before you want to serve it,' was Susan's repeated advice to her. 'So much better, because if you turn your caramel custard out too soon it will stay in the bottom of your ramekins . . .' Calli didn't even know what a ramekin was, nor did she care, when she first started living with James, and she was certainly not going to be cooking anything the day before. But she decided that if once in a while she was willing to make James's beloved dessert, she must ensure at least that she had a few ramekins in case he refused to eat it in anything else. He was quite particular about that. 'Not that your mother spoiled you or anything,' she'd tease him. She didn't really mind, it didn't happen that often and she made it pretty clear that that was where her housewifely duties and indulgences would end; she tried to leave most of the pampering to his mother. 'I'll learn to make your crème caramel if you learn to make me my Greek coffee,' she bargained.

Calli finished going through a batch of photos and turned off her computer for the day. She walked downstairs to the kitchen in search of her mother-in-law's recipe.

For a much richer taste add an extra two yolks to the eggs, Susan had added as a footnote to the recipe. Calli started with the caramel custard, thinking that if she made it in plenty of time there would be less chance of it sticking to the wretched ramekins. The thought made her smile; her mother-in-law had little more to weigh on her mind other than making the perfect dessert or three-course dinner. But she, Calli, was different; she was occupied with her work, no time for all of that. She always referred to Susan as her mother-in-law even though she and James had never married. 'After ten years of me living with her beloved boy she has earned the title,' Calli would joke to James, 'and in any case she's stuck with me whether she likes it or not.'

She poured herself a large glass of chilled Sauvignon Blanc and chose a Greek CD from a pile she kept in the kitchen – she found cooking with Greek music in the background inspiring and mood enhancing, and since she was still alone she could listen to whatever she chose. She gathered her ingredients, placed her mixing bowl on the counter and reached for the eggs. She cracked the first four and then separated an extra two as in Susan's instructions. Watching the golden yolks land softly in the bowl, her mind turned to those other eggs inside her own body.

James sat back on his chair, reached for the bottle of wine and filled his glass to the brim. Calli watched and waited. She had been speaking for some time without interruption while James sat silently listening. That was not how she had envisaged the discussion. What she had hoped for and wanted was a conversation between the two of them, an exchange of views, not for her to deliver a monologue.

Dinner had been a pleasant affair with animated talk full of anecdotal chit-chat and laughter, mainly about James's day at his law firm; he always liked to take centre stage, be the centre of attention. The crème caramel was consumed with satisfied exclamations and praise. 'Mmm! Nearly as good as my mother's,' he had said, which was approval enough for her – so long as he was happy and enjoyed it, that was fine by her. But after they had finished eating and Calli started to speak, the mood gradually began to change; whereas just a short while ago she couldn't stop him talking, all of a sudden James seemed to lose the power of speech. The more silent he became, the more Calli continued, nervously explaining how she was feeling of late about her ageing eggs and how maybe it was time to consider seriously what it meant to grow old childless. He sat mutely, listening and watching her. When she stopped, James reached for his wine and gave her a long silent look.

'Well? Say something, James, for God's sake!' she burst out. 'Surely you have something to add on the matter?'

Still he said nothing. Calli gritted her teeth and waited. Finally he leaned forward, put his elbows on the table, looked her in the eye and spoke.

'Calli . . .' he began, his ice-blue eyes never leaving hers. Her heart started to pound. If ever James opened a conversation with her name, she knew that whatever it was she hoped would happen, wouldn't.

'Calli,' he said again and lifted the wine to his lips; he took a sip then replaced the glass on the table, as if in slow motion, before speaking again. 'I had believed, and correct me if I am wrong' – his voice an octave lower than usual – 'I had believed,' he repeated, his eyes never leaving hers, 'that you and I have always been on the same page when it came to the issue of parenthood.' He paused for a second before going on. '*We*, Calli, and by that I mean you and me, not just one of us but *both of us*, have never wanted to go down that path in life. Correct? Or not?'

The shock of his response made the blood rush to Calli's head; she was lost for words. This pompous side of James was his least endearing characteristic in her view and the last thing she had expected from him that night. She had observed it at times, but if it was ever directed at her she would cut him short; he knew well enough how she felt about it. He could be quite petulant and difficult and occasionally a little controlling, which Calli put down to his job as a barrister – in her opinion it gave him an air of haughtiness that got on her nerves.

'Yes, James.' She struggled to steady her voice. 'That is correct, but life is fluid and beliefs and feelings can change over the years.' She took a deep breath, held it for a moment, then continued. 'And please do not patronize me or try to intimidate me, you're not in court now.'

She reached for her glass, trying to remain calm before speaking again. 'The thing is, James, if you were actually listening to what I was trying to tell you, you would have realized that my feelings right now are in transition, which means I don't know exactly what I want *or* feel.' Calli leaned forward to face him directly, disappointment evident on her face. 'What I had expected from you was respect . . . not this! I expected that you love me enough to engage in a conversation about how I feel and what I think, not just dismiss me without any discussion. We are not children anymore, James, we are grown-ups and that's what adults do. We discuss things.'

'I'm sorry, Calli' – his voice was hard – 'I am not open to discussion where this matter is concerned.' His words were directed at her with breathtaking finality. She sat motionless, letting them hang in the air as she tried to take in what he had said. Neither of them spoke for a long while. Then, slowly, Calli stood up from the table, turned around and silently walked out of the kitchen.

That night she slept in the spare room. She needed time to digest what she had heard and wanted her fury to subside before resuming any form of conversation with him. She had never been a woman given to impulses, huge confrontations or hysterics. Throwing crockery and heavy objects around the room at each other was never their way as a couple, although they knew others who had violent arguments on a regular basis. But that night Calli feared that if she hadn't removed herself from James's presence, he would have run the risk of having a ramekin land on his head.

The next day, sitting at her desk and still brooding about the night before, Calli started to reflect. As she had expected, her fury did subside by morning; she could never sustain anger for too long. Even so, every time she remembered James's harsh words a wave of resentment washed over her. But then the part of her that always tried to give everyone the benefit of the doubt took over and she began to look for reasons to justify his behaviour. Perhaps, she reflected, these things took time. *She* might have been thinking about babies lately and ruminating and obsessing about her body and the future, but he hadn't reached that stage. Surely with time he would be willing to discuss the subject. She had just caught him off-guard with her unexpected change of mind. She always thought that James could be a little immature at times and, like a child, she needed to give him time to think about what she had said. Her mind worked overtime trying to find excuses. To be fair, she finally told herself, he might even have a point: they had always been in agreement about babies. What she needed to do was to step back and let things be, and who knew? Maybe he was right. Perhaps the two of them weren't cut out for parenthood.

2

She didn't slip up on purpose; or if she did, the slip was surely subconscious.

They had spent the evening at a wonderful party after an awards ceremony. Calli was nominated for photojournalist of the year and although she hadn't won, she was highly commended for her work for the Sunday magazine, so celebrations were in order. They did have a glass or two or three too many – she could never resist when champagne was on offer and since they weren't driving home that night they both indulged. They danced and drank and laughed and it felt like old times.

Over the past few months since their uncomfortable conversation they had both been on their guard, and although they never broached the subject again, Calli felt that while it was left hovering in the ether James might have a change of heart. They continued as before, following the way of life they enjoyed, plus a few more visits to their friends with babies and children, instigated by Calli, sometimes joining them for walks on Hampstead Heath with prams and dogs and toddlers.

Sex had never been a problem between them, indeed it was an important element in their relationship – you could say it was the glue that kept them together. However, since the night of the discussion something shifted in their love-making. James was almost hesitant if Calli initiated sex, wary of her motives, and Calli's sexual appetite was like-wise affected. But that night, the elation of her success, the flattering attention from her colleagues and their consumption of champagne had heightened their desire and finally in the back of the black cab on the way home they both let down their guard.

'Oh baby, that's what I love about you,' James breathed into her ear, 'you are such a minx!'

'Wait till I get you home,' she said, feeling like her old playful self again.

She had been oblivious, had thought nothing of that evening until she missed her period, which always arrived like clockwork. She hadn't been taking the pill for a couple of years – her gynaecologist advised her to take a break from the regime – so they had been using the rhythm method and condoms. The two together worked well and they never had problems or mishaps with the arrangement – not until now, that is.

'Maybe you're pregnant,' her mother told Calli when she mentioned her concern about a possible medical problem. 'Have you considered that?' Eleni asked, wondering why her daughter didn't think of the most obvious reason for a missed period.

'Well, *no*, Mum!' Calli replied. 'Because we take precautions for that and it has never failed before.'

'In my experience there is always a first time for everything,' Eleni replied.

The confirmation that she was indeed pregnant filled Calli with a jumble of emotions and concerns. Would she cope? Would she be a good enough mother? How would James react and what sort of a father would he make? But her initial and strongest response was one of absolute elation. '*YES!*' she shouted, punching the air with her fist as she sat on the loo with the test kit and a huge smile across her face. 'My eggs are healthy and well and haven't gone to seed!' she rejoiced. So much for her Greek aunt, whose words had haunted her for nearly ten years. Calli disposed of the kit, pulled herself together and walked into the living room in search of her mobile to call her mother. James, she decided, needed to hear the news in person, not over the phone. With that thought Calli took a deep breath and told herself that surely this time James would come round to her news. This was different. Planning to have a baby, trying to make a conscious decision to start a family, was harder to accept but now that it was a done deed it was out of their hands. The decision was made for them and they would cope.

This time she didn't prepare James's favourite dessert or cook dinner for him. Instead she met him in town at their favourite restaurant, the one they always chose for celebrations, around the corner from his law firm in Soho. She was early – excited and a little nervous, she ordered a Virgin Mary and some bread and olives while she waited. She watched him walk down the stairs into the restaurant looking handsome in his dark work suit, his eyes searching the tables for her.

'There you are!' he said, crossing the room to her table and beckoning the waiter as he bent down to give her a kiss. 'I'm famished and I need a stiff drink. What a day I've had,' he complained in typical James fashion, loosening his tie as he dropped down beside her. 'What's the occasion?' he asked, popping an olive into his mouth. 'Have you been nominated for another award or something?'

'Let's have a drink and order first,' she replied, 'and I'll tell you.'

The return of the ice-blue glare sent shivers down Calli's spine. Again that stubborn silence, the grim expression, the tightly set mouth. *Oh no, no!* her brain screamed inside her head, *not again, no!*

'Oh, Calli, Calli . . .' he finally said, shaking his head, his voice almost inaudible. 'How could you do this?' he hissed now. 'What part of *I have never wanted this*, not now not *ever*, did you not understand from our last conversation, and from living with me all these years? Did you really think that hanging out with your friends with children was going to change my mind?'

She tried to speak but had no voice. She kept her eyes as wide as she could to stop them from flooding as she looked silently at him.

'What do you have to say for yourself?' he went on, staring coldly at her.

His words, like a slap across her face, made her snap out of her state of speechlessness and she hit back with force.

'I do not have to say anything for myself, James!' she hissed back at him. 'I did not do this behind your back or on my own!' Her fury was quickly getting the better of her and her tears finally found their way down her cheeks. 'You were fully present when it happened, or have you forgotten?' She turned her head away from him; she couldn't bear to look at him any longer.

'It's no good, Calli. I never signed up for this.' His voice was harder than she had ever heard it before. 'If you wanted a baby, you should have chosen a different man. You knew that from the start. If you want us to stay together, you choose. It's either me or *it*.' And with that, James stood up, drained his glass of wine, put a handful of money on the table and stalked out of the restaurant, leaving Calli with a pain like a sharp blade in her heart. Eventually she picked up her handbag, pulled out her mobile and called her mother.

'Get in a taxi and come over immediately!' Eleni's worried voice instructed. 'Or, better still, your father will come and collect you.'

'No, Mama, don't send poor Dad into town,' she replied in a small voice. 'I'll be fine, I'll make my own way,' she added, even if at that moment all she wanted was to fall into her parents' arms and have them take care of her. But no, she thought, she could manage; she was a grown-up.

Sitting in the back of the black cab, tears streaking her face, she remembered the last time she and James had shared a taxi and how the passion flowed between them. She was partly to blame for this, she told herself. James had shown his *true stubborn colours* to her on so many occasions, yet she had always chosen to ignore them. Now she could have no doubts, he had revealed them in glorious Technicolor and with such clarity that no more excuses could be made for him. As her best friend Josie always used to say, 'When a person shows you their true colours you'd better believe them.' Josie often told her this, especially when someone or other had let her down, but given her nature, most often Calli turned a blind eye.

'The trouble with you, my friend,' Josie would scold her, 'is that you choose to see what you want to see in people, and it so often leads to disappointment.'

Now at long last it was time to open her eyes and see James for who he really was.

*

'Selfish, that's what he is!' said Keith, Calli's father, as he listened to his daughter explain what had happened earlier that evening at the restaurant. Keith was a solid, dependable, loving family man, who found it beyond him to understand why anyone would shun their responsibilities in such a way. His private opinion of James had never been high – he thought the young man rather pompous and full of himself – but he believed that if his daughter was happy, he had nothing to say on the matter, until now.

'What sort of a man would behave like this?' Eleni added, glancing at her husband.

'Incredibly selfish,' Keith repeated. 'And with no soul,' he muttered under his breath.

'What really hurts me after all these years of being together,' Calli told them, 'is that at no point did he ever stop to think about me . . . about what I might want.' She looked at her parents. 'I guess it's my fault for always going along with whatever he wanted, always trying to please.'

'None of this is your fault, my girl.' Her mother reached for her hand. 'Remember what I told you once? What matters is that you are now pregnant. Provided you are happy about it that is all that counts, because it means you *know* that you want your baby and that the time *is right* for you regardless of James . . .' Eleni got up from the table and with open arms walked round to where Calli was sitting. 'Your father and I and your brother will be here to

support you and love you and the baby, no matter what.'
She bent down and took her daughter in her arms. 'And if
James is fool enough to turn his back on you both, then he
is not worthy of our love. It is his loss.'

3

Calli returned to their flat just once, to collect her possessions with her father's help when she knew James was at work. She could never share a home with him again, she considered his behaviour unacceptable. It was true that they had both spent years rejecting the notion of a child but then they were both in agreement. Now there was neither a choice nor a decision to be made by her about the baby, the choice was James's. From now on, she promised herself, she would face this alone; as far as she was concerned the relationship was finished.

'I know you have always been independent, Calli *mou*,' Eleni had said, 'but while you are pregnant it will be good for you to stay here with us. Later on you can decide what to do.'

Returning to the bosom of her family temporarily suited Calli well. She needed their support, not only because of the pregnancy – she was healthy and robust – but also to recover from the blow of James's rejection, which had left her reeling emotionally. She had always been good friends with her mum, and her dad was a good listener. When her younger brother Alex, a martial arts instructor, first heard what James had done, he offered to go and punch him on the nose.

'He's an idiot,' he said. 'Someone needs to teach him a lesson!'

'Thank you, Alex, but I don't need you to teach him anything.' Calli laughed at her little brother's demonstration of solidarity. From as young as five or six he had declared himself his sister's protector even though he was four years her junior. Everyone rallied around Calli, not only her family but friends too, her own and others she had shared with James as a couple.

'I know he used to say kids weren't his thing,' Nick, a mutual friend, said, while trying to fathom how a man could turn his back on his partner at such a time, 'but I never really believed him. I know I wasn't so keen on the idea at first but as soon as Sarah fell pregnant, I came round to the inevitable.'

'It's true,' added Sarah. 'Nick was pretty shaken at first but as soon as Lucy was born he was over the moon and wanted another one straight away. I'm truly surprised at James's behaviour.'

'Well, I'm not surprised at all,' Josie had told Calli when she first heard the news. 'I always thought of him as a supremely selfish person, but then I wasn't the one living with him.'

'I guess for a long time we were both selfish together . . .' Calli replied. She paused before continuing, 'It's when one person changes and the other doesn't that the trouble begins.'

'And the trouble of course began because *you* actually grew up,' Josie said, 'while James remained, and probably will always remain, in a state of arrested development.'

'I don't know, Josie . . .' Calli hesitated. 'I do now see that James is selfish, but not necessarily because he didn't want children . . . There are many people who don't want to be parents, for whatever reason.' She stopped for a moment to gather her thoughts. 'The fact is,' she began again, 'the more I think about it, the more I accept that it was as much his right not to want the baby as it was mine to want to keep it. But what I *can't* accept is his behaviour towards me after all these years, his refusal to even enter into a discussion, his utter disregard of me. For that I can't forgive him.'

'Well, you don't *have* to forgive him,' Josie replied, reaching for her friend's hand. 'Do you think he'll want to have anything to do with the baby when it's born? Will you allow him access?'

'Yes, if he wants it,' Calli replied. 'It's still his child.'

'Have you asked him?'

'Not yet. I can't bear to speak to him at the moment, but I will at some point.'

Living with her parents again felt strangely pleasurable for Calli. Her brother lived nearby and when he came to visit, which was now often, they would regularly eat their evening meal together as they had before they left home. Eleni and Keith were delighted to have their two children to themselves again after all this time.

'She will be fine,' Eleni told her husband. 'She's strong, our girl, a regular Cretan woman just like my mother. I always said that Calli is more like her grandmother than me.'

'She's got a lot of you in her too, my love,' Keith said, slipping an arm around her slender waist. 'You are one strong woman, my darling. It's that Cretan spirit of yours that bewitched me, don't you know?' he said again and kissed her full on the lips, the chemistry and love still evident between them even after all their years of marriage. Every time Keith thought about James and his 'treacherous' behaviour, as he saw it, his anger flared. He was a passionate husband, loyal to his wife and children: they were his world, he would defend and protect them to the end. 'How could that man abandon our girl?' he would protest to Eleni. 'And the baby too, what more could anyone ask from life?'

Keith had met and fallen in love with Eleni while on holiday in Crete, having taken a year's sabbatical to travel around Europe in the summer of 1980. He had completed his PhD at Oxford and wanted a break before starting his first full-time position as a university lecturer in London.

He and two of his friends had spent a couple of months travelling all over Greece and ended up in late August on the island of Crete. They had hired a car, determined to explore the entire island, especially its archaeological sites. Moving from place to place, they finally arrived at a remote village surrounded by mountains, with an equally remote beach by a sea more crystal-clear than any of them had ever set eyes on. Enchanted, they set up camp there and stayed far longer than they intended, not only because of the physical beauty of the location but also because Keith had fallen under the spell of a pretty girl who worked in the local grocery shop. Eleni was a teacher at the village primary school and was helping out at her family's shop for the duration of the summer holidays.

'He's really got it bad,' the other two boys, John and Tony, joked to each other when Keith would walk back from the shop laden with groceries that they didn't need.

'Can you at least wait till we eat the last watermelon you bought yesterday before bringing another one?' they would tease. But Keith couldn't let a day go by without seeing Eleni. The girl too was eager each day to see the English boy with the green eyes, golden suntan and long hair, until eventually, Keith, urged by his friends, summoned up enough courage to ask her for a date.

'You can't keep up this love-sick act for too long,' John told him, 'it's a real downer on everyone! For heaven's sake ask the girl out.'

'She's guarded within an inch of her life by some fierce-looking types in the shop . . . maybe her father, uncle, brother, cousin, I don't know,' Keith complained.

'Well . . . in that case you'd better watch out. They have quite a reputation, these Cretans!' Tony laughed. 'You've seen *Zorba the Greek*, haven't you?'

But Keith was braver than he appeared and his crush on Eleni was greater than his fear. He did approach her, and they did start talking, and when he realized that she liked him too he made a point of chatting to the uncle or cousin or whoever was in the shop while he was spending his money on groceries. And, as it turned out, they were all perfectly friendly and polite. The fact that he took the trouble to speak to them in Greek, even if his vocabulary was limited, went a good way towards their acceptance of him. Having graduated with a first in Classics from Oxford together with three years of modern Greek, the English boy's command of the language was reasonably good. He was something of an oddity, unlike the usual hippy types they were used to seeing backpacking on the island. The first time they heard him speak they fell about laughing, making no attempt to hide their mockery and amusement, but Keith was determined.

'*Kalimera sas*,' he said, bidding good morning to all present in his strong and, to their ears, comical English accent. '*Poly zesti simera*,' very hot today, he continued, causing more hilarity as he looked around the room.

'*Kalimera*,' Eleni replied sweetly, ignoring her male relatives and their teasing. She was touched that the boy was making an effort. From that day he would sit and practise words and sentences from his Greek dictionary and phrase book before setting off to the shop. Eventually the men stopped mocking him, and when he suggested to Eleni that she go out with him one evening she told him that she would have to ask permission from her father.

'I don't want to cause offence. I know things are done differently here from the way we behave in England,' he had said to her. 'If you would like me to speak to your father, I shall be glad to do so.'

'No need,' Eleni replied, 'it's fine, I've already asked him. He's seen you coming to the shop every day and he likes you, my brother and uncle too.'

When Keith eventually had to return to London the romance continued at a distance for several months. He wrote to her in Greek and she started to take English lessons. The following spring at Easter he returned to Crete and asked for Eleni's hand.

'He's a good boy, and a teacher too, you know,' Eleni's mother, Calliope, told the neighbours when it was obvious that her daughter had made her choice for a husband.

'Good for her!' her unmarried elder sister Froso said approvingly. 'She is a modern girl! Remember how she used to tell us when she was little that she wanted to marry for love?'

'I do, I do!' her mother laughed. 'When she was five years old she announced that when she grew up she would marry that boy Georgos because she was in love, remember that?'

'How can I forget?' her daughter replied with a chuckle. 'She had a wild spirit, that girl.' Froso, who was significantly older than both Eleni and their brother Androulios, was still living with her parents in the family home. Despite offers of marriage she had always been reluctant to enter into matrimony, preferring to stay at home with her father and mother and help bring up her siblings. Now she was considered past marriageable age.

Eleni and Keith married in the village directly after the Easter celebrations, thus continuing the feasts and festivities for a few more days. The trestle tables and chairs which had been laid out in the square for Easter remained in place to accommodate the marriage celebrations. The spring lambs that had been cooking on the spits for Easter were replaced with new ones several times over for the duration. Eleni was a young woman very much loved by her community, and the Mavrantoni family was well respected, so this wedding was not going to be celebrated only by friends and relatives but by the entire village, young and old. It wasn't every day that one of their own was marrying an Englishman, soon to be whisked away from them. The celebrations continued for three days and the music and singing echoed around the hills and mountains while the dancing put Keith's stamina to the test. Knowing of the Cretan custom for traditional dancing at weddings he tried his best to learn a couple of them and practised diligently, but there was no competing with the local men who were born and raised on the moves.

Since Keith's new university post allowed him a month for the vacation, which as luck had it overlapped with the Orthodox Easter, he stayed with Eleni's family after the wedding. On his return to London he immediately set about making arrangements for her to join him. He rented a little apartment near Mornington Crescent close to central London, booked a date at the register office for them to marry according to British law and then returned to Crete to collect his new bride.

Life in London was as exciting as Eleni hoped it would be, and Keith was as loving and supportive as she knew he would be. His job provided well for both of them, although Eleni was not content to stay at home. She was used to working and enjoyed it. She applied for a job at the Greek embassy and was taken on as a part-time receptionist. Her fluency in Greek was an asset and she soon made enough contacts to start giving private tuition to the children of compatriots living in the capital who wanted them to grow up speaking their language. This would keep her in work for many years to come – her calling as a teacher was ever useful. As her sister Froso had said, Eleni had a mind of her own; she was an enterprising young woman and managed to settle successfully into the life of the metropolis.

'It's a long way from my village,' she told Keith one Sunday afternoon as they walked arm in arm in the park. 'It's hard to believe this is my home now! Thank you for bringing me here!'

'I was afraid that you would miss the sea and the open spaces, and your family,' Keith said, concerned for her.

'So long as you are here with me, I'm happy,' she replied, leaning closer to him.

'I'll always be here.' He kissed the top of her head.

'When I was little, I used to have these recurring dreams,' she told him, her arm linked in his. 'I was living in a busy place full of noise and buildings and cars, people I didn't know all around me, yet I wasn't scared at all.' Eleni looked up at Keith and smiled. 'I didn't feel afraid because there was always someone with me . . . I didn't know who, but I felt secure. I used to think that maybe it was my grandmother watching over me . . .' she tightened her hold on his arm and looked up at him again. 'I felt safe, like I feel now with you!'

'You obviously had a premonition you were going to meet me,' he smiled and bent down to kiss her.

'I know! I did . . . it's not a joke!' she replied. 'My mother always said I had some kind of gift of prediction . . . just like when I first met you. I had a feeling you would come into the shop, and then when I saw you, I knew you!'

It was through this gift of foretelling the future that Eleni believed she had known the very moment she had conceived. They had discussed having a family at some point and had agreed to wait a year or two, but not long after arriving in London she fell pregnant. Calli was born on the twenty-seventh of January 1982, which Keith discovered to his delight was the same date as the birth of his great hero Wolfgang Amadeus Mozart – and of course he couldn't help but announce it to all the nurses and to anyone else who'd listen. 'What an act to follow!' the midwife told him, laughing, as she placed baby Calli in Eleni's arms.

Being in London in the depths of winter with a newborn, away from her family and friends, was hard for Eleni. But both she and Keith embraced parenthood wholeheartedly and counted themselves lucky. Thinking back to those days was another reason why, now, Calli's rejection by James hit them both so hard. Neither of them could understand his motives and they struggled to see how he could turn his back on their daughter at such a time.

'When we had our babies there were just the two of us – no one to help – but we managed,' Eleni would lament privately to Keith lest she upset Calli by raising the subject again.

'Yes, but we had love in our hearts, Eleni,' Keith said,

shaking his head. 'Unfortunately it seems that our daughter chose the wrong man for a life partner. End of story! We should all try to forget about him!'

Nonetheless it wasn't easy for Calli to forget ten years of her life without regrets. But the baby she was carrying made up for all the heartache she was feeling and gave her strength to continue and look towards a new future. Her work kept her busy too; support from her family and friends did much to help her heal emotionally, and to her surprise she appeared to have more energy than ever.

'It's your hormones,' her mother told her, 'if they don't make you feel nauseous, they sometimes give you a boost and you can feel even better than before.'

'I couldn't get out of bed from throwing up,' her friend Sarah told her when she came to visit, 'and look at you, all glowing skin and shiny hair . . . I hate you!' she laughed. Calli's due date was early November; a baby girl, she had learned after her last scan. She had had doubts about finding out the sex but eventually decided that the knowledge confirmed the baby's presence and made the event all the more real and exciting.

'Ah! Look, Mum!' she said, pointing at the screen. 'A little Eleni!'

Following the Greek custom, Calli had announced that if the baby was a girl she would be named after her beloved mother. 'Just as you named me after *Yiayia*,' she said. Mother and daughter had gone to the hospital together for the scan and when the doctor told them she was carrying a baby girl they both burst into tears.

'She's going to be another little Cretan thunderbolt,' Calli said, squeezing Eleni's hand.

4

Eleni was pushing the overflowing supermarket trolley down the tea and coffee aisle when she heard her mobile phone ring in her handbag.

'I must remember to stop dumping my bag in there,' she muttered under her breath, diving among the groceries to retrieve it buried under a heap of shopping. Now that she had the whole family to feed again, her trolley was always more loaded than when she shopped for herself and Keith.

When eventually she found the phone it had switched to voicemail. It was Keith. *He must want me to buy something*, she thought, waiting to hear the message.

'Don't worry, love, everything's fine,' she heard her husband's anxious voice reverberate in her ear. 'Don't panic, keep calm,' his voice continued, 'but Calli's been in an accident. Can you come home please . . . straight away!' Without a second thought and of course in a panic, Eleni abandoned the trolley in the middle of the aisle and ran out of the supermarket to her car.

*

'She wasn't the one driving,' Keith began, anxiously trying to explain what had happened as they set off for the hospital. 'John, you know, her assistant . . . he called me from the hospital just before I phoned you . . . He told me that he had been driving . . .' Keith's speech faltered in his attempt to keep calm. 'He apparently had to swerve to avoid hitting a cyclist who came out of nowhere, and ended up having a head-on collision with a car coming the other way. But . . .' he paused to take a deep breath before continuing, 'but luckily they were both driving slowly, so it really wasn't as bad as it might have been.'

'Never mind all that!' Eleni interrupted, cutting him short, her impatience getting the better of her. 'Do we know how badly she's hurt?' she said, her heart thumping in her ears as she turned to look at him through tear-blurred eyes. Keith's face was as pale as her own. 'And the baby?' she asked, again holding her breath and dreading the answer.

'I don't know, love. I feel so stupid for not asking, but when I got the call from the hospital, I was so shocked I just couldn't think straight . . . all I heard . . . all that mattered at that moment was that Calli was all right.'

When they at last located Calli's bed, they found her fast asleep, sporting a nasty bruise on her right shoulder and arm, and one on her forehead; she looked pale and drawn but otherwise less badly injured than they had feared.

'We gave her a sedative to calm her,' the nurse told

them. 'Don't worry, she's fine now. The doctor will be along soon to speak to you.'

Eleni looked at her daughter and tried to fight back her tears. She reached for Calli's hand and sat by her side. Gently she brushed her hair off her forehead and bend down to kiss it. She had woken that morning with one of her strange premonitions, but Calli was in such a buoyant mood that she had tried not to dwell on it. A few hours ago the two of them were having coffee in the kitchen, waiting for John to come and drive Calli to the photo shoot.

'She was so cheerful this morning.' She turned to Keith, who appeared as miserable as she felt. 'Poor baby, look at her now.'

'She was lucky to have escaped with minor injuries, no broken bones,' the doctor told them when he finally arrived, 'and she was quite conscious when she was brought in.' He picked up the clipboard from the front of the bed. 'She will be fine,' he paused while reading her notes, 'but unfortunately,' he continued, looking up at them both, 'we couldn't save the baby.' Eleni felt her knees buckle beneath her and put an arm on the bed to steady herself. The impact of the collision, he informed them, had been enough of a shock to cause the placenta to become detached, thus causing a severe haemorrhage which sent Calli into premature labour; the baby was stillborn. Eleni looked from the doctor to Keith, unable to speak, the colour drained from her face. All she could think of was how matter-of-factly the young doctor had delivered those devastating words.

She was already five months pregnant and the baby had been due in November. Calli was inconsolable. The ordeal of what happened to her physically and emotionally left her bereft and traumatized. The shock and loss of her relationship had now faded into unimportance in comparison with the loss of her baby. The grief she was plunged into had no measure and its intensity overwhelmed her. She reached the depths of despair on the date baby Eleni was due. Her mother worried for her safety; she had never seen her daughter so broken.

'You have been through a lot,' her friend Josie told her. 'I think it would be good to talk to someone other than just us . . . someone who knows how to help.'

'Maybe if she accepted some work,' Eleni said to Keith, at a loss as to what else to suggest. 'It might do her good, take her mind off things . . . You know how she loves her job.'

'She will go back to work when she is ready. She needs time, what she needs now is help,' Keith replied.

Her world was dark, it took several months of therapy and the best part of a year with all her family and dear friends rallying around her before Calli started to find herself again. By then, spring was well on its way. The long sad nights were at last behind them and the smell of freshly cut grass scented the air. Calli took a deep breath, literally and metaphorically, and with her exhalation she blew away some of the sadness she had held inside herself for so many months. It was time now to pick herself up and rejoin the world.

The next time her phone rang with a work assignment, instead of declining the call she accepted the offer with pleasure, with a certain relief at the prospect of employing her mind again. During the next few weeks she eased herself into work with a few small commissions, and then started to look for an apartment. It was time to leave the refuge of the family home and launch herself into an independent life, as she had promised herself she would do. James was out of her thoughts now for good and it was time to move on.

'He's got a bloody nerve!' Josie had said when Calli told her that after she lost the baby he had tried to see her. 'I hope you told him where to go!'

'Don't you worry, my friend,' she replied. 'It was fine, James is history, I can handle it.'

She was now well on her way to recovery and once again ready to embrace life with something approaching her usual zest. Calli knew that the loss of her baby was a sorrow she would always carry with her, but she refused to give up. There was a world out there waiting for her. She was finally ready to embrace life again and as it turned out this came in the form of an assignment, a job proposal from her Sunday paper.

'There's an island in Greece called Ikaria,' David, her commissioning editor, had said when he telephoned, 'and I'd like you to go there and do a story for us.'

'Sounds great! What's the story and where is it?' Calli asked.

'Somewhere . . . let me think . . . in the Aegean . . .' he replied, distracted by interruptions competing for his attention in the office; Calli could hear someone in the background trying to talk to him.

'What exactly do you want me to do, David?' she asked, trying to focus his attention on their phone call.

'Well . . . apparently people are living for an awfully long time on this island,' he struggled to explain, 'but no one really knows why . . . It's a bit of a phenomenon.'

'Is that so different from other Greek islands?' she persevered, hoping for more information. 'Don't most people live to a ripe old age in Greece?'

'Well, maybe, but they say this is different . . . something to do with the environment that makes them live even longer . . . Look, just come into the office tomorrow and I'll tell you everything,' he finally said, exasperated. 'It's crazy busy in here and I can't hear myself think.'

As soon as Calli was off the phone, she looked up Ikaria online.

*

'I've been given a commission to go to Greece to follow up a story,' she told her parents over dinner that night.

'Where in Greece?' her mother asked, leaning forward to hear more.

'The island of Ikaria – do you know it?' Calli looked at them both.

'Isn't that the island where everyone lives for ever?' mused Keith.

'Kind of . . .' Calli said, wondering why *she* hadn't heard about it before now. 'How did I miss this?'

'Perhaps because you've been a bit busy lately?' Eleni replied.

'I heard a programme on the radio about it the other day,' Keith told them. 'It sounds a fascinating place.'

'To say the least!' Calli reached for a chunk of bread to soak up the olive oil and lemon dressing from her plate. 'They've named it *the island where people forget to die!* Did you know that there are only four other places in the world that have the same record of longevity?'

'Do they know why?' Eleni asked.

'Well, it *must* be something to do with the healthy lifestyle, but apparently from what I've been reading there's more to it than that . . .'

'Well . . . there's all the mythology too,' Keith added, 'hence the island's name – you know, the story of Icarus flying too close to the sun and falling into the sea and all that?'

'Exactly!' Calli said. 'Not that that can have anything to

do with people living a long time – but it does add to the mystery, don't you agree?'

'When do they want you to go?' Eleni reached for the bottle of wine and filled their glasses.

'Soon, I think. I'm going into the office for the briefing tomorrow.'

'Will you still take the flat?' her mother asked. Calli had at last found an apartment that she quite liked and was considering putting down a deposit. Over the last few weeks she had viewed several possibilities, but nothing that she thought suitable until now. *No point moving somewhere you don't like for the sake of it*, her parents encouraged her. *Stay until you find the right place.*

'I probably won't, Mum,' she replied, 'It wasn't that brilliant. If you don't mind, I'd rather leave my things here while I'm away?'

'Of course we don't mind!' Eleni said, relieved that her daughter was not about to move out yet. 'You can start looking again when you return.'

'You know . . .' she looked at her parents, 'I was thinking I might stay on a little longer after I finish the job, take a break . . . have a holiday . . . spend the summer in the sun. I mean, I don't really have to rush back, do I?'

'Ikaria is part of the north Aegean islands,' David informed her the next day when she went into the office for her briefing, 'and it has been declared one of the five "Blue

Zones" in the world. The other four,' he continued, more informed and much calmer this time than the day before on the phone, 'are Nicoya in Costa Rica, Okinawa in Japan, Loma Linda in California, and Sardinia in Italy.'

Calli of course already knew that – she had done her homework – but she still wanted to hear what David had to say. 'Research shows that the environment in these five areas is conducive to old age.' He continued with his explanation.

'Do you think it's due to the easy pace of life and to eating habits?' she asked, musing that as far as she knew most of rural Greece was conducive to old age.

'Well . . . not only . . . Food and lifestyle obviously are both factors, but more causes than that seem to be involved.' He reached for his laptop and turned it round so that Calli could see his screen showing images of the island.

'I know, I've googled it and I've seen the pictures,' she told him. 'It looks like paradise – but to me most Greek islands *are* paradise.'

'The thing is, Calli' – he peered over his glasses at her – 'apart from people living a very long time, research on the island indicates that on Ikaria instances of cancer, diabetes and heart disease are much lower than other places, and dementia is almost non-existent. But they don't really know why.'

The more Calli was learning about the place, the more

her interest was aroused. She loved Greece. She had spent most of her childhood summers on Crete with her grand-mother, and what better opportunity to ease herself back into her old life than a trip to an Aegean island? She liked nothing more than a travel story with bite.

'So, what do you say? Interested?' David asked, treading carefully. He was aware of Calli's recent problems and her reluctance to take on lengthy assignments. 'What do you think?' he added hesitantly. 'Are you up for it? Do you feel well enough?' He smiled gently, gauging her reaction. 'I can't think of a better person than you to go and discover the secret of Ikaria.'

5

Calli arrived in a small, noisy plane around the time when, apparently, all of Ikaria's inhabitants were taking their siesta, except for a few taxi drivers outside the little airport. She had taken an impossibly early flight from London to Athens, where she then boarded a plane the size of a bus for a connecting flight to the island. From the air, Ikaria looked like no more than a massive rock rising from the sea, yet once on land and starting to explore, Calli was to discover an altogether more interesting world.

Her hotel, which had been booked by the newspaper, was a good hour and a half away in the village of Armenistis, and the taxi driver who approached her as soon as she walked out of the terminus was more than eager to drive her there.

'*Kalosorisate,*' he greeted her, using the polite plural tense but quickly adding an English *welcome,* unaware that Calli spoke perfectly good Greek. Her response in Greek caused his face to break into a broad smile and he reached for her hand.

'Very nice to meet you, miss,' he said with evident delight. 'I am Theo.'

'Very nice to meet you too, Theo. I am Calli,' she said, returning his vigorous handshake and relishing this island familiarity which she knew so well from her visits to Crete. If ever she had to get a taxi to her grandmother's house the driver would invariably try to find out everything there was to know about her in the hour it took to drive to the village.

She liked to travel light for her work; she had only two small cameras, her laptop, a notebook, and her mobile as a recording device. 'I like to feel free and not be weighed down with too much gear . . .' she would explain when people were surprised that she carried so little equipment with her. 'The kind of photography I do is spontaneous, not very technical, I could do it on my phone,' she would laugh.

'Are you on holiday, Miss Calli?' Theo enquired right on cue as she settled herself in the back seat. 'Most young people come here as couples for a romantic holiday – or old people come in groups from Athens for the therapeutic waters.'

'I'm here to do some work . . . take photographs,' she replied, wondering if perhaps she should start her investigations with Theo, but too weary to ask any questions.

'Well, there's a lot of things to photograph here,' he said, gesturing out of the window towards a steep precipice falling to the sea beyond. 'I hope you don't feel carsick,

Miss Calli,' he added cheerfully, 'there are many bends on this road.'

'I think I'll be fine,' she replied, sinking into the seat, her eyelids suddenly heavy with exhaustion. She was quite used to 'bends on the road', Crete was full of them. She longed to close her eyes for a few minutes to combat her fatigue after the early morning start but what she now saw out of the car window was so spectacular that she couldn't bear to shut it out; sleep would have to wait.

'No matter how many times I make this journey I am always amazed by these views,' Theo told her, 'especially on a clear day like today when you can see so far!'

The journey to the village – a bone-shaking drive, since Theo was not the best of drivers, which lasted almost two hours – proved to be breathtaking and kept Calli wide awake and on the edge of her seat. One moment they were high in the hills, only to plummet down into a valley the next, then climbing steeply again to reveal through crystal-clear air a panorama of the shimmering sea stretching across to neighbouring islands.

'Look, Miss Calli' – Theo gestured eagerly to her – 'you can see Samos over there, and the other one is Fourni . . .' His excitement was equal to hers, as if he was seeing everything for the first time through her eyes.

Theo delivered Calli to her hotel safe and well, if a little rattled, in good time for her to collapse into bed for a well-deserved siesta of her own. When she woke the sun was already sinking fast towards the west. She stepped out barefoot onto the balcony and rested her eyes on the un-interrupted line of the horizon. The sky, a swirl of faded pastels, was alive with the flight of swallows skimming the surface of the sea in a last attempt to snatch whatever insects they could find hovering over the water before nightfall. The warm sea breeze on her naked arms and legs felt like a welcoming Grecian caress. *It can't get much better than this*, she told herself and filled her lungs with sea air.

In no time at all she bathed, dressed, grabbed a camera and ran outside to catch the last of the light. She needed to explore, to walk around, see what was there. She didn't need a map, she didn't even want any information from the hotel reception just yet, she was sure she would find her way around.

No sooner was she outside and down the front steps onto the road than she was cheerfully greeted by a young couple in high spirits dancing their way barefoot towards a small crowd, also apparently in a celebratory mood.

'What's happening over there?' Calli asked, gesturing towards the animated group.

'We are all going down to the beach,' the young woman replied in English. 'Come with us,' she said, taking Calli by the hand. 'My name is Sylvie and he is Christian, what's your name, are you staying at the hotel, have you just arrived?' she asked in one long sentence.

'Did you come here in time for the festival?' The young man hurled another question, giving Calli no time to reply.

'I'm Calli,' she finally said, extending her hand. 'I didn't know there was a festival . . . But possibly yes, maybe I have come here for that,' she murmured, more for her own benefit than theirs. It occurred to her that a festival was just what she needed now for a multitude of reasons, but chiefly because it was high time for her to start enjoying herself again.

'Well . . . it's not exactly a festival but more of a celebration—' Christian started to explain before Sylvie cut him short.

'Come *on*!' she called, pointing towards the waterfront. 'Let's go! We'll talk about all of that later.'

'Why is everyone here?' Calli asked once they reached the beach.

'We've come to see the moon rise, we do it every evening,' an older woman in a red bikini and a colourful sarong replied, turning to look at her; she smiled broadly, flashing even white teeth.

'Calli has just arrived,' Sylvie explained as a way of introduction.

'Nice to meet you, Calli.' The woman extended her hand. 'My name is Maya. Welcome to Ikaria, you will love it. The moonrise is a magnificent sight at this time of year.' She cupped Calli's hand with both of hers and held on to it for a long moment.

'Of course she will!' enthused Sylvie. 'How could anyone not fall in love with this place?'

'Do you practise yoga?' Maya went on as Calli settled down beside her, taking off her sandals to feel the warm sand between her toes. 'We gather here every day at dawn.' The woman gave Calli a long persistent look. 'Join us, you look as if you are in need of some sea air in your lungs and some colour in your cheeks.'

'Erm . . . well . . . I haven't done yoga for years . . .' Calli mumbled, taken aback by the woman's candour. 'Pilates is more my thing,' she added lamely, darting a glance at Sylvie for support. She was well aware that she looked pale and fatigued, she hardly needed a stranger to point it out. Then again it wasn't a lie; she was indeed in urgent need of more than sea air in her lungs and sun on her skin and she had to admit that nothing was *her thing* these days; it had been a long time since she had done anything that resembled physical exercise.

'That's OK, Pilates is not so different,' Sylvie chirped. 'Come, you'll enjoy it, no better way to start the day.'

'Especially on this beach,' Maya added, 'you can feel the presence of the angels at dawn.'

Calli sat chatting with her new acquaintances for some time while they waited for the moon to rise and as they did so, she fancied that she was in the company of good friends instead of complete strangers. They talked and laughed and drank ice-cold beer as the waves lapped at her feet in the warm evening breeze. And as time passed, Calli discovered that this crowd in which she so unexpectedly found herself was a friendly gathering of men and women of various nationalities and ages, all with a shared love for this small Aegean island.

'Christian and I come from Berlin,' Sylvie told her. 'We leave our busy city lives behind and come here to feel free . . . Enzo over there and Maya are Italian . . .'

'Actually, I am *partly* Italian,' the older woman protested, 'my grandmother was Greek! I consider Greece my spiritual home . . .'

'We don't see each other from one year to the next,' Christian took his turn to explain, 'but in the summer months we all gather here, come what may. See the two guys over there?' He gestured with his chin. 'Bruce and Andrew come all the way from Australia . . . We try to keep in touch via email but even if we don't, when we meet, we all pick up from where we left off.'

'Early morning yoga on the beach,' Maya went on, 'is the one activity that we all like to follow together to keep mind and spirit healthy – meditation too, but generally speaking we mostly go our separate ways.'

The group came and went individually at different times over the summer months, Calli was told, occupying themselves with voluntary tasks such as working in the vineyards with the picking of grapes or assisting elderly folk in their gardens or fields. This year, Christian explained, they had agreed to gather at the same time in order to witness all together the lunar eclipse which was about to take place in a few days.

'It's the longest total lunar eclipse of the twenty-first century, and I can't wait!' Sylvie said with evident excitement. 'It will be spectacular to watch it from the beach. Christian is an amateur astronomer and he has everything ready to capture the event on film, and a state-of-the-art telescope for all of us to use.'

'It's a very special event for us all. That's why we are celebrating,' Maya added. 'This year most visitors have come to the island for this experience alone.' She turned her eyes quizzically on Calli: 'Is that why *you* are here?' she asked.

To her embarrassment Calli had completely forgotten about this celestial phenomenon, despite having heard and read about it during the past few weeks in London. Her own concerns had been so all-consuming that everything else had an annoying habit of slipping her mind.

The moonrise that evening was breathtaking, equal only to one or two spectacular evenings she had witnessed with her mother and grandmother on beaches in Crete many years before as a child, although then its impact had been lost on her youthful self.

This time Calli watched closely in anticipation as the

moon announced its appearance in the form of a yellow glow on the horizon. She sat motionless, waiting. Within moments, as if in a spectacular conjuring trick, an enormous amber globe began to rise from the sea towards the heavens. Calli held her breath and as she looked on, she was engulfed by a sense of wonder so powerful that it caused the tears to overflow from her eyes and her heart to ache. She sat on the warm sand for as long as it took for the moon to travel high in the sky and turn into a silver disc so bright that it lit up the restless sea. She followed its slow upward journey with her eyes, and her mind began a journey of its own, taking her back to the events of the past year which had caused her such pain. To her surprise she discovered that the sting in her heart was one not of sorrow but of joy. She looked around her and was filled not only with gratitude to have been transported to this blessed island, witnessing this awesome spectacle of nature, but also, for the first time in a year, with a positive anticipation for what the future might hold for her.

Gradually and without haste as the time passed, a few people rose from the beach and ran into the sea for a moonlit swim while others started to make their way towards the local taverna. Calli stood up, wiped away her tears, walked to the water's edge and stood in the shallow surf. *Tomorrow night I too will bathe in the moonlight*, she promised herself.

*

Her companions all strolled unhurriedly to the taverna and sat in the scented night air at tables surrounded by pots of basil and geraniums, under a vine laden with juicy black grapes hanging over their heads. That first evening on Ikaria Calli found herself in the midst of this unconventional, likeable and most easy-going group, the likes of which she had never encountered before. These people, she was glad to discover, apparently took pleasure in leisure and gave merit to life's simple joys of the moment, unlike herself and most of her driven friends back in London who valued work and its rewards above anything else. With a sinking heart her mind also turned to James, the man she had lived with for more years than she now cared to recall, whose principles and values she now found abhorrent. She looked around at all the new faces she had just met and her old life in London seemed as distant as the moon itself. They say that people are the same the world over, Calli thought, but it wasn't really true. She saw something in the folk she was with now that she hadn't seen since she was a child in Crete – a diversity in age that was quite uncommon among social groups in London. This group, she guessed, ranged from their mid-twenties to their sixties and more, and their age seemed to be irrelevant. Their common interest of nature and this island united them.

'I hope you are not too fussy with your food,' Sylvie said, laughing when she saw Calli searching for a menu, 'because you'll get what *Kyria* Erini gives you, which will be whatever she's cooked.'

'If she's prepared fish, you know it was caught that very morning,' Maya said, stretching across for the wine carafe in the middle of the table.

'That's fine by me. I'd eat anything, especially if it's Greek,' Calli replied, picking up her camera and leaning forward to take a photo of the earthenware carafe and the several glasses that *Kyria* Erini had piled on the table when they arrived.

'So, Calli . . .' Maya said, looking at her while filling everyone's glasses. 'If you are not here for the lunar eclipse, then what *are* you here for?'

Once more Maya's direct approach caused Calli to raise an eyebrow.

6

Calli's introduction to Ikaria and the people she met there proved to be as fascinating as she'd hoped the island would be. Sylvie and Christian were delightful, and she found Maya intriguing; once she had explained the reason for her trip, she found plenty of offers from volunteers to show her around and help with her story by introducing her to remarkable old people.

'Apart from the obviously healthy life they lead here,' Maya observed, 'they are also a spiritual people. The island's history sees to that – those ancient Greeks knew a thing or two about mysticism.'

'In a way, that's the reason why most of us are here,' Sylvie added. 'To absorb the aura of this place and perhaps learn something valuable about life from its people.'

'When I am on this island, I feel more connected with the cosmos than anywhere else in the world.' Maya turned her eyes on Calli once again. 'What about you, do you feel this power that emanates from here?' she asked.

Calli had never considered such matters before. Spirituality or mysticism were concepts she had never dwelled on – she considered herself a thoroughly grounded and pragmatic person.

'I am very excited for you to meet him,' Sylvie said a few days later as they made their way to visit an old couple she knew, who had agreed to talk to Calli about her subject. Socrates and his wife Sophia lived close to the beach and Sylvie was now eager to introduce him to Calli; she had been helping him with his grape harvesting for the past few summers and had grown very fond of the old man.

'He is a super amazing guy,' she enthused on the way to his house, 'you'll see. Not only does he look twenty years younger than he really is, he has more stamina than I do sometimes.'

'Did you know that, compared to Americans, two and a half times as many people on Ikaria reach the age of ninety?' the old man told her when they met. 'And I should know, I lived in Chicago for fifty years.' He gave a chuckle. 'I'm eighty-seven and I don't feel any different from how I was when I left Ikaria as a boy.' He smiled broadly, showing a set of teeth that a far younger person would have been glad to own. 'But when you get to my age – and I aim to live to be over a hundred – it's time to return to your home.'

Calli and Sylvie were sitting with the old couple in their garden, shaded by a large walnut tree, drinking their home-made wine and feasting on black olives, village bread, ripe red tomatoes, freshly laid eggs and cheese. When Sophia was told they were having visitors she insisted with typical island hospitality that despite being unexpected they must stay and eat with them.

'No one comes to my house without being fed,' she told her husband and busied herself laying the outdoor table.

'I know you probably think this is very late to be having lunch,' Socrates told them, 'but we don't wake up early here, we don't rush, we take our time with everything. We don't even have a clock in the house. Who cares about time, eh?' he laughed. 'In America they eat their dinner the same time we wake up from our siesta.' He spoke in English, his heavy Greek accent tinged with American, betraying the many years he had spent in the USA.

'We like to drink some wine with our lunch every day,' he told them, 'and then of course we have our siesta; we always go to our bed, we never go without our after-lunch nap.' He smiled and turned to give a mischievous glance at Sophia, who in turn leaned across, cupped his face with both hands and gave him a tender kiss on the cheek. That was something that Calli was to encounter often during her meetings with people on the island. Apparently a healthy sex life well into old age was normal practice on Ikaria.

'See? What did I tell you?' Sylvie said with delight after they left the old couple to their desired afternoon bedtime and made their way to a bar on the beach. There they had arranged to meet Maya, who along with Sylvie had taken a keen interest in Calli and her assignment.

'They are the age of my grandparents, those two, and they act as if they are newly-weds! I never saw anyone that age behave like this in Germany!'

'Could it be that that's the secret of Ikaria?' Calli laughed.

'I wouldn't be surprised! We should all be having more sex!'

'It's more like the Red Hot Zone around here rather than the Blue Zone!' Calli added, smiling.

They met Maya sitting on a bar stool in cut-off jeans and blue T-shirt, drinking ice-cold mountain tea as she talked to Stavros, a young local man who was serving behind the counter. She was a good-looking woman, Calli thought, about the same age as her own mother she guessed. Her hair, a rich chestnut woven with natural strands of grey, fell on her tanned shoulders while her dark eyes and strong nose gave her a classically Grecian air. In fact, Calli mused, something about Maya reminded her very much of Eleni. The easy smile and the straight speaking were not unlike the Cretan women in her family, whose manner she had encountered so many times in her grandmother's village. It wouldn't surprise her if Maya didn't start asking her why she wasn't married or had had children yet. That familiarity, she decided, was the reason why she didn't take offence at the woman's blunt approach; in fact she rather liked and was amused by it.

'Joking apart,' Maya said after the two women told her about their morning visit, 'we are all too quick to underestimate the power of sex.' She took a sip of her drink and continued, 'It definitely keeps you healthy, and I firmly believe it has something to do with the longevity of people here. Not just the sex but the *love* too . . . you feel it everywhere on this island.'

Calli could not deny that even after a short time on Ikaria, so far she had encountered nothing but goodwill and warmth.

'One thing I've heard repeated on the island over the years,' Maya went on, 'is that this is not a "me" place but an "us" place . . . They look after each other, these folk, nobody feels alone here.' She gave a sigh. 'Take all of us in the big cities – there is so much loneliness, especially among the old. We don't take care of one another, so how can we thrive into a ripe old age?'

'This acceptance of strangers goes back a long way,' Sylvie added, reaching for her coffee. 'Look at the story of Icarus, look at us – we are strangers from all over the world – we come here year after year and they welcome us as if we were locals.'

Maya nodded in agreement. 'It's true. I believe the kindness and love on this island travels across millennia. Mythology was based on truths.'

Like most people, Calli knew the legend of Daedalus and his son Icarus, who plummeted to his death into the sea fringing Ikaria after disobeying his father, but she had always believed it to be a cautionary tale of youthful defiance. She had read the story many times as a child and had done so again recently after accepting her assignment. But she didn't follow why it was relevant to what they were discussing now. She was struggling to understand the implications of love and kindness to which Maya and Sylvie were now alluding, until the older woman began to explain.

The journey of escape from cruel King Minos in Crete, which had started with such ingenuity and hope for father and son and which ended in tragic disaster, Maya claimed, indicated not only the extent of compassion and care among the citizens of Ikaria but also their tolerance for strangers.

The curious alien pair who disturbed the inhabitants' peace one summer's day arrived at their shores not by sea but from the sky, like two giant birds of prey flapping their wings. People stood on the shore looking up at the cloudless heavens, blinded by the bright scorching sun, witnessing a sight so inexplicable and disturbing that a more hostile people would have reached for their weapons in fear of their safety. Yet they did no such thing; instead of launching an attack they stood and waited in order to establish who or what the unearthly phenomenon approaching their land might be. Once they realized that the 'giant birds' were in fact men and that one of them had begun to spiral dangerously towards the sea, they rushed to this stranger's aid. One after another, they dived in turn into the sea in an attempt to save the curious bird-man, but by then all that remained floating on the water were the wooden wings and feathers which the boy's father had so lovingly crafted for their escape.

Unable to save him, the locals did their best to retrieve the drowned youth from the seabed and respectfully set about attending to his body before burying him in accordance with the island's rituals; the inconsolable father was given refuge and solace. Maya often brought up the story of Daedalus and Icarus as an example of the island's legacy of compassion and acceptance.

'I have always believed that this tale is one of the reasons why the angels favour this island . . .' she said and gestured towards the sea. 'I know they are here, I see them everywhere, and I often feel the boy's presence.'

'Did you know there is a monument to Icarus on the island?' Sylvie turned to Calli.

'Yes, I do . . . Is it far from here?'

'Nothing is that far from here.' Maya smiled. 'I will drive you there on Friday, but not to the recently erected monument, beautiful as it might be, but to the ancient rock that stands in the sea on the exact spot where the boy fell.'

Calli gazed at the older woman, perplexed. How on earth could anyone know the exact spot where Icarus fell? Not to mention the fact that the story was a myth . . . But saying nothing, she put her logic and pragmatism to one side for once and allowed herself to be swept along by her new friend's magical thinking.

'Have you noticed all the rock formations on the land, Calli?' Maya asked. 'To me, each and every one looks like a monument and not only for that poor foolish boy. I will show you tomorrow.'

'Be sure to be back in good time on Friday.' Sylvie turned to them both. 'I would like to come with you, but I promised Christian I'd spend the day with him, preparing for the evening. He is setting up the telescope on the beach.'

On Friday morning, the day of the eclipse, just as the sun was appearing above the line of the horizon, Maya picked up Calli in her yellow open-top Citroën 2CV and set off for the village of Vaoni, to visit the fated spot where Icarus had lost his wings. Equipped with her camera, notebook and swimsuit, Calli could hardly believe her luck. The most she had expected for this trip was to find a taxi driver who would be willing to drive her to some places on a budget, or to hire a small motorbike and find her own way around. Finding new friends who were not only willing but wanted to help her was not what she had anticipated.

'Glad to see you didn't forget to bring your bikini,' Maya shouted cheerfully over the car engine as they chugged along the twisting country roads. 'Every beach we'll drive past you'll want to dive into,' she added, pointing towards an emerald cove just beneath them.

'It's wonderful to know that this ancient amphitheatre is still in use,' Maya said when they arrived at their destination. 'Can you imagine sitting here to watch a performance?' She gestured to the semicircle of steps around them and then pointed out to the shimmering sea, towards the stone marking the spot where Icarus fell.

Calli stood mutely gazing at the rock. The sight of that monolith rising from the sea no more than fifty yards from where she was now standing made her head swirl and her vision blur. She had no warning of the impact this would have on her: the noise of the wind sighing through her ears, the hot sun beating down on her and the sunlight playing on the water, flickered like the wings of a thousand birds. She closed her eyes and stumbled back. Maya rushed to her aid; with her arm around her shoulders she led her to the steps of the amphitheatre. They sat together for a long while without words.

The older woman was the first to break the silence. 'You have much pain in your heart, my friend.' She reached for a bottle of water in her bag and handed it to Calli. 'I sensed it from the moment I saw you . . .' She hesitated. 'You are grieving for your loss, I know, like the father of this wretched boy grieved for his loss, so long ago.'

The younger woman sat mutely with her eyes tightly shut. That rectangular column emerging from the sea had looked nothing less than a tombstone to her. A humble monument marking the death of a beloved child, any child whose life had been cut short. When she opened her eyes again, two large tears ran down her cheeks.

7

Calli wiped her tears with the back of her hand and turned in disbelief to look at Maya. She had never spoken about the loss of her baby, the break-up of her relationship or about her grief, to her or to anyone since she arrived on the island.

'How did you know?' she asked almost in a whisper.

'It is who I am,' the older woman said softly and reached for her hand. She held it tightly for a few moments before continuing. 'I would like you to know, Calli dear, that there is someone who is by your side, someone who is looking after you . . .' She hesitated for a second, then shifted a little closer. 'That someone,' she continued, 'is Raphael. He is your guardian angel.'

Calli turned sharply to look at her with unblinking eyes.

'Don't look so shocked, my girl.' The older woman gave a little laugh. 'I know what I am saying; Raphael looks over you, *always*.'

Calli stared silently for a long while until finally she managed to speak. 'If that's the case,' she said under her breath and pulling her hand away from Maya's, 'then he isn't doing a very good job of it, is he?'

'You might not think so now, my friend,' she replied solemnly, 'and you may reject what I am about to say . . .' Maya paused again for a moment to think before continuing, 'But things always happen for a reason and—'

The younger woman's response cut her short, coming fast and sharp. 'What possible reason do you suggest there was for me to lose my baby and for my life to be turned upside down?' Her cheeks were blazing, her voice raised.

'I know it's a harsh and painful thought . . .' Maya paused again, unsure if she should continue. 'But you see . . . you had to be *free*.' She hesitated again before speaking. 'And now there is *nothing* that ties you to that man . . .'

Calli leapt to her feet before Maya had a chance to finish; her eyes flashing with fury, she looked down at the woman still sitting on the step. There was much she wanted to say but no words could come out of her mouth. Her thoughts were jumbled, uncertain. She knew James was not worthy of loyalty or mercy and it was true she wanted nothing to connect herself with him. But that poor innocent soul – what harm had she done?

'What I am saying,' Maya said gently, trying to soothe her, 'is that it just wasn't meant to be, my friend, not any of it.'

Calli continued to stand facing her defiantly, her emotions jumbled, her head aching. Having spent a couple of days with Maya she had come to realize that she had never encountered anyone quite like her before. This was a woman with a different slant to the world, a different reality and vision from her own. Until now Calli had found this intriguing, but now she felt that Maya's attitude had gone beyond her acceptance.

'You see, Calli dear' – Maya continued in the same gentle tone of explanation – 'it's a chain of events and the loss is truly tragic. But some things must happen, no matter how painful they are, before others follow, before change will occur. Believe me, my girl, I know what I am speaking of. Out of sadness will come joy for you, I promise. This lunar eclipse we are about to witness tonight, it will bring change, it is a given, and change never happens without the loss of something.'

The drive back to Armenistis was subdued. Calli had been shaken by her experience at the monument, and the conversation with Maya disturbed and confused her, giving her much food for thought. Maya, concerned that her earlier rhetoric had contributed to her friend's agitation, refrained from saying more. The two women sat in the car in reflective silence until a rock formation in the distance on a small hill by the roadside caught Calli's eye.

'What is that ahead?' she pointed, leaning forward for a better look. 'Is that another monument?'

The stones, or rather giant boulders, which were rapidly coming into closer view looked as if they had been arranged intentionally in such a way as to resemble some kind of memorial site or shrine.

'No, it is not,' Maya replied. 'This is one of those natural formations of stones I was telling you about yesterday, remember? Isn't it magnificent?'

'Can we stop?' Calli asked, reaching for her camera. Earlier she had been too preoccupied and disturbed to think about taking any photographs, but now with her camera poised for action she was halfway up the hill, intrigued by the sight ahead of her. Calli stood in the shade of the rocks and looked up. If not for their size they could be a pile of pebbles balanced one on top of the other, but these ancient boulders rose to a height of some twenty feet. No one could have arranged them one above the other without the aid of modern technology. As she snapped away, she fancied that the hand of a giant had playfully piled them up in a childish game.

They arrived back at the village in the early afternoon, in good time for a siesta before the evening celebrations on the beach. They had stopped for lunch at a roadside taverna, Maya relieved to see Calli's mood restored, and feasted as usual on whatever had been cooked that day. They drank Maya's preferred infusion of ice-cold herbal mountain tea whose benefits she was always praising.

'Mint is an antioxidant, rosemary stimulates the immune system, dandelion cleans the liver . . . I could go on and on,' she laughed, 'but no one else seems to drink it cold here,' she told Calli as the old man serving them pulled a face when Maya asked for iced tea.

'We don't keep cold tea,' he told her, 'we have to boil the water to make it.'

'By the time you bring us the meal, the tea will have cooled down . . . Put some ice cubes in it and a little honey, that will do it!' She gave the old man a broad smile. 'Just wait and see,' she turned to Calli, 'they will be so slow in bringing us the food, the tea will be cold whether I wanted it so or not!'

Like everything else on the island, nothing was done in a hurry, but when the food eventually arrived it was well worth the wait. A Greek salad of home-grown vegetables and feta cheese, black olives and chunks of sourdough village bread were the first dishes to arrive on the table. *Kyria* Elpiniki, the owner and cook, was a little slow at preparing the food today, the old man told them, so they would have to be patient. It wasn't difficult, and above all it was expected. The new friends were content to sit in the gentle breeze, shaded by the ubiquitous green canopy of a vine, and snack on whatever they were given.

'There is no rush,' Maya told Calli, 'this is Ikaria. We have all the time in the world.'

Next came a large bowl of chickpeas cooked in a tomato sauce, followed by a plate of *horta* – field greens – in olive oil and lemon dressing. By then Maya's sage tea had arrived, chilled and fragrant. They ate at a leisurely pace, drank and chatted for as long as it took and by the end of their meal the blues and sadness Calli had felt earlier had totally lifted. For the second time since arriving on the island, she was infused with a sense of hope for what might be ahead of her.

When Calli awoke from her siesta the preparations for the lunar eclipse celebrations on the beach had already begun. She felt refreshed even though it had taken a while for her to fall asleep, her head whirling with the dazzling and confusing events of the day. Maya was indeed a strange woman; Calli wanted to reject her reasoning and her words which echoed confusingly in her ears, but she found she could not. Eventually she fell asleep and dreamed of Icarus and angel wings.

She stood on her hotel balcony and watched the stream of people carrying food, drink and preparations down to the shore. She dressed quickly, remembering to wear her bikini for a moonlit swim under her shorts and T-shirt, and hurried to join the others. She found Christian and Sylvie, the telescope already in place, filling a cool-box with drinks and snacks.

'What can I contribute?' Calli asked, aware that she had been a guest since she arrived.

'Nothing,' Sylvie told her, 'it's all in hand, just enjoy yourself.'

'It's going to be a long night,' added Christian, 'so we are making sure we have everything we need.'

'Why? How long will the whole thing last?' she enquired, curious to see people arriving on the beach with yet more baskets of food, drink, and blankets to lie back on, in order to gaze at the night sky. She had assumed that this evening's event would last two or three hours maximum, about the same time as the previous moonrises.

'The entire phase of the "blood moon" eclipse will take less than two hours,' Christian explained, 'but the whole celestial event will last for many more.'

'More than four, actually,' Sylvie added, handing Calli an ice-cold beer. 'But that doesn't mean we go home after it ends – no way! We'll party till dawn!'

'Bruce over there,' Christian gestured with his chin, 'is taking care of the music. We've each chosen one song we like. I'm sure it's not too late to put in your request.'

The longest total lunar eclipse of the twenty-first century proved to be every bit as magnificent, magical and as awe-inducing as had been promised. At first the moon rising from the sea was no more spectacular than the other two ascents Calli had witnessed on the island, but as the upward journey progressed, so did its audience's excitement and anticipation. As the hour grew late, Maya leaned close and whispered into Calli's ear.

'When the eclipse begins, you must enter into the sea and make your wish.'

'What? Why? What wish?' she stammered, confusion evident on her face.

'The wish you want to make, you know . . . the one that always brings the tears to your eyes,' she replied. 'You must walk into the water facing the east,' Maya instructed mysteriously, 'and ask Raphael to grant you your wish. But be specific. Don't be vague. Ask for exactly that which you desire, and he will hear you.'

Calli, once again thrown by Maya's words, said nothing. Her head was swimming with unfamiliar thoughts, as it had done earlier at Icarus's rock. She sat silent and motionless, gazing at the constellations in the night sky for a long while. Then, as the earth's shadow slowly began to pass over the moon, masking and transforming it into a dark crimson globe, Maya's words suddenly became clear. She scrambled to her feet, stripped off her shorts and T-shirt and ran towards the water.

She stood for a moment in the shallow surf, looking up at the 'blood moon', then slowly started to walk into the sea, murmuring words almost like prayer. The evening breeze blew through her hair and caressed her arms which were raised to the sky. She stretched them higher and felt weightless: the wind seemed to pull her up effortlessly by her extended arms towards the moon; the deeper into the sea she waded, the more the sensation of being lifted increased, until she was floating above the water as if she had grown wings.

'Please, Raphael,' she whispered and looked down at a silvery beam of light illuminating the sea. 'Please, Raphael,' she repeated into the hot night air and closed her eyes, 'by the power of this moon send a good man to love me and a baby in my womb.'

8

When she reopened her eyes, Calli was lying in her wet bikini on a blanket on the beach. She had no idea how much time had lapsed. She turned to prop herself on one elbow and watched her companions joyfully singing and dancing to the dulcet sounds of Carlos Santana's 'Black Magic Woman'.

'Calli! Calli! Come!' she heard Maya call as she ran towards her. 'It's time to dance,' she cried and seized her arms to pull her to her feet.

By now the moon had once again resumed its normal silver glow and was hovering above them, illuminating the beach like an enormous spotlight. Calli held on to Maya's hand to steady herself and then, lightheaded and elated, joined the dancing crowd.

'They must be singing about you!' she called over the music to Maya, laughing, and wrapped her arms around her shoulders. They danced barefoot on the warm sand through the night, song after song, Greek, English, French, Italian, melody after melody, voices and laughter mingled together, drifting into the night air; once in a while one or two dancers would break away and run into the sea for a refreshing dip before returning to the party. As if they were a single organism not separate individuals, the company stayed on the beach until the faint light of day started to break. Only then did some people begin departing; many stayed on the shore for their early morning yoga.

'My bed is calling me,' Calli yawned, bending down to pick up her flip-flops and discarded clothes.

'What! No yoga?' Sylvie teased, giving her a playful nudge.

Later, by the time Calli walked down to the beach bar for her morning coffee, the hour was well past midday. She had had a fretful night; it was way past sunrise before she finally fell asleep, and even then she hovered between dreams and wakefulness. She was eager to see Maya and to discuss the strange events of the night before, but her new friend was nowhere to be seen.

'*Kalimera*, Miss Calli,' Stavros greeted her as she climbed onto a stool, looking subdued. 'Was a good night last night, no?' he continued, looking from her to a man sitting where Maya normally sat.

'Ciao, I'm Paolo,' the stranger said cheerily and offered his hand. 'I saw you dancing last night but it was all such a big *casino* I didn't get a chance to speak to you . . .'

'Casino . . . ?' Calli looked perplexed.

'Ah! Yes! Sorry,' he laughed, 'I mean a big noise, a

big . . . how do you say . . . too many people! This is what means *casino* in Italian.'

Calli smiled, shaking his hand and her head in agreement.

'Are you staying at the camping?' Paolo swivelled round on his stool to face her better.

'No, at the hotel – and you?'

'Yes! Me I do!'

Evidently Paolo's English needed some improving, but his accent and smile made up for it. He lived in Verona, he informed her, and had arrived the night before just in time for the eclipse.

'Do you know Maya and Enzo? They come from Italy too,' she asked.

'Of course, we are old friends! We meet here every summer.'

It didn't take long for Calli to find out that Paolo was a yoga instructor and travelled twice a year, first to Greece, spending three weeks holidaying at the campsite in Ikaria, then to India for longer over the winter, teaching yoga at an ashram in Goa. He chatted easily, sometimes asking questions but mainly volunteering information about himself.

'Yoga is easy to learn if you are already used to Pilates,' he told her when she informed him that she wasn't really a follower. 'I teach you if you like,' he offered with a smile so charming that she found herself agreeing. The yoga discipline he practised, he began to explain, if possibly with a little too much detail for her liking, was called the *pancha-kosha* system which, he said, restores natural health and balance to those who practise it. Calli, surprising herself, sat attentively listening to Paolo explain the benefits of this school of yoga. His deep-set brown eyes and good looks, she realized with some amusement, were of more interest to her than the subject itself, although the idea of regaining her health and balance wasn't entirely disagreeable. 'If you had a past trauma or live stressful city life you lose the balance,' he continued his monologue, edging a little closer to her while he spoke. 'And this can cause . . . how do you say, many *psychosomatic* illnesses. But then you see, Calli, yoga wakens the body's ability to heal itself.'

Did she see? She was doubtful. Nor did she follow all of Paolo's explanations, despite the fact that his English when talking about his preferred subject seemed to improve miraculously. Nevertheless, Calli did understand one aspect at least, which was that once again since arriving on this island she was talking to somebody with an alternative lifestyle and view of the world that until now had been unfamiliar to her.

'So, you come tomorrow at dawn for yoga?' He leaned in a little closer. 'Or you prefer this evening when moon rise?' He smiled again, and two intolerably attractive dimples formed on either side of his cheeks making her incapable of saying anything but *yes*!

*

Calli spent the rest of the day interviewing and photographing islanders who had been recommended to her for her story, meanwhile counting the hours until her return to the beach to see Paolo again. She had met Sylvie for a quick coffee before dashing off to meet the owner of a local taverna and his family and took the opportunity to ask her about her new acquaintance.

'He is the best yoga instructor I have ever met,' Sylvie enthused, 'and not only that,' she giggled, 'he's pretty hot too, don't you think?' Calli, suddenly flustered, picked up her coffee cup and averted her eyes. Yes, she had to admit, Paolo was pretty hot! This Italian man made her heart race and her cheeks flush; he had caught her attention in a way that she had long forgotten. She had agreed with Maya that her face needed more colour, but she had hardly expected to acquire this by meeting a sexy cosmically attuned Italian. She could hardly believe herself. She had never been remotely interested in any of the alternative hippy stuff that she was now meeting in Ikaria – and that, apparently, despite herself, she was starting to enjoy.

'Paolo has offered to teach me some yoga,' Calli said, looking at Sylvie over the rim of her coffee cup. 'I'm meeting him on the beach this evening.'

'Lucky you!' her friend replied with a mischievous smile. 'What was it we were talking about before . . . Something about the secret of longevity around here?'

*

When Calli arrived on the beach Paolo was already there waiting for her; he had just finished his own yoga session and was sitting on a mat laid on the sand, evidently the one he had been using earlier.

'Come, Calli,' he said kissing her on both cheeks and taking her by the hand, 'first we take breath . . . fill our lungs with sea air . . . feel the energy.'

They stood side by side facing the water and as they did, she stole little glances at him. He looked strong, with wide shoulders and slender limbs; his eyes were closed and his arms lifted to the sky as if in prayer. She raised her arms too and as she did, she remembered her plea to Raphael the night before. Could it be that her guardian angel had something to do with sending this fabulous man to her so swiftly? She closed her eyes, smiled to herself, dismissing the thought, and silently thanked the angels and the moon for this moment of peaceful bliss, whatever it might be.

'The physical, the mental and the soul are all believed by many spiritual traditions to be part of our true selves,' Paolo began to explain again as she lay on the mat while he knelt beside her. 'The ancient Greeks called this the *soma*, *psyche* and *nous* – maybe you know this, Calli, as these are Greek words?' But Calli was oblivious; all she knew or was conscious of at that moment was his hand on the small of her back.

It didn't take long for Paolo to recognize the effect that

he was having on Calli. It was hard for her to hide it. She hadn't been exactly blatant, she thought with a slight sense of embarrassment back in her hotel room later that night, but she hadn't been too subtle about it either. *But* she was a grown woman, for heaven's sake. She was free. She had no need to justify her actions. She could do anything she wanted. Above all, she told herself, it was time she felt the surge of sexual desire run through her veins – she had been too long without it. If sex was one of the secrets of longevity, then she wanted plenty of it. She wanted to live again, and she intended to do that for a good while yet.

She'd had plenty of boyfriends when she was younger but it had been a while since then, she'd been with James so long she had forgotten the thrill of a new romance. Besides, Paolo was no 'boy', he was very much a man. He was forty-two, he told her, and although he had never married, he had a seven-year-old daughter called Anna, with a woman who was now one of his best friends.

'Serena and I lived together for three years after the baby was born,' he said later that evening as they sat under the vine with the circle of friends during their usual dinner at the taverna. 'Then we realized we want different things: I want to go to India, she wants to be in Milan; I want to teach yoga, she wants to paint . . . It is better to be free – now it is good for all of us.'

Calli sat silently absorbing this information from him

as alarm bells began to ring in her head. *How is that good?* a voice in her head nagged. *What of the child? How is that good for* her *without her father? Is Paolo another irresponsible quitter?*

'Well, yes, freedom is good, but it also has its price,' Calli suddenly heard Maya interrupt as if she had read her mind. 'I know that you and Serena do the best for your girl, my friend, but there are many who don't, and there is always a cost.'

Paolo sat back in his chair, and before replying he gave Maya a long lingering look. 'I think *you* of all people, as Anna's godmother and my good friend, must know very well that my daughter always comes first.'

'Yes,' the older woman retorted with a smile, 'I do know that, but then I believe you are something of an exception, my friend.'

Calli, watching them, wondered if perhaps Maya's little sermon had been for her benefit. Had she sensed Calli's attraction to Paolo and wanted to make a point of emphasizing that Paolo was a good man? She wouldn't have been surprised if that was true. The woman seemed to sense so much else about her, she was a regular little sorceress – so why not this? Her mother always boasted that she could predict the future in dreams and in the coffee cup, but Maya was something else. Her name alone, Calli suddenly realized, sounded like the Greek word for *magic*. This new friend of hers, she thought with wry amusement, was like a modern-day Circe, goddess of magic, the daughter of the mighty Titan Helios.

'Drink up, everyone!' someone suddenly called out and stood up. 'A toast to the moon!' he cheered, lifting his glass.

'And to love!' a voice from the other end of the table added. And they all raised their glasses in agreement, eager to continue with the previous night's festivities, putting an end to the conversation which was beginning to become a little too sombre for the occasion. More wine was brought to the table, after which *Kyrios* Tassos, the owner of the taverna, appeared from the kitchen carrying a guitar in one hand and a bottle of *raki* in the other. Not long after he was followed by his son-in-law, who had an accordion slung over his left shoulder and was dragging a couple of chairs to the table.

'Time for song,' the old man shouted, and sat down.

'We are all in for a treat.' Sylvie clapped her hands, shifting to make space for the two men.

As soon as the music and singing began, a sweet wave of nostalgia washed over Calli, bringing to mind warm Cretan evenings under the stars in her grandparents' garden. Aunts and uncles, cousins and neighbours, all eating, drinking, singing and dancing. There had been countless memorable nights like that during her summer visits to her beloved grandmother's house. Children playing hide and seek with a myriad of places to hide, women diving in and out of the kitchen with plates of food while the men, when enough *raki* had been consumed, would bring out the musical instruments and the assembled company would sit down and start to sing – the Cretan harp, she remembered, had been her brother's favourite. The little boy was capable of sitting transfixed, listening to his uncle play for hours; later, when he was older, he tried to learn it.

Eleni would take the children to stay at her mother's house for the entire summer. Sometimes Calli and her brother would be sent on ahead while Keith would join them later with Eleni and stay for as long as his work permitted. Calli remembered her excitement as the summer holidays approached, knowing she would be spending carefree weeks in the sun and sea and have her every whim granted by her *yiayia*. In the absence of Keith's mother, who had died before she was born, the little girl adored her Greek grandmother, so much so that when she died Calli refused to go back to Crete for years, much to Eleni's despair.

'What about your *bappou* and *Thia* Froso?' she pleaded. 'They want to see you.' The old man and her sister were still living in the family house, but Calli couldn't imagine the house or the village without her *yiayia*. She loved her grandfather well enough and her *thia* Froso was nice, if a little overbearing. In fact, the sadness of losing her *yiayia* followed Calli through to adulthood and she maintained a warm affection for old ladies, always looking for a grand-mother substitute.

'You can share my grandma if you want,' Josie had offered when they first met at school, sealing their friend-ship for life. Josie's Jamaican family seemed not unlike Calli's own Cretan relatives, and her friend's grandmother ran the household and looked after Josie and her siblings in a familiar way. There were plenty of similarities in the generous meals, love, laughter and the old women's ample size.

That balmy Ikarian night brought Calli's childhood mem-ories flooding back, and when *Kyria* Erini finally freed herself from her kitchen duties and joined them, she fancied that one of her older relatives could be sitting across the table from her. A plump, lively and mischievous-looking woman, she sat as close to her husband as she could, their knees touching as she joined in the singing with as much *kefi* – zest – as the two men. 'We eat well, we sleep well, and we love well here,' she had told Calli with a wink earlier that day when she interviewed her. This woman had many characteristics that were reminiscent of the women in Crete, Calli thought, especially her easy way of exploding into laughter, making the younger woman all the more nostalgic. Perhaps it was time to pay them a visit – it had been a long time since she had last visited her relatives there. Her grandfather was long gone but her *thia*

Froso was still living on her own in the old house. She felt a pang of guilt when she thought of her aunt – a kind woman who had shown far more love towards her than she had ever reciprocated. Ikaria wasn't so far from Crete. She could easily pop over once she had finished her assignment, perhaps persuade her mum to join her. They could make the return journey to the island together. Mother and daughter both deserved a break.

There was much genial bonhomie at the taverna that night; the group seemed to linger on even longer than usual, reluctant to break the spell, until the musicians at last decided it was time for them all to head for their beds.

'Shall we take a walk on the beach?' Paolo asked Calli, reaching for her hand as they stepped onto the road. The silver moon played on the water, and high up in the sky Mars glowed like an orange beacon of light.

'Do you remember ever seeing Mars so clear and so bright?' he asked, slipping his arm around her waist as they walked along the shore.

9

The attraction between them was electric. They strolled along the shore holding hands, talking and laughing and sat until late under the night sky. Calli felt like a young girl again, the pain and heartache that had been weighing so heavily on her for so many months seemed to wash away, cleansing her like waves over a rock.

As the night wore on, her earlier concerns that Paolo might perhaps be made from similar stuff to James vanished, blown away by the night breeze. The more he spoke of his life, the more Calli was reassured that he bore no likeness to her ex.

'You see, Calli,' he said, folding his arms behind his head and lying back on the warm sand, 'when I'm not working, I spend most of my spare time with Anna.'

'But you are not working now,' she challenged him, 'so, why isn't she with you?'

'When I come here, it is the time when Serena takes our daughter to see her grandparents in Tuscany. But when I go back to Verona, she will be with me,' he began to explain, his voice pensive and serious. 'When we realized

Serena was pregnant, we both knew that our lives would change for ever. It was a question of duty and responsibility . . . I believe when there is a child, we must grow up, we are not the children anymore.' He sat up to look at her. 'You understand what I am saying, Calli?' She understood perfectly well, she didn't need to ask or he to tell her more.

When at last they left the beach, Paolo walked her back to the hotel but neither of them wanted the night to end. They sat on the terrace and continued talking till the first blush of dawn appeared on the horizon.

Paolo seemed to be as taken with Calli as she was with him. This half-Greek, half-English woman was unlike any other he had been involved with. She had the look of a Mediterranean woman – soulful dark eyes, a mass of dark curls which framed a pale face, giving her an air of fragility and vulnerability. Yet her appearance belied her manner of quiet confidence and assurance. He liked that contrast. She was creative, she came from a different world from his, unlike most of the women he had been romantically connected with in the past who had been from his circle, interested in spiritual matters, needing reassurance, searching, looking for the elusive. Calli's feet seemed firmly connected to the ground, she seemed to know what she wanted from her life, and where she was going.

Earlier in the evening she had been curious about him and had encouraged him to talk about his life; now it was his turn to find out who she was.

'A child is a precious gift,' he told her softly after she had finished talking. He moved closer and took her hand. 'It is a gift that should be cherished,' he said again, visibly moved by her story, and gave her a tender kiss on the lips.

She woke to the sound of laughter and the insistent ringing of her mobile. Flicking open the handset, she heard her editor's raspy voice invading the bedroom.

'Hey, Calli, how's it going?' David asked, causing her to wake instantly and snap into action. 'Got a suntan yet?' he jested.

'Yes . . . fine, all good,' she replied, trying to control her first-thing-in-the-morning voice, hoping it sounded less croaky down the phone than it did in her head.

'How's the piece going? Found out some secrets yet?' he continued cheerfully.

'Yes, well . . . some,' she said, trying to sound professional. 'Should have the piece finished soon.'

'Cool! No worries, it's not due till the end of the week. I was just checking how you are,' he told her. Calli hadn't been on the island that long, yet London seemed to be a thousand miles away from her physically and mentally.

Looking at the clock on the TV facing her bed, she was shocked to discover that once again it was way past midday. No wonder David had called, thinking she must be up and about and working. Throwing the bedclothes aside she ran to the balcony and stepped outside. A jovial group of people were drinking coffee on the terrace below, evidently it was their laughter that had woken her. Before parting with Paolo she had agreed to meet him for a swim, for which she now realized she was all too late. She scanned the beach in the hope of spotting him but all she saw was a group of elderly men and women in high spirits who were noisily emerging from the sea after completing their daily dip. Calli had been told about this ritual, which was apparently observed without fail by most elderly Ikarians.

'This island is full of wonder and magic,' Paolo had told her the night before. 'Not only does it have in my opinion the most pure beaches in the Mediterranean; some areas are like natural spas which are a cure for many ailments.'

Apparently, Paolo had said, in some places around the coast hot mineral springs flowed into the sea from the shoreline, creating natural therapeutic spas. 'Another reason why these people all live forever here,' he laughed.

The enticing aroma of coffee and cheerful chatter wafted up to her room from the hotel terrace, urging Calli to make haste and get dressed. She might have been too late to go swimming with Paolo, but she was still in plenty of time for her next interview, with the local doctor, which Maya had volunteered to arrange for her. 'Talking to a medic could be interesting for your story,' she had suggested during dinner, and Dr Demitriou, who was a great believer in herbal medicine, was in her opinion the perfect candidate.

Calli threw on clean clothes, gathered her equipment in record time, and dashed down to the lobby to meet her friend as arranged, anxious not to keep her waiting as well as eager to talk to her about Paolo.

'Dr Demitriou is a very personable man,' Maya said as they made their way to see the doctor, 'and although he is the only physician around for miles, he always has time for everyone.'

They found him waiting by the front door of his surgery-cum-office. The doctor was taller and younger than most of the people Calli had interviewed so far. He had sparkling eyes, a friendly face and a head of unruly brown hair.

'Welcome! Come in, please!' He greeted them with a broad smile and ushered them into a large room flooded with sunlight and sound from a host of cicadas that had taken occupancy on every tree and bush in the vicinity of the house, and seemed to have decided at that very moment to start singing in unison. Calli smiled to herself: how unlike this surgery was from any she had ever visited in London. The picture window facing the garden was wide open and let in not only the sounds from outside, but also a warm breeze that drifted in, carrying with it the sweet aroma of jasmine and herbs. Yet, looking around, she observed that it was as well-equipped as any surgery she had ever seen.

'It is quiet at this hour,' Dr Demitriou explained, offering the women a couple of chairs under the ceiling fan. 'It is of course the hottest part of the day and even with the breeze from the window we still need more air,' he said apologetically. 'If you had come just a little earlier you would have met some of my patients waiting to see me – not that I have many in any one day.' He smiled. 'By now everyone is getting ready for their siesta after their lunch, or perhaps their breakfast if they got up late,' he chuckled. 'You might have guessed that nobody is in a hurry here, taking it slow means fewer accidents, fewer falls or broken bones.' He smiled broadly.

This easy slow pace of life, Dr Demitriou claimed, was a significant reason why people lived such long and healthy lives on Ikaria. Their love of sleep and their diet, he also believed, were the two main causes behind this phenomenon.

'Everything they eat is organic, and they consume a lot of olive oil, honey and local wine,' he explained. 'They grow all their own produce, and above all,' he said with certainty, 'I am convinced that this local mountain tea which they drink on a daily basis is a huge factor.'

'I have always been a strong advocate of this,' Maya said, glancing at Calli and nodding in agreement.

'There are many varieties of local mountain tea, or perhaps a better word is infusions,' the doctor continued, 'and they all have their particular qualities. What I find amusing is that people drink it and relish it as a delicious beverage without consciously thinking it is medicinal, but then again I believe they *do* know. They know it instinctively and that is the beauty of it and the reason why, if they are suffering from a certain ailment, they always recognize which herb to use as a remedy. I honestly think this knowledge is in their collective consciousness, passed down to them through the generations.'

'What did I tell you?' Maya said as they left the doctor's surgery and made their way to the beach bar. 'He knows the local people better than anyone.'

Calli was in complete agreement that Dr Demitriou's stories of local life would be an excellent addition to her article. All the same, just now she didn't want to talk about him. What was topmost in her mind was to ask her friend about Paolo – after all, she seemed to know him better than anyone else there.

'He is a good man,' Maya told her with sincerity in her voice. 'We've been friends for many years, and I love him as if he was my brother. He is an old spirit, that one, he's been on this planet many times before.' Calli stared at the older woman with perplexity, wondering, as so often since they had met, what she was talking about.

'Er . . . yes, well . . .' she murmured, ignoring Maya's cryptic words and eager to continue with her questions. 'What I wanted to ask you was . . . you know what you told me the other night?' She hesitated, her tone tentative. 'Remember that wish you said I should ask Raphael?'

She reached for her drink and took a sip, her mouth suddenly very dry. 'Do you think this . . . I mean Paolo might be the answer to my plea?' she heard herself say – and could hardly believe her own ears as the words came out of her mouth. Could this be the same Calli who had always approached life with firm logic and pragmatism, for whom metaphysical fancies and the supernatural had no place in the world?

Maya swivelled round on her stool and fixed Calli with her eyes before answering.

'*You*, my friend, don't know it yet, but *you* have been granted a rare gift. What you experienced the other night was a potent and rare thing. Paolo has come into your life for a reason. When I first met you, all I saw was pain and loss in your eyes. Now I see something else, something quite different.'

Calli held her breath and waited for her to continue.

10

Maya inhaled deeply, shifted a little closer and reached for the younger woman's hand.

'What I see now, my friend, is a fruitful journey ahead of you, a long and winding road with gain and reward at the end of it.' Calli sat listening, rooted to the spot, her senses on edge. 'I am well aware that you are by nature an inquisitive and thoughtful person; it is your trait as an Aquarian.'

Once again, the younger woman stared in disbelief; she did not recall ever mentioning her date of birth or her horoscope to anyone since arriving on Ikaria.

'Don't look so amazed, Calli, my dear,' Maya burst out laughing, 'I just know these things. But the point I am making is that although by nature you are sceptical you are also able to pick up things quickly and you have an innate curiosity for that which you don't quite understand, which is a great asset.' As with so much that Calli had been exposed to since arriving on the island, astrology was of no interest to her and she was at a loss to understand how her date of birth was relevant to the question she had just posed.

'I suppose what I am saying,' Maya continued, seeing the impatience in Calli's eyes, 'is that given your natural curiosity about people, and Paolo's good heart, spending time with him will be beneficial and enlightening for you.'

Calli hardly needed to hear more. This was all the validation she had wanted. Her Ikarian oracle had spoken and had just given her, even if a little sketchy, the go-ahead to trust her instinct. Horoscopes, roads ahead and cosmic journeys were other matters that could wait: all she heard was that Paolo was a good man and, what's more, that he would be good for her. She was a grown woman, but to herself at that moment she felt like a teenage girl about to embark on her first sexual encounter and it was all too thrilling. Lately she had been stuck in the past and apprehensive about the future; it was time for her to start enjoying the here and now.

The two women sat at the beach bar for a little longer until Calli made her way to her hotel room to work, and Maya to an olive grove to help with the picking. Calli had been transcribing each interview and editing photographs each day as she gathered her material. Now the piece was beginning to take shape and she was able to assess that before too long the process would be complete. She had made up her mind that as soon as the article was finished and had been emailed to David, she would have a splendid holiday, the kind she hadn't had for a long, long, time.

*

She met Paolo at the beach for their allocated yoga lesson. She had tried to take a siesta after she stopped working but found it impossible to fall asleep or relax. Her mind swirled with unsettling thoughts, not the kind she had been experiencing recently that had made her ache with sadness – no. The thoughts that flashed through her mind now were making her body tingle with what she recognized as sexual desire, fuelled further by images of Paolo's hands on her body. Eventually she gave up trying to impose sleep on herself and made her way to an empty beach; it was the time for rest, and there were still a couple of hours before she was due to meet Paolo, so she welcomed the opportunity to be alone for a while. For days now Calli had been surrounded by people and although she enjoyed the distraction and relished the company of her new friends, she realized that she also needed a little time alone.

She paced along the deserted shore and plunged into the warm waters of the Aegean. She let herself drift, arms outstretched, eyes closed, surrendering her body to the sea, which in turn evoked a sweet childhood memory. As a child she had had trouble allowing herself to float on the water until her father took it upon himself to teach her. 'Relax, Calli, trust me,' Keith's voice drifted to her ears in the wind. At first her child's body, tense and afraid, refused to relax and float. 'I am right here, I'm holding you, don't be afraid. I would never let you go!' Keith reassured, banishing her fears. How comforting those words of his had been, and true to his words her father had never let go of her, nor had he ever let her down. Floating now in the calm water, the hot sunlight beating red through her closed eyelids, Calli was filled with a surge of love towards both of her parents; having Keith as a father, she realized, was not only a blessing but also the reason why she had always been able to trust so readily. James might not have been worthy of her trust, but others were, and she would not. allow him to change that which was her nature.

That evening's yoga session was a deeply charged experience. The stretching, relaxing and breathing made her acutely aware of and in tune with her body. She was no stranger to sensuality, having always been a physical sort of woman, and looking back she realized, perhaps all too late, that sex had probably been the strongest bond between her and James, along with their single-mindedness about their work and self-indulgent lifestyle – hardly a basis for building a family life together if that's all there is.

After yoga was over, Paolo took Calli by the hand and led her away from the beach. 'Come,' he whispered, 'I know another place where we can see the moon rise . . . just you and me.' She followed in a hypnotic trance, her body tense with anticipation. Holding her hand tightly, he led her up a small hill where a pile of giant stones heaped on top of one another stood in much the same way as the boulders that Calli had found so enthralling a few days earlier.

'We have a perfect view to the sea from here,' he said, sitting at the foot of the rocks, pointing to the horizon where the moon would soon be making its appearance. He reached for her and gently pulled her towards him; as she fell, his arms engulfed her, and they rolled onto the soft earth.

Paolo was a gentle and thoughtful lover, all the while they made love murmuring words in Italian, tender, sensual, inaudible words which she wouldn't have understood even if she could distinguish them, but all adding to her pleasure.

The days that followed were blissful. They spent as much time with each other as they could and when Calli at last concluded that her article was finished, he helped her to choose which photographs she should email to the paper.

'You are a very talented woman, *tesoro*,' he said, kissing her bare shoulder as he sat next to her in the hotel bedroom in front of her laptop. 'Beautiful and talented, what an intoxicating combination!' Paolo was doing wonders for restoring Calli's self-esteem and confidence; she had been badly bruised, and he was like a healing balm to her wounds.

'Must you go now your work is done?' he asked, taking her hand. 'Can you stay with me until I leave?' his eyes pleaded. When she first met him, she had said that she would be there for as long as it took to complete her assignment; now he was hoping he might entice her to stay longer. He needn't have worried: Calli had already made up her mind she was not going anywhere just yet.

'Yes, Paolo. I shall stay until you leave,' she replied and turned round to kiss him. 'Besides, my editor has asked for a few amendments to my article so I'm not free of this work just yet, another day or so and I'll be done and then I'll be totally free.'

Once her work was completed, Calli was able to focus on having the holiday and pure enjoyment she so badly needed. She continued to stay in the hotel but would spend some nights in Paolo's tent which made their liaison feel all the more youthful and exciting. The only time she had ever been camping was during the summer when she had finished her A-levels. She had set off with a crowd of friends to a camping site in the Costa del Sol. It was rough and ready, disorganized and chaotic, but it was the best fun she had ever had and the first time she tasted the joys of sex. Steve had been a friend who she quite fancied and who apparently lusted after her, so when they had found themselves in the heady atmosphere of sun, sea and alcohol, seduction and falling in love wasn't difficult, and Calli decided that by the time she returned home she was not going to be a virgin any longer.

Sex in Paolo's tent had all the erotic nuances of 'first

love', and when they wanted a little more space and a soak in a bathtub like grown-ups they would transfer to Calli's hotel room. The days followed one another effortlessly and the two lovers basked in each other's proximity. Maya and his other friends often joined them for a swim in the bay and each evening they all had dinner together in *Kyria* Erini's taverna.

Paolo suggested that the two of them hire a couple of bicycles and volunteered to show Calli some remote parts of the island that she could simply enjoy at leisure now that David had approved her article. When they weren't soaking up the sun on some hidden cove and swimming with dolphins, he involved Calli in his allocated jobs around the island – picking grapes, watering vegetable gardens – and continued teaching her yoga.

'You're getting pretty good, *tesoro*,' he praised her. 'Do you see how the natural balance returns when you practise often?' It was true; Calli was indeed enjoying her daily lessons on the beach and could see that she was improving, but she couldn't in all honesty say which factor was restoring her equilibrium. Was it the yoga or the sex that was making her face glow and left her feeling like singing most of the time? Whichever it was, the effect was spectacular. She hadn't felt so alive, so carefree and joyous in years.

'So, *tesoro*,' Paolo had said one day as they sat under the shade of an olive tree, taking a break from watering a plot

planted with cucumbers, courgettes and succulent tomatoes, 'when you go back home will you come and visit us
in Verona? It is beautiful, it is the city of passion, the city
of Romeo and Giulietta, and I know Anna will love
you . . .' he continued cheerfully. 'Then later me and Anna
can come visit you in your London too, no?'

'Er . . . yes . . .' Calli started to reply. 'I'm sure I would
love her too . . .' her voice trailed off as she reached down
by her side for her bottle of water, aware that a surprising
hesitancy stopped her from saying more. As she drank,
buying a little time before continuing, she knew that her
reluctance had not been because she didn't want to meet
Paolo's daughter, but because England at that moment felt
further away than the moon and she had absolutely no
desire to think about London or make any plans for the
future.

Sensing her hesitation, Paolo too reached for his bottle
of water, took a sip, then sprang to his feet and with a
smile took Calli's hand and pulled her up.

'OK! Let's go,' he said cheerfully, putting an end to the
awkwardness of the moment. 'We must carry on with
the watering, there's still much to do.' They spent the
afternoon in good humour working on the land and
neither of them mentioned the subject again. However,
over the next few days they both considered their reaction
to what had been said that morning. Paolo found that he
was as surprised by his suggestion as Calli had been by

her reaction. As a rule, he was not a man given to making too many plans and certainly not, where his daughter was concerned, with other people. There had been very few women with whom he had been romantically involved that he considered fit to introduce to his family. Calli, he mused, had apparently touched him in a way he did not expect, but Paolo was an intuitive man and understood that what he felt was not necessarily reciprocated. He hadn't spent decades studying eastern philosophies and self-awareness not to detect another person's feelings.

For her part, given her initial enthusiasm about Paolo, Calli was equally perplexed at what it was that held her back from venturing further into his life. Meeting his daughter didn't feel right. She considered it to be a big commitment, a step too far, and she was not ready for it. She loved spending time with Paolo – he was good company, she found him kind, good-natured and intriguing and enjoyed making love with him – but she had come to realize that her feelings went no further than that. If there was one thing she had learned recently, it was to listen to her inner voice. She had spent too many years going along with what she *thought* she needed, what she *willed* herself to want, confusing sexual attraction with love, too eager to please others, imagining that by doing so she was also pleasing herself. Paolo was a good man, he was indeed the healing salve to her wounds. He was helping her to recover, he was the transition from sadness to joy and she was loving spending a carefree summer with him. Yet her inner voice was telling her that what she now needed and wanted was something different, something else, and Paolo was not *it*. From now on she pledged to follow her instinct and hear that inner voice which so often spoke to her but which she had mostly chosen to ignore.

11

'Do you remember what I said when you asked me to give you my assessment of Paolo?' Maya asked Calli while they walked along the beach one afternoon. 'Does it make sense to you now?'

'I *do* and it *does*,' Calli replied, linking her arm through her friend's as they splashed their way through the shallow surf. 'It took me a little while, but I now understand. As you said, Paolo has been both *beneficial* and *enlightening* for me. I see that now.'

'I am pleased, Calli dear; you have learned to listen to yourself,' Maya replied. 'You have learned to understand, not so much what you want, because often we don't know that until we find it, but what it is that you don't want. Paolo has been good for you, that's obvious. You've blossomed through your friendship with him and your spirit has returned . . . but you have discovered that he's not what you are really looking for, is he?' Calli could not disagree. Talking to Maya, being able to voice her feelings, brought clarity to her thoughts.

She had enjoyed every minute of her time in Ikaria but

now in less than a week this summer idyll would end. Paolo would be leaving for Italy to collect his daughter and continue with his life, and Calli, who had been thinking increasingly of delaying her return to London, was now wavering between island-hopping for a few weeks longer, or perhaps going to Crete. Her decision was finally made for her when she received an unexpected email from her mother while sitting in a cafe.

Calli darling, your dad and I are on our way to the Lake District but just this morning I got a message from my cousin Eleftheria to tell me that my sister is not well at all. You know your thia Froso, she wouldn't tell us anything about it, not wanting to trouble us – but as you are not so far away, could you please go and visit the family in Crete and find out what's going on? I'll come immediately if you think I should . . .

As soon as she was back in her hotel room, Calli called Eleni. Of course she would go, no question about it. Besides, mother and daughter had talked of taking a holiday together after Calli recovered, had discussed the possibility of a joint trip to Crete to visit *Thia* Froso and the rest of the family.

'Do you know what's wrong with her?' Calli asked.

'Not really, Eleftheria didn't elaborate. Probably Froso swore her to secrecy. I can't imagine it's *that* serious. If it was, she would have contacted us earlier.'

Perhaps this wasn't quite how Calli had envisaged the rest of her holiday, but Crete was only a hop and skip away from Ikaria and it made perfect sense; she had to go, of course she would, and Eleni would follow. Meantime, she thought, she still had some days left to spend with Paolo and the rest of her new friends and she wanted to make the most of them. She had met some extraordinary people on this enchanting mythical blue zone of an island, and the friendships that had been formed during her time there she was certain would continue for a lifetime.

'So, tell me about Crete,' Paolo said to Calli one morning as they lay languidly after a swim on a smooth white rock that jutted into the sea like a pier. 'Is it beautiful like Ikaria?'

'It's beautiful, but different,' she replied, raising herself on her elbow to turn and look at him. 'It's quite wild, the landscape I mean, and the village where my relatives come from is quite remote. There is sea and there are mountains and you can go to both with equal ease. And the people are all . . . How can I describe them? I guess intense is one word, but loving, too.'

'Tell me more about the people,' Paolo said, rolling onto his side too, their faces so close their noses were almost touching. He moved even closer and gently kissed the tip of her nose. 'I shall miss you, *tesoro*,' he said, his voice a whisper.

'I will miss you too,' she replied and meant it. What she

felt for Paolo was great tenderness and more. In the past, when she had fallen in love, sex would inevitably follow and when sex came into the mix her feelings would become charged: more anxious, a little insecure and unsettled. But with Paolo, what followed after making love with him and what she sensed at that moment was a tranquil affection, of a kind that comes with untainted friendship. She could not remember ever having such relaxed and tender emotions for someone that she had been sexually involved with. He, she decided, had been sent to her not only to help her heal but to show her another way. She looked at Paolo's face and tried to take a mental photograph, to imprint his features in her memory one by one so that at some point in the future, wherever she might be, she would be able to recall them *and* this moment.

'I feel that our paths will always cross, our friendship will last,' he said as if in agreement, as if he guessed her thoughts, and pulled her to him. They made love on the smooth white rock surrounded by the blue Ikarian sea to the sound of the seagulls circling above them and the breaking waves around them.

'So, tell me about the people in your grandmother's village?' he asked again afterwards as they lay sleepily in each other's arms, heat emanating from the rock, limbs heavy from their love-making.

'There are many relatives . . . you know how it is, you are Italian!' she laughed. 'But most of the old ones have gone now . . . my grandmother was the head of the family.'

'Yes, my *nonna* too,' Paolo said, 'from my mother's side, she was a wonderful wise woman; she died when I was seventeen.'

'I was almost twelve when mine went,' Calli mused.

'What about cousins, do you have cousins?'

'Yeah, plenty of those too.' She smiled with the memory of their multitude. 'My brother and I used to play with some of them when we were young, but I haven't seen any of them for ages.'

'I know,' Paolo let out a sigh. 'My family live in Villa-franca di Verona. It's really close to Verona, but I don't go as often as I should; always too busy, always travelling . . .'

'It's my auntie, my mother's sister, I feel guilty about,' Calli said as she stretched her arms above her head. 'She is getting old and all alone and now she is not well. I haven't seen her in years.'

'It is good that you will make the journey then,' Paolo said and reached across to stroke her hair.

The days that followed, before everyone departed from Ikaria, were as celebratory as the 'blood moon' festivities had been when she first arrived. Each evening's gathering on the beach became a boisterous party with food, drink and music and promises always to keep in touch. Calli would be the first to leave, now that she had made new travelling arrangements. Although she was excited about the second part of her journey, she was also sad that this surprising voyage of hers had come to an end.

'You are heading towards a new adventure, my friend,' Maya told her as they sat with Sylvie and some others on the beach the night before she left. 'You are going to the place where Icarus and his father started their journey. The Ikarian myth does not end here . . . it follows you.'

'I'll miss you, dear Calli,' Sylvie said. 'Meeting you has been such a pleasure. You must come and see us. Berlin is not Ikaria, but it's a wonderful city.'

'No need for heavy hearts, my friends,' Maya told them both, 'we shall all meet again soon . . . I know!' Calli turned to look at her and, as always, wondered what it was that this extraordinary woman professed she knew. 'We will all be visiting you in Crete before too long,' Maya continued with a beaming smile, 'by next spring we will all be together again, I am sure of it.'

'Count me in!' Sylvie said and clapped her hands. 'I've always wanted to visit Crete.'

'OK then, let's make a deal, let's shake on it,' Calli told them with delight and stretched out her arm. 'Let's promise that wherever we all are and whatever we are doing we will meet up in Crete next spring.'

'It's a deal and I promise,' Sylvie said, shaking Calli's hand vigorously.

'The friendships that blossom on this island are for keeps,' said Maya and put her arms around the two women sitting on either side of her. 'Spring in Crete, then, it is!'

The next morning the older woman insisted on taking Calli to the airport in her little car.

'You really don't have to do that,' she protested.' It's a long journey and I can take a taxi just as I did when I arrived.'

'I won't hear of it,' Maya reassured her. 'Besides, we can enjoy a few more hours together and it will give me a chance to look around the town after I've dropped you off.'

The return journey to the airport proved to be much more enjoyable than Calli's arrival. Maya's driving was a far cry from old Theo's, and since the two friends had allowed plenty of time, they stopped for a picnic. Maya parked the car and led Calli down a gentle slope towards a giant boulder invisible from the road.

'I find this particular rock formation very majestic,' Maya said, spreading a cloth under its shade. She delved into the picnic basket and brought out freshly baked village bread, cheese, black grapes, ripe red tomatoes and juicy green olives. They ate with relish and after they had finished their meal they lay back on the warm earth, savouring the gentle breeze and the sound of the cicadas. Suddenly Maya sat up and turned to look at Calli. 'You must walk forward and only look ahead,' she said, snapping the younger woman out of her gentle drowsiness. 'Turning back will do you no good. Look only to the future,' she told her and reached for the flask of coffee to pour them both a drink. 'Until we meet again, my friend,' she said, smiling, and raised her cup to her lips.

12

Crete, 2018

Calli's flight touched down at Heraklion airport in the early evening. The sky was streaked in swirls of pink, the air fragrant and familiar. Whenever she and James had arrived on the island, they would either take a taxi or hire a car and drive to the village, although it would have given Calli far more pleasure to see some of the familiar faces of her family waiting at the Arrivals gate as they had always done when she was a child. He had never wanted that – he couldn't be doing with their intensity, their fussing, their emotional reunions – so she complied.

This time her cousin Costis was there to greet her. She had sent a text to tell him she was coming and his jubilation at the news of her arrival was touching. *I hope you are not going to refuse me again*, he replied immediately. *I'll be there to collect you. Send me your flight details.* She had been out of touch for a long time and guilt rose in her throat as she messaged him back. Costis was not much older than Calli and she had always been fond of him; after her grandmother he was her favourite relative. They had been close as children, had spent each summer together when his two 'English' cousins visited Crete. He had been protective of both Calli and Alex, who were something of a novelty among the other children in the village; he had felt proud and privileged to have such exciting relatives visiting from England. Even though both siblings spoke perfectly good Greek, Costis relished teaching them the Cretan dialect spiced with certain words deemed unsuitable for children of their age. 'Where did you learn to say that?!' a furious Eleni would often shout, inevitably turning to scold the rascal culprit. But that was all such a long time ago – Costis had a wife she'd never met and two young children now and was running the family grocery store in the village. Yet whenever the cousins met their childhood connection was ignited and Calli could spot that same mischievous glint in his eye.

'Calliope! Over here!' she heard Costis call out her name in full, the Greek way, the name of her grandmother. He spotted her looking around for him among a crowd of visitors and ran smiling towards her. 'Welcome back, my little cousin,' he said, engulfing her in a warm embrace and landing a loud kiss on each cheek. 'How long has it been?'

'Too long!' she said, kissing him back.

The drive to the village reminded her of the taxi ride

she had made a few weeks previously in Ikaria. As they left the airport and headed for the hills the sea behind them shimmered in the evening light, reflecting shades of gold, and the undulating land was covered with olive groves as far as the eye could see. The city of Heraklion stretching across the valley rose like a concrete forest and she was glad to leave it behind and begin the ascent through the hills towards the village. When she was young her grandfather would pick them up from the airport along with her *yiayia* and *Thia* Froso, who would often insist on coming along too. Then they would all be squashed into the car like sardines and either she or Alex or both would have to sit on an adult's lap, with the result that as the road snaked through the mountains one or other child would start to feel carsick. But of course, as soon as they arrived at their destination the discomfort was all worthwhile and both children forgot about their nausea. On those summer visits long ago, as they drove into the village, more often than not some of the local kids who considered Calli and her brother a source of curiosity and amusement would spot the car and start running after them. They would chase them up the hill to the house, where other relatives and friends would have gathered to welcome them.

'So please tell me, how is *Thia* Froso?' she asked Costis, surprised that he had not yet raised the subject.

'You probably don't realize it, but you couldn't have

come at a better time,' he replied as he masterfully manoeuvred yet another hairpin bend over a steep ravine.

'I think I do . . .' she replied, not sure if he was referring to her aunt's illness. 'It's *Thia* Froso, she's not well, right?'

'Oh! You know about it . . . I wasn't sure if you did,' he said as he flicked his cigarette ash out of the open window. 'My mother spends quite a lot of time with her lately, taking her to the hospital etc.'

'Yes, I know, your mother sent my mother an email about it. That's why I am here now . . . I thought I mentioned it in my text.'

'You probably did, but I was so pleased you were coming I forgot.'

'What's wrong with her?' Calli asked, wondering why her cousin seemed so unconcerned. 'Will she be all right?' Calli tried to extract some kind of information from him.

'I don't know. She seems fine to me,' he replied, turning to look at her. 'I tell you one thing: she was over the moon when she heard you were coming.'

They found Froso waiting in the yard, sitting at the wooden table under the shade of two old olive trees in front of the house. She knew that Costis was picking Calli up from the airport and was anxiously waiting for her. She had been up since early morning baking and preparing all of her niece's favourite food. She had a soft spot for Calli, who reminded her of her own young self before life became a hardship. She had always thought that as a child her sister's daughter possessed the same energy, the same defiant spirit that both she and Eleni had had at that age. But Froso's spirit had been crushed early; she had to grow up fast and learn to be responsible. Being so much older than her brother and sister, she had to pull her weight around the house and help her mother with bringing up her siblings.

She loved both children, her niece and her nephew, in equal measure; little Alex was always tender and sweet and displayed his affection for her openly, and although young Calli reserved her love exclusively for her grand-mother it made no difference to her aunt.

'She'll grow out of it,' Eleni would tell her sister when the girl refused to come to Crete with her anymore and she would arrive only with Alex. 'She'll come when she's ready. You know how stubborn she is.'

When Calli did at last return, she had just completed her first year at art school and had taken a month off to travel around Greece with a couple of friends to take photographs for her college project. Crete had been on their itinerary and their arrival on the island flooded her with a sweet nostalgia, reminding her of the happy summers she had spent there with her family. Calli's decision to leave her friends behind and head for the old village was spontaneous and easy to make. She hadn't seen any of her relatives since she was twelve, and while the half-a-dozen years that had passed since then might not have made a significant impact on the place or on her aunt and grandfather, for Calli they had been transformational. The old man was a little more lame and a lot more hard of hearing. Her uncle Androulios, her mother's brother, had died in a car accident a couple of years before but *Thia* Froso was there, still good-looking and robust even if her hair was now flecked with silver. Calli, on the other hand, was a brand-new person. Gone was the lanky girl on the verge of moody teenagehood or the lively seven-year-old who would have swum in the sea from morning to dusk if they had allowed it. She was now a beautiful, composed young woman with a camera around her neck and regret in her heart for leaving it for so long to visit these good people who loved her.

After that first trip Calli would return regularly, until she met James; then her visits became sparse once more.

'There are so many other places in the world to visit apart from Crete,' he would complain to her, and she, like a fool, would indulge him as ever.

Seeing her aunt now under the familiar olive trees in that fragrant garden of her childhood, she felt a sense of belonging, a sense of freedom. All she had to think about now was herself, no James and his preferences, his idio-syncrasies and his capricious demands on her time, always feeling responsible for him. Now she was free to do as she pleased, be with whom she wanted to, go wherever she chose and stay as long as she desired.

'Calliope *mou*!' her aunt called as soon as she caught sight of her approaching the garden gate. Rising to her feet she hurried towards her visitor with open arms. 'Welcome, my blessed child,' she said, embracing her and showering her with kisses. 'Come, sit, let me look at you, you are as beautiful as ever.'

Thia Froso looked well, Calli thought, stealing glances at her while they talked. As her aunt stood up to go into the house to fetch some refreshments, she watched her move without effort and stride towards the kitchen door.

'She looks perfectly OK.' She turned to Costis with relief. 'I was fearful of how I would find her.'

'I only know what my mother tells me,' he replied with a shrug, 'and she told me she hadn't been too well, but who knows? People exaggerate, don't they?'

Froso reappeared, walking steadily towards the two cousins, carrying a tray with three small glasses, a mini-carafe of *raki*, three tiny silver forks and a plate of orange peel slices in syrup – the customary citrus *glyko* and the perfect accompaniment to the white spirit. This offering, Calli knew, was the traditional welcoming drink in those parts and something she remembered her father was particularly fond of; Keith always looked forward to this Cretan custom with relish.

'Before everyone else arrives we will drink a toast,' *Thia* Froso said to the two young people as she poured the *raki*. 'Welcome back to us, my girl, we have been waiting for you,' she said, turning to Calli, and raised her glass.

13

Calli had indeed returned, in more than one sense. She could hardly remember the last time she had sat under the olive trees with the people she loved, and her mind free of anxiety and concern for anyone apart from those she had come to visit. Her aunt had been cooking for the evening's gathering and promised that she would be preparing more of the dishes which she deemed unavailable in England and which she knew that her niece especially enjoyed.

'Remember Manolis, the old fisherman?' she asked while the two of them started to set the table under the trees for the feast. 'He has promised to catch some *barbouni*, red mullet, tomorrow. But tonight, we will eat what I prepared this morning, I don't want to spend all my time in the kitchen on your first evening.'

Gradually neighbours, friends and relatives close and distant started to arrive, bringing their own gastronomic offerings to the gathering. In no time the table was groaning under plates of steaming *moussaka*, *stifado*, salads, fava dip, *tzatziki*, village bread, and a huge platter of *briam*. This dish, a vegetable stew of aubergines, herbs, peppers, potatoes and courgettes cooked in flavoursome tomato sauce, was a special favourite of Calli's; though akin to the French ratatouille it was enhanced, she was sure, with some kind of Cretan magic. She couldn't identify what made it different from its French or mainland Greek counterpart, perhaps it was the potatoes, she just didn't know, but in her view the Cretan recipe decidedly had the edge.

'It's because I make it with love, that's why you love it so much,' her grandmother used to say when Calli as a young girl had come back for more.

Everyone that evening had been invited to the house to welcome the new arrival and one by one took their place at the table. Several of Froso and Eleni's cousins and their grown-up children with their wives and husbands were present, and Calli was delighted to see among them Andreas and his sister Vasiliki, whom she was very fond of even though, she remembered, Vasiliki had mostly refused to join in their rough-and-tumble games, preferring to stay home by her mother's side. How many summers had she and her brother Alex spent playing with their cousins and kids in the village, all galloping across the neighbouring hills and beaches until sundown? How could she have neglected these people, she asked herself; how could she have put that part of her life to one side for so long? Manolis had come too, promising to deliver fresh fish for her every day.

'I remember your mama always asked me to bring her some *Maridaki* whitebait, because it's your papa's favourite,' the fisherman told her. 'Where can she find such fresh fish for him in your London now, eh? Tell me!' he demanded with a hearty laugh.

The local wine flowed, the food was eaten with relish and everyone's spirits were high; when all was consumed and the table cleared, the *raki* was once again brought to the table and all glasses were filled. No feast was ever complete without a bottle of *liquid fire*, as Calli referred to the drink, to mark the end of the meal. All the guests stayed until late except for Costis's wife Chrysanthi, who had to take the children home to bed but who promised to return the next day.

'You've done well, my cousin,' Calli goaded him after Chrysanthi had left. 'Your wife is a beautiful person . . . Where did you find her and how did you manage it?' she teased.

'She comes from the other side of the island, and she hasn't done too badly herself to find me, either,' he protested, laughing, and poured himself another shot of *raki*.

That first night, after everyone left, Calli, Costis and *Thia* Froso sat together under the olive trees in the night breeze, chatting quietly until sleep started to get the better of them.

*

The next morning, she woke early. She had slept deeply and soundly in the old bed she used to occupy as a child. Her good-sized bedroom on the first floor of the house had two picture windows, one at each end, looking to the sea in one direction and in the other to the mountains. The two single beds against the wall had been for herself and Alex when they were children, both facing towards the sea. When Calli had started to visit the house with James her aunt would always push the beds together and lay her best cotton sheets edged with lace over them – but this wasn't good enough for James. 'This is so uncomfortable, I haven't slept in a single bed since I was a child,' he whinged.

From a young age Calli loved to rise early, throw open the wooden shutters and then climb back into bed to lie and look out of the window to the sea; that morning was no exception. Both the early breeze from the shore and the evening one from the mountains always found their way into that room, never did she feel the stifling heat of high summer which engulfed her the moment she walked downstairs to the kitchen or living area.

She stretched back on the cool sheets, folded her arms behind her head and through the open window feasted her eyes on the vast blue of the Libyan sea, following the perfect line of the horizon which never ceased to enchant her. There she lay until she heard her aunt's footsteps out in the back yard. *She must be collecting eggs from the chicken coop*, she thought and sprang to her feet to look out of the window.

She loved that morning ritual, which her grandmother Calliope also used to observe, and which her young self had eagerly anticipated. 'Come, come my little one,' her *yiayia* would call out to her each morning. 'Let's go and hunt for eggs,' she would call again, raising the girl from her sleep. Calli could think of nothing more thrilling or more precious than the discovery of a new-laid egg, which she would hold in her child's palm like precious treasure. She would keep it for a moment, feeling its warmth and brushing off the tiny feathers clinging to the shell, before gingerly placing it in the basket with the eggs her grandmother had already collected. Once they had finished, they would return to the kitchen and breakfast would be cooked. 'Full of goodness,' her *yiayia* would say lovingly. 'Fresh eggs, they will make you grow up healthy and strong, my little one.'

She missed the old lady; the memory of her voice and especially her laughter lingered on in Calli's mind. She was aware that she had resisted poor *Thia* Froso's attempts to be something of a substitute but in her child's mind all those years ago her loyalties lay with her grandmother who was irreplaceable. She now remembered with a sense of guilt, how soon after *Yiayia* Calliope passed away Froso tried to entice her into collecting the eggs with her, but the more the aunt tried to replace her grandmother, the more the result was to push the little girl further away until eventually she refused to visit the village any longer. The memory made her feel bad and a regretful fondness for her poor aunt flooded her thoughts.

The news about Froso's ill health had worried Calli, but since her aunt appeared to be well and had made no mention of it, she decided to leave it to her to raise the subject. Leaning out of the window now, looking at the top of her aunt's head, she fancied it was old Calliope walking back to the house with a basket of eggs. *I suppose in the end we all end up looking like our mothers*, she mused, aware that she too was starting to resemble her own mother these days. Grabbing a long T-shirt she threw it on over the cotton shorts she was sleeping in, and without bothering to look for shoes ran downstairs to join her aunt.

'*Kalimera*, Calliope *mou*,' Froso said, turning round to look at the young woman standing on the stone floor in her bare feet. 'How about some eggs for breakfast?' she said smiling, pointing at the basket in her arms.

'Perfect!' Calli replied; although she was not in the least bit hungry after the last evening's feast, she could hardly refuse.

'They said it's going to be a scorcher today but it's still cool outside,' Froso said, gesturing towards the back door with her chin. 'Why don't you go out to the garden while it's still fresh and pick some tomatoes while you're about it?'

Her aunt was right, it felt refreshing in the garden; the early morning dew which had drifted from the mountains in the night was still visible on the leaves, though Calli knew that in an hour or so it would be gone and replaced by the blistering summer heat. She wandered around the back garden, paying a visit to the hens and the rabbits which again as a child she would spend hours petting, only to discover at some point that one of the furry animals that she adored had ended up in a *stifado* stew. She had refused of course ever to eat it; it took years to persuade her even to taste the dish and then only after her grandmother promised to replace rabbit as the main ingredient with lamb or octopus.

The unmistakable aroma of fried eggs wafted through the kitchen window out to the yard, making her salivate and instantly transporting her once again to childhood summers. She walked back into the house with a handful of red tomatoes and sat at the table.

'Good to have you here, my girl,' her aunt said, turning around with the frying pan ready to dish out the food, 'and soon we'll have your mama here too, the three of us all together like old times. It's been too long since I've seen my sister.'

'Good to be here, *Thia*,' Calli replied and meant it more than ever.

She tucked into a morning feast: goat's cheese and

olives, fried tomatoes and eggs and chunky village bread for mopping up the bright orange yolk. Then, just as she sat back in her chair having eaten more than enough, Costis's wife Chrysanthi breezed through the door carrying a plate of *mizithra* and a pot of heather honey from her own hive. How could Calli resist one of her favourite dishes? This soft fresh cheese served with a spoonful of honey and a sprinkling of cinnamon was in her opinion more delicious than the best ice cream she had ever tasted in London.

'*Kalimera!*' her cousin's wife greeted them cheerfully. 'Costis told me how much you love *mizithra* with honey, so I brought you some.' She drew up a chair to join them. This too was another fond memory for Calli. She loved the impromptu visits from friends and relatives, especially from the women, who would gather during the day and sit under the shade of the trees, drinking coffee and gossiping until one or the other would jump up and run home to prepare the table for the midday meal before the men came home from work. No one lived far away; they could call to each other across their gardens or from their kitchen windows, and if they were visiting, they could even keep an ear and an eye out if food was cooking on their stove.

Calli liked her cousin's wife, a primary school teacher, an open-hearted cheerful young woman with large round eyes the colour of roasted chestnuts and an equally large, full-lipped mouth that seemed to be perpetually set in a smile. Her hair, Calli noticed, was lighter than that of other young local women, who mostly seemed to possess velvety coal-black tresses. Chrysanthi's hair framed her face in soft light-brown curls with shades of gold when catching the sun.

'Costis often talks about you and your brother,' she said, busying herself with the food. 'He even talks to the children about the two of you,' she continued as she poured honey over the cheese. She paused for a second and then looked up with smiling eyes. 'I feel so happy to meet you at last, Calliope!'

'And I'm very happy finally to meet you too, Chrysanthi,' Calli said with genuine sincerity, struck for the second time that morning by a pang of regret for the lost years.

'Costis told me they call you Calli in England. Do you prefer me to call you that?' the young woman asked, spooning a portion of cheese into a bowl for her.

'You can call me whatever you prefer,' Calli replied with a smile, and reached for the bowl. That morning the three women sat in the kitchen talking cheerfully, until Froso announced that she had errands to do in the village.

'You girls sit and chat,' she told them, reaching for a basket hanging on a hook behind the door. 'I need to go and see Manolis for the fish.'

There was no shortage of conversation between Chrysanthi and Calli that day; they sat at the kitchen table over their cheese and coffee until the heat in the room banished them to the garden, where a breeze was blowing from the shore.

Calli felt as comfortable with her cousin's wife as she had done a few weeks previously with Sylvie and Maya on that other enchanting island in the Aegean.

'I love being a teacher,' Chrysanthi said at one point when they were discussing their work. 'Apart from the children, I also love having the summers free,' she giggled apologetically. 'Mind you,' she added, 'they say it's *free*, but between looking after my own kids and the house it's not exactly a holiday.' Calli couldn't quite imagine what the responsibility of running a home and a family was like. She loved her work too and kept a fairly neat apartment with the help of her cleaning lady once a week. But with no children to look after she could work whenever she liked, sometimes well into the night if she had a deadline. Without the restrictions of a family, she and James could please themselves.

'Tomorrow night you will come to our house,' Chrysanthi suddenly declared enthusiastically. 'I shall cook dinner for all the family and friends. I want everyone who doesn't know you, to meet you. We must celebrate your homecoming.'

Calli was sure that if this woman had grown up in the village during those long summers of her childhood, they would have been good friends. She had always longed for a girl as a playmate – her cousin Vasiliki, she remembered with amusement, was her only female cousin and she hadn't been that much fun. *Better late than never*, she smiled to herself; if she had lacked a girl friend then when she was growing up, maybe she would find one now.

14

The second night Calli spent in the village and in the old house was probably the first time that she had spent alone with her aunt without a crowd of relatives and friends around them. They sat at the table under the olive trees breathing the fragrant air which blew down from the hills mingling with the salty breeze from the shore and ate what Froso had prepared – Manolis's freshly caught *barbouni*, fried in shallow oil just as Calli liked it, with thickly cut potato chips and served with the ever-present mixed salad of seasonal leaves.

'These rocket leaves are so peppery, *Thia*,' Calli said with her mouth full. 'And these potatoes are just like *Yiayia* used to make them.'

'How else did I learn to cook them, if not from my mother?' her aunt replied, visibly pleased as she refilled Calli's plate. 'Your mother always loved them too when she was small. So happy that you are enjoying them, my girl.'

'I'm not sure what size I'll be by the time I leave here, but I'm very happy you cooked them for me,' Calli laughed.

'Would you like to go over and see Costis and Chrysanthi now?' Froso asked after they finished their meal and cleared up. 'It might be more fun for you there with the children than here with me.'

'We are both going to see them all tomorrow, Auntie,' Calli replied. 'Tonight it's just you and me, so let's get the *raki* and some of your delicious *glyko* out now, please!'

The two women sat caressed by the evening breeze, enjoying the cool that comes with nightfall under a sky filled with more stars than Calli thought could be possible.

'I always forget about how a moonless sky looks here,' she told her aunt and took in a lungful of air.

Suddenly *Thia* Froso reached across the table and cupped her niece's face with her palm. 'Your mother has told me about what happened this past year, Calliope *mou*,' she said, looking into the young woman's eyes. 'I am so sorry about what you have gone through, my beloved girl.' Her aunt's unprompted words and loving gesture caused a surge of emotion to rise in Calli's throat. She swallowed hard and reached for her glass of *raki*.

'Yes . . .' she struggled to say and took a sip of the hot liquid, feeling it slide down her throat, releasing the tightness.

'Do you want to talk about it?' Froso asked gently.

Calli of course knew that her mother would have discussed the events of the past year with her sister but given the nature of her relationship with her aunt and the lack of communication with her, Calli herself had mentioned nothing of her troubles as yet. In many ways since leaving London she had hoped to escape from the sadness and had managed to do so despite the rush of emotions that had floated to the surface in Ikaria with Maya. However, Calli was beginning to understand that to face her sorrow was not the same as to wallow in it. She had found that out during her sessions with a therapist, realizing that the talking had actually encouraged the process of healing.

As Calli began to speak and her aunt sat quietly listening to her, she concluded that this was not unlike her therapy back in London. The only difference now was the warm night air and the several glasses of *raki* she was consuming, which were making her open up and talk more candidly than usual. She spoke of her worries that she might never have a child, and of the joy in discovering that she was pregnant, of James and his harshness, of her decision to keep her baby, and of her parents' support and her grief after losing her baby girl. 'We were going to call her Eleni, you know,' she said, fighting back tears.

When Calli fell silent, Froso stood up and took her in her arms.

'Oh, my girl,' she said, her voice catching in her throat. 'Oh, my girl . . .' she said again and sat heavily back in her chair. 'There is no end to what we women have to suffer at the hands of men.' Froso let out a deep sigh. 'Eleni told me about what you went through but hearing it now from your mouth breaks my heart further.'

Calli looked at her aunt and wondered how many women she had known in her life who had gone through experiences like her own. 'Life has always been hard on a woman,' Froso repeated, 'no matter how many years come to pass the story gets repeated.' She sighed again and opened her mouth to say more, but changed her mind and remained silent.

'What? What, *Thia*?' Calli asked. 'What were you going to say?'

'Eh . . . no matter, another time,' Froso said and started to get up. 'The tune of the lament is always the same,' she said, looking at her niece, 'it's only the words that differ.'

Calli reached for her aunt's hand. 'Thank you for listening,' she said. 'I didn't want to upset you.'

'Life is upsetting, my girl,' her *thia* said, picking up their glasses and plates from the table and placing them on a tray. 'There is life and there is death but there is also joy, we must never forget that.' She gazed at Calli fondly and started to head towards the kitchen door with the tray.

'Tomorrow will be even hotter,' she said, changing the subject, 'so you must go for a swim, Calliope *mou*. You missed it today.'

Once again Froso was right; the sun had only just risen when Calli woke the next morning, yet the temperature seemed already higher than the day before. Did her aunt instinctively know what the weather was going to be like each day, she wondered, or did she consult her radio in the kitchen? Whichever it was, Froso was proving to be a good meteorologist.

Leaping out of bed, Calli threw open the wooden shutters, stretched her arms to banish sleep from her limbs and took a deep breath. No time today for her usual morning reverie; she would run straight to the sea for an early swim.

She dressed quickly, wearing her swimsuit under her sundress, and headed down the path towards the beach. This early hour was her favourite; people were hardly starting to stir in their homes and the few summer tourists from mainland Greece or from Heraklion would still be tucked up in their hotel beds. She walked unhurriedly towards the seafront, trying to decide if she would just take a dip or stay out for the whole morning. If she was going to spend the day at the beach, Calli preferred to continue along the shore towards some rocks jutting out into the sea. Climbing over them, she would reach on the other side a small secluded little enclave of a beach almost like a lagoon. Most people couldn't be bothered to make the extra effort in the heat, preferring to take the easy option of lying under an umbrella belonging to the two or three cafes in front of the long beach. Once Calli made her way to her private enclave, she would spend the day undisturbed, swimming, reading, sunbathing, and even do some of the yoga moves that Paolo had so expertly taught her. Although at first she was uncertain about partaking in the yoga ritual of Ikaria, Paolo's coaching and influence had changed her mind. From now she decided that each day she would dedicate a short time to doing her stretches. This morning, because of the early hour, the shore was deserted so she decided to stay closer to home; besides, the prospect of her aunt's breakfast would soon be beckoning her back to the house.

She plunged into the cool refreshing water and swam vigorously for several minutes, then, covering her face with her straw hat, she lay back on her towel and surrendered her body to the early morning rays of the sun. The previous evening's conversation with *Thia* Froso came to mind and she berated herself for not taking the opportunity to show more interest in her aunt's health. She had called her mother to say that the situation was evidently not urgent, much to the relief of Eleni, who had been fretting about not being there. 'Your dad's gone and sprained his ankle and I really should stay with him,' she told her daughter anxiously. 'It's OK, Mum, everything is under control,' Calli reassured her, 'no need to rush here.' But all the same, despite her aunt's reluctance to talk about herself, Calli still thought she should ask about Froso's state of health. *Last night would have been the time to do that*, she told herself and made up her mind to raise the subject when she got back.

*

'There you are! You are even more of an early bird than your mother,' her aunt said as Calli walked into the kitchen. 'Ready for some eggs now?' She pointed to the table laid out with breakfast.

'There wasn't a soul on the beach today,' Calli replied, pulling up a chair. 'I had it all to myself.' She looked at her aunt and started to spread some butter on a slice of thickly cut bread.

'The heat will drive them all out there soon enough,' Froso replied, pouring out the coffee. Calli reached for her cup and breathed in its revitalizing aroma. 'You are really spoiling me, *Thia*,' she said, taking a sip. 'You must let me do things for you, too, while I'm here.' She glanced at her aunt over her cup, gauging if this was a good time to find out about her health.

'I hear you haven't been so well,' she began. 'But you look more than fine to me,' she added quickly.

'I am well enough, my girl, and even better now you are here,' she replied and reached for her coffee, too.

'Yes, Auntie, I am here!' the young woman replied cheerfully, 'and I'm not going anywhere for a while. I'm here to help you, and if you ever want to talk to me about anything, I am here for that too.'

'I will, my girl. There is plenty of time for that – but now don't forget we have things to do this morning after you finish your breakfast,' she replied, reminding her niece that they had some obligatory visits to pay around the village.

Calli knew that on arrival in Crete one always had to spend some time paying visits to various relatives, calling from house to house. In the past, her mother told her, when a visitor arrived at the village the locals used to compete with each other on who should offer the most hospitality to the newcomer, even insisting on putting them up for the night, and would sometimes be offended if the visitor refused.

Although her cousin's wife had arranged a big gathering that evening in her honour, Calli knew that there was no avoiding the individual house calls too and the last thing she wanted was to cause offence. By the time the two women returned home from their social rounds it was almost time for the midday meal.

'What would you like for lunch?' Froso asked Calli, who was stuffed with as many sweet delicacies, cups of coffee and home-made lemonades as she could endure. All that she could possibly manage or wanted now, she told her aunt, was to collapse into her bed for a long, well-deserved siesta.

The gathering at Chrysanthi and Costis's house was a crowded affair with not only many of the relatives she had already visited that morning but also quite a few people she had never met.

'Costis wants to show you off to some of his friends,' Chrysanthi told her. 'He is so proud of his talented cousin.' She smiled broadly and ushered Calli towards a crowd of men tending to a fire in a stone-built barbecue at the edge of the garden. 'They are getting ready to cook the *pagithakia*, the lamb chops.' Chrysanthi pointed to a pile of meat ready for the hot coals. 'Come, let me introduce you. Your cousin has been boasting about you, he's even shown his friends your website.'

Should she be embarrassed, irritated or touched by Costis's enthusiasm? In the end, Calli opted to ignore it.

As expected, Chrysanthi had gone to great lengths to prepare a feast for the party, and all the women and girls were busy laying everything out on long trestle tables under the vine canopy. Once again, more food was brought along by many of the guests and Calli thought that not since she was a child had she seen such a marvellous family celebration – but then again it had been so long since those days, perhaps she had forgotten.

'Your cousin thinks highly of you,' Michalis, one of Costis's friends said after Chrysanthi introduced them. 'I believe your work takes you all over the world. It must be very interesting.'

Standing in her cousin's garden in the early evening light with a glass of chilled white wine in her hand, making polite conversation with a man she had never met before, talking about herself and her work, struck Calli as incongruous and amusing. Her memories of such events were always dominated by older relatives, parents, grandparents and old folk from the village who had known her from childhood. This was an altogether different crowd: much younger, around her age, men and women, some with young children who had all come to meet her.

'I saw you walking to the beach today,' Michalis continued as they stood by the barbecue. 'Do you always go for a swim so early?'

'The place was completely deserted this morning,' she replied, surprised, having noticed no one apart from a couple of dogs and some cats out and about on her way to the sea.

'I was just getting into my car to go to work, so you wouldn't have seen me,' he explained. He too liked to be up with the dawn, he told her, and would often start his day with a swim.

'You're so lucky to live in a place where you can plunge into the sea whenever you want to, especially before going to work,' she said, remembering with distaste how she would often push herself to visit her gym's chlorine-infused pool before starting her day in London.

'I agree,' he replied. 'I feel that I'm blessed to live on this island. I wouldn't change it for anything.' He turned to gesture around him. 'I used to live in the village over that way when I was a boy.' He pointed to the mountains behind them. 'That's where I was born, but the sea beckoned me, so now I have the best of both.'

They were indeed blessed, Calli thought, those who lived on Crete: mountain or sea, you are never too far from either.

'When did you move to the coast?' she asked, her curiosity aroused.

'First I moved to Heraklion, got a job there,' Michalis replied, 'but it didn't suit me – too many people, too many buildings, not enough nature.'

She tried to guess what he did for a living. Chrysanthi had said that a couple of Costis's friends had their own business and she tried to imagine what that might be. She observed him as he talked and decided he was handsome in an earthy sort of way: muscular arms, sunburned skin and wiry black hair – so different from Paolo with his slender suntanned limbs, yoga-honed body and smooth silky hair.

'I've travelled a lot,' Calli told him, 'but this island, this landscape' – she turned around to point towards the hills as he had done – 'the people, the culture, are locked in my heart. If I was writing about Crete and I hadn't been here before I think I'd be describing it as *the land of mountains and canyons, sea and olive groves*!'

'It's true, though don't forget all those ancient sites too.' He smiled. 'But, yes, I'd agree. In fact, these olive groves are my passion and my life's work.'

His passion, he told her, was his acres of olive plantations. His work, he explained, was running his small but prolific olive-oil distillery near the village of his birth, some twenty kilometres from the sea. 'My father and grandfather had a few olive groves and we used to produce oil just for the family. Then I decided to come back and take on the business and develop it further. Cretan olive oil is the best in the world, you know,' he said with pride. She didn't disagree; she knew that Greek olive oil was superb, and if Michalis considered his island's to be the best then so be it. 'I always bring several bottles for your *thia*, when we make the first pressing; she says my oil is the only one to her liking.'

'I know she *loves* her olive oil,' Calli replied.

'I bring a bottle to all the friends in the village when we do our first pressing but for *Kyria* Froso I bring more.' As he talked, Calli could see Michalis's pride and pleasure written all over his face and in his eyes. His eyes, she thought, were as deeply black and bright as those beloved olives of his.

As it was a Saturday evening with no work the next day, the party continued until the early hours of the morning. Once the eating was finished and the plates and food had been cleared away, the tables were moved to one side, the musical instruments were brought out, and then the singing and dancing began.

'Who is going to feel like getting up for church tomorrow?' one of the old uncles called out, laughing raucously as he poured himself another shot of *raki*.

'*You* will!' his wife said, snatching the bottle away from him, 'because I'll be getting you out of bed whether you like it or not.'

Calli, who had learned some of the traditional dances, was able to join in with the women. Linking arms, they danced in a circle to the tune of an old Cretan melody and the intoxicating combination of drums, *laouto* – lute – and the unmistakable sound of the Cretan *lyra*. Some dances, Calli knew, could traditionally be performed only by men; one of these was the *Pentozali*, a very old dance which was said to hark back to ancient times when it had originated as a war dance. According to one myth, it had been performed by the war hero Achilles, who danced around the funeral pyre of Patroclus, his beloved friend and wartime companion. Another story she was told about the dance was that it symbolized the five attempts of Cretans to liberate their island from the Ottomans, hence the dance's name *Pentozali*, which translates as 'five steps'. Calli had always loved these ancient myths and legends, learning about such stories, and as she watched the men follow the intricate steps of the dance with its athletic, acrobatic moves she could easily understand why it should be considered a war dance. The men, standing boldly in a line and holding one another firmly by the shoulders, oozed raw combative masculinity. They stood upright and proud, following the music with intricate foot movements – apparently a warning to the enemy – progressively picking up speed, becoming more hectic as they kept up with the pace of the instruments. Michalis was among the dancers and Calli watched him as he took his turn to move to the front of the line to lead the dance, his limbs and body gyrating to the frenzied rhythm of the music by leaping and jumping in an impossible show of fitness.

Once again, as she stood watching among the other onlookers, Calli felt a sense of belonging, a sense of place. She was filled with gratitude to be able to immerse herself in the joy of the moment, without the niggling sense of responsibility when someone she was with was not having fun. Smiling to herself, she looked across the room at all the faces, young and old, family and strangers, breathed a sigh of relief, and joined in with the rhythmic clapping of the bystanders.

15

'You put me to shame!' Calli called out the next day as her aunt opened the garden gate and came towards her. Despite the late night, Froso had got up at her usual hour and made her way to the early morning holy liturgy, as she did every Sunday.

'Don't be silly, my girl, you went to bed about the time I got up to go to church,' her aunt laughed and pulled up a chair to join her. Calli was sitting under the olive trees drinking her first coffee of the day and musing over the previous night's events.

She had stayed up into the small hours at her cousin's house, talking and drinking with them and their friends, including Michalis. The musicians had long gone to their beds taking their instruments with them, but Costis brought the CD player into the garden and the party continued. Calli liked all of her cousin's friends and she willingly agreed to a suggestion that they should meet again the next day. Aside from Michalis and his friend Demitri, it was Katerina and Spyros, a newly married couple with no children as yet, who came up with the idea of a day trip. 'Let's take Calli somewhere in your car,' Katerina proposed, looking pointedly at Michalis, knowing that he had a four-wheel drive and the largest car by far.

'We can drive up to the hills, maybe up to my village,' Michalis willingly offered, approving Katerina's suggestion.

'We did have a fine time, last night, didn't we?' Calli said to her aunt, who had joined her at the table.

'You enjoyed yourself, eh?' Froso asked with a mischievous little smile as she handed Calli some *koliva* wrapped in her white lace handkerchief.

'I did!' the young woman replied, reaching for the little bundle. 'Was there a *mnimosino*, a memorial service, today?' she asked as she started to unknot the handkerchief, eager to taste the contents. Froso knew how her niece loved this sweet concoction which was always offered to the congregation after a memorial service: the cooked wheat, pomegranate seeds, almonds, sugar, sesame seeds, raisins and cinnamon, which, although a mournful offering in memory of the dead, was also a delicacy for everyone to enjoy.

'Yes, there is usually one most Sundays,' she replied. 'Today was for old Nicholas, God rest his soul.'

'Oh, I remember him, he lived up the hill from here,' Calli said, already tucking into the *koliva*.

'So, you had fun last night, eh?' Her aunt was eager to return to the subject of the previous night's party.

'I did!' the young woman replied through a mouthful, 'and how about you? Did you have a good time?'

'Seeing you enjoying yourself was all the pleasure I needed,' the older woman said, smiling, 'and as I saw, you made quite an impact on the young men!'

'Really?' Calli looked up in surprise at her aunt. 'What *exactly* did you see?' she laughed.

'I could see our Michalis was rather taken by you . . .'

'Ah! Michalis!' Calli said, taking another handful of *koliva*. 'He's really nice, I liked him.'

'Me too, he's a good boy. He comes to visit me sometimes and brings me olive oil,' Froso said, a little smile playing on her lips. Calli was surprised by her aunt's light-hearted comments, having always found her rather serious and earnest and not given to playfulness, but this Sunday morning she was in a lively mood.

'He's single, you know,' Froso continued, smiling.

'And what's that supposed to mean?' the young woman replied and burst out laughing. 'Are you going to arrange a match for me by any chance?' she said, trying without success to suppress her mirth.

'You were always able to make me laugh,' Froso said with a giggle, her own amusement evident on her face.

'If the truth be known, *Thia* Froso, it is *you* that's making *me* laugh,' Calli said and leaned across to give her a tender kiss on the cheek.

'I am so glad you came, my girl,' she said, delighted

with this display of tenderness from her niece and happy to finally have her all to herself for once. 'Now tell me,' she continued cheerfully to Calli before turning her head towards the kitchen, 'what should I make for lunch?'

'Oh no! No, Auntie! No lunch today,' she pleaded. 'I'm still full from last night *and* all that *koliva* – no room for lunch. Besides' – she gave her aunt a playful look – 'you might like to know that I've been invited by Michalis and his friends to spend the afternoon with them today.'

As much as Froso would have enjoyed preparing lunch for Calli, since feeding her niece was one of the main ways that she could express her love for her, Calli managed to convince her aunt to forgo the ritual once again. She couldn't think of anything less appealing than to sit down to another large meal, the past few days of feasting having exhausted her appetite.

'They are not picking me up till three o'clock,' Calli told her aunt cheerfully, 'so let me look after you for once. You sit in the shade and I'll make coffee for us. Maybe we can eat together later when I return. We'll enjoy supper so much more then.'

To Calli's surprise and relief, Froso agreed, and to her further surprise nobody called unexpectedly to see them that morning either. Since everyone had already paid their respects to the newcomer over the last couple of days, they were now content to leave the two women alone to their Sunday.

They had a blissfully quiet morning in the garden, aunt and niece relaxing in the shade on two old deckchairs that Froso kept in the outhouse, while the thyme-scented breeze that blew from the hills kept them from over-heating, and the relentless song of the cicadas lulled them into a kind of doze. It was marvellous not to have to think or talk for a while but just to bask in the sleepiness and tranquillity of the hot day.

Neither of them knew how long they lay there, but judging by how refreshed they both felt when returning to a state of wakefulness, it must have been some time.

'Goodness me,' Froso said, sitting up, 'I have no idea how long I was asleep.' She looked at Calli. 'I can't remember the last time I was relaxed enough to close my eyes under the tree . . . I don't sleep so well these days.'

'It's wonderful, isn't it?' Calli replied, remembering that the last time she had fallen asleep al fresco was in the arms of a man on a white rock perched above the sea, having just made love. She really had been having the most extraordinary time of late, she thought. After more than ten years of her life when nothing too remarkable had occurred to change things, suddenly everything had happened at once, everything turned upside down with no sign or warning; yet she was feeling more alive, more vibrant, more present than she had felt during most of her adult life. *Things always happen for a reason*: Maya's words floated into her mind. When her friend had told her so, she had resisted its validity, but now she was starting to believe it.

Since weekends and especially Sundays were the only days of the week when the beaches were busy, it had been decided unanimously the night before to give the seaside a miss and instead head to the mountains, as Michalis had suggested, towards his family's village. 'Even the people in the hills run to the sea on a Sunday,' they told her, 'so we'll have the place to ourselves.'

Calli had never ventured into that region of the mountains before, or if her mother and father had taken her as a child she had no memory of it. The car followed narrow roads snaking precariously above steep ravines towards the mountains. After climbing the tortuous route for about forty minutes, at last they arrived at an almost deserted village. Michalis parked the car in the small piazza dominated by an ancient plane tree whose hollow trunk was sheltering a sleepy dog that had taken refuge in its coolness. They made their way to some chairs and tables belonging to the village *kafenio* and sat under the leafy branches that covered the entire square. It was a good thing she'd skipped lunch, Calli thought, because the tray of sweet delicacies and coffee ordered by her new friends in her honour and now being carried to the table could not be resisted.

They spent the afternoon exploring the village, strolling through its streets paved with cobbles, before venturing into the cool green shade of a fruit orchard where orange and lemon trees grew among fig, olive, pomegranate and medlar, all mixed together in perfect discord with each other.

'My great-grandfather planted a few of these trees,' Michalis told them, becoming animated, 'and then, other members of my family added more.' His eyes sparkled as he spoke and Calli found his passion both touching and appealing. 'I remember when I was a child this orchard was the perfect playground for all of us kids in the village. If you like' – Michalis turned to Calli – 'next time, I'll take you to one of my olive groves.'

'I *would* like very much,' she said and was conscious that she was blushing.

Gradually, as the late afternoon turned to early evening, where day greets dusk and the cicadas' song is temporarily replaced by the darting flight of birds preparing to roost for the night, the five friends decided it was time to return to the coast.

'I have an early start tomorrow,' Katerina said. 'Maybe next time we can all go out on a Saturday.'

'Next time,' Michalis said, turning to Calli, 'I will show you some beaches you never knew existed, and we can go to a small taverna I know in the hills that makes even better *briam* than your auntie.'

I can't wait, she thought to herself as she nodded her agreement.

Michalis's suggestion, which was noticeably directed at Calli, implying that his offer was for her alone, filled her with delight.

Froso was sitting at the wooden table in the garden doing her embroidery, one of the neighbourhood cats curled at her feet, her brow furrowed. She looked deep in thought. The sound of Calli's footsteps made her start.

'Sorry to startle you, Auntie,' the young woman said apologetically as she approached her.

'It's not you, my girl,' Froso replied with a sigh, 'it's me . . .' Embarrassed by her reaction, she added, 'I was miles away.'

'And where were you, *Thia*?' Calli asked lightheartedly, drawing up a chair beside her to look at her.

Froso put down her embroidery and turned to face her niece. The expression Calli saw in the older woman's eyes was so unexpected, so haunting, that it caused her to reach for her hand.

'What's wrong, *Thia*?' she asked, alarm in her voice.

'Why, nothing,' Froso's reply came swiftly and with a sweeping gesture of her free hand banished the darkness that had clouded her gaze. 'Nothing . . . nothing wrong, my girl,' she repeated, trying to smile. 'How was your trip?' she hastened to add. 'Did you have a good time?'

'Yes, Auntie, it was wonderful,' Calli replied in confusion.

'Good!' Froso said and stood up. 'I'll just go inside for a minute, then you must tell me all about it,' and picking up her needlework she made her way towards the kitchen.

Calli sat alone in the garden for a long moment, trying to decipher what had prompted her aunt's dark mood, when she emerged into the yard holding a tray.

'Don't tell me you are still not hungry,' Froso said, the gloomy cloud replaced by a smile, a plate of cheese, bread and a bottle of wine on the tray. 'I suggest we have a little snack now and then I'll make us something more for supper. What do you say?'

'I say *yes!*' Calli replied without hesitation and got up to help her.

That evening, after the two women had finished their supper in the garden and the heat of the day had given way to cooler air from the sea, *Thia* Froso sat back in her chair, looked her niece in the eye and began to speak.

'Since you spoke to me the other night, my darling girl, since you confided in me about all that you have suffered, I have thought of little else . . . You and I haven't spent much time together over the years, despite my longing to do so, and I was touched and honoured that you chose to open up to me.' She took a deep breath. 'I know that my cousin Eleftheria mentioned that I have not been too well lately . . . I didn't want to burden you with all of that, certainly not as soon as you arrived . . . but now I feel the time has come for me to talk to you.'

'But you look so well, *Thia*.' Calli reached for her aunt's hand. 'What exactly is wrong?'

'I haven't said anything to your mother either,' Froso replied, holding her niece's hand tightly. 'When I was diagnosed with cancer the only thing that concerned me was that I might die without being given the chance to tell you and your mother everything that I needed to say, but I didn't know how.'

'People don't have to die from cancer these days, Auntie,' Calli interrupted her fervently. 'There are many treatments for it, not like in the past.'

'You can never be sure, my girl,' Froso said calmly, 'and then it might be too late . . .'

Calli held her aunt's hand more tightly now and waited for her to speak.

'Perhaps . . .' she hesitated, 'all that I want to say should remain unsaid.' She looked into Calli's eyes, faltering a little before going on. 'But . . .' she continued, 'lately I have been deeply troubled and the prospect of going to my grave without speaking to you and Eleni has been tormenting me.'

'My mum will be here too, Auntie. I know she will come soon; the only reason she's delayed is because of Dad's twisted ankle,' Calli reassured her. 'Having that stupid fall has given him more trouble than expected. I'm sure he'll be fine soon and she'll be here in no time.'

'I know, my girl, it couldn't be helped. Your mother told

me when she called . . . but you are here, that's good enough for me and Eleni will soon come . . .' She hesitated, took a deep breath, and continued. 'After you spoke to me of your sorrow it made me want to speak, too. They say, and I don't know if it's true, that if we carry a heavy burden inside us it can be like a cancer which in the end will devour body and soul.' Calli sat motionless, holding her aunt's hand, eyes unblinking, waiting to hear more, not knowing what her maiden aunt could possibly be referring to. Long moments went by in silence. Froso took Calli's hand in both of hers and held it, her eyes downcast, as she tried to summon the courage to begin.

'My life hasn't been as simple and straightforward as you might have thought . . .' She looked up at the young woman's face and fell silent again as if she was considering whether to go on. 'I have had my share of pain,' she finally said, her voice faint and sorrowful. 'I, too, lost someone once.'

Part Two

1

Crete, 1936–1950

Calliope gave birth to her firstborn, a baby girl named Froso, in the depths of winter in 1936 while the highest peaks of the mountains were covered in snow and the sea battering the coast roared like an angry beast. Giving birth was no more difficult for her than if she were climbing a rock to pick wild sage and thyme, with little fuss and bother and hardly enough pain to remember. But she wasn't to know that the pain she had escaped in bringing her baby girl into the world would be bestowed on her many times over later on in her life. 'Next time I'll give you a son,' Calliope said to Nikiforos, her husband, when he peered with slight disappointment into the cradle. But even if baby Froso hadn't been the boy her father had hoped for, she was growing up to be as strong and tough as any boy, despite her feminine good looks. As an infant she was healthy and robust, with a mop of hair black as jet and eyes to match, strong lungs and an equally strong grip. Calliope did eventually give her husband the son he desired to help him in the fields, drink *raki* with him when he grew up, and fight by his side when needed, as fighting was an essential part of life in Crete. The island had seen much of it over the centuries, from the Saracens to the Venetians, from the Ottoman Turks to the Germans in World War Two. Readiness to fight was as fundamental to Cretan men as passion, heroism and honour; it ran hot in their blood in equal measures.

But although Calliope and Nikiforos Mavrantonis's first-born had been a daughter, she was the one who stood tall by her parents' side, helping both mother and father in every way until the boy was old enough. Androulios was born long after Calliope had given up hope for another child.

'I thought the Holy Virgin had turned a deaf ear to my prayers,' she exclaimed after she discovered she was pregnant. 'I lost count of how many candles I lit, begging her to grant me a boy.'

'I don't know how you know it's going to be a boy, Mother,' Froso said with irritation. She could never understand this obsession with sons. As far as she was concerned, most boys were a nuisance. A baby sister would have been more welcome.

'Whatever it is, so long as it's a healthy baby I'm happy,' her mother replied, feeling a sense of shame for expressing her preference. 'You are right, my girl,' she hastened to add. 'Look at you! I couldn't be more proud to have a daughter such as you, as good as any son, and I would be more than happy if God granted me more daughters.'

By the time Androulios was born Froso was eight and she took a loving maternal role towards her baby brother; by the time she was in her early teens, she was already blossoming into adulthood.

'He is luckier than the luckiest, this baby,' her mother would tell her as the young girl helped with taking care of her sibling. 'He has two mothers to look after him.'

By then Froso had stopped going to school, which she had attended for six years. A group of children would gather at the square where a bus would pick them up, take them to school in the nearest larger village in the hills and bring them home each day, until they completed their last and sixth year. Most of Froso's childhood had been spent with World War Two raging in the background; then, after it ended at last, a bitter civil war broke out throughout the whole of Greece, prolonging any return to normal life.

The village up the hill, although not much larger than the village by the coast, was considered something of a centre for the region, having not only a school but also a post office, a small bank and two larger general stores as well as a weekly market. Once a month Calliope would accompany her daughter on the bus to do her errands and wait for Froso to ride back home with her. As the young girl grew, so did her good looks, and there were plenty of lads who were sweet on her. Calliope watched over her like a hawk, keeping any unwanted attention at arm's length and her virtue intact, but it was the girl's father who was ferociously protective, and made sure no male came near his daughter. Any marriage proposals had to be vetted by him and kept at bay until the girl became of age.

The young girl would have liked to continue her education after elementary school. But life was already hard for Nikiforos, trying to make enough of a living from his little grocery shop to feed not only his wife and children but his old parents and parents-in-law, too.

'She's a girl, what does she need more education for?' he said to Calliope when his wife tried to put the case for keeping Froso at school for a little longer. 'No sense in that. When the time comes and we find a suitable match we'll marry her off. In the meantime she stays at home with you.'

Calliope had no option but to agree. Besides, those were hard days: schools were disrupted, male teachers had to go and fight, and children who reached the age of twelve or thirteen were deemed old enough to help their families. Girls stayed at home with their mothers to learn the ways of domesticity, knowing that before too long they would be married, while most boys would either go on to learn a trade, work in the fields, or follow in the footsteps of their fathers and grandfathers as fishermen.

Froso knew better than to complain for long; in any case she loved looking after her little brother, and since she could read and write she could find all the information she desired in books, which she could access from her old school library. Once or twice a month she would take the bus up the hill and pay a visit to her former teacher, *Kyria* Demitra, who was especially fond of her bright pupil. The teacher would always be ready to lend her a new book to take back home, which she considered a way of contributing to the girl's further education. It was a rare thing to find a child in those parts who was eager to learn past leaving school and formal education. Froso enjoyed these little outings, which aside from collecting her books gave her the opportunity to escape from her parents' watchful eyes for a short while. Calliope was loath to let her daughter out of her sight, but after the first visit, when she insisted on accompanying her, and after the reassurance of *Kyria* Demitra that visits to the school were beneficial for Froso, she reluctantly agreed to allow the girl to travel alone; besides, apart from everything else she had to do she had a young child to take care of too now.

'It won't be long before the marriage proposals will start flooding in, my girl,' Calliope would tell Froso. 'In fact some already have,' she'd inform her, without giving too much detail as at her age there was no need to be concerning herself with such matters. There was one young man by the name of Mitros, from a well-to-do family in the upper village, whose family had already expressed interest in her, but it was not something that

Froso needed to know about just yet. Calliope and Niki-foros's desire was to make the best match for their daughter when the time came, but this was not the time; besides, they preferred to keep their options open, and wait and see if there might be an even better offer for their girl. The Mavrantonis' answer to Mitros's family was that their daughter was too young for marriage but in a year or so they would be considering their proposal. 'Virtue and modesty are the best attributes for a girl. They are as good as a dowry, if not better,' Calliope would insist, concerned that some boy might turn her head. But she had no reason to worry; Froso was a good girl, and the family was her main concern – until a boy called Kosmas came into her life. He was a couple of years older than Froso, and a fisherman like his older brothers, father and grandfather before him.

When Froso left school she was happy with her books as well as looking after her little brother and helping her mother take care of the house. Until the moment she became aware of Kosmas, the young girl had no interest in boys and romance, or anything much else apart from her family; but this particular youth captured her heart in an unexpected way. It was during a *Panigiri*, feast day: it was *Agios* Theodoros's holy name day and the celebrations were to last three days.

Down by the sea, along the narrow strip of road running beside the coastline where all the *kafenios* and small tavernas were to be found, the vendors from the small nearby villages in the mountains had set up their stalls selling all kinds of sweet delicacies and local produce as well as trinkets for the girls, colourful bangles and necklaces, silver crucifixes and lucky charms. A band armed with Cretan musical instruments was set up outside one of the tavernas; as soon as dusk fell they started to play, and then the festivities commenced. The young lads and girls in their traditional costumes lined the street to take turns with dancing; the sound of music and the tantalizing aroma of meat cooking on charcoals filled the evening air.

Of course, this was not the first time Kosmas had seen Froso; the village was not a large place. But that day, when the girl's eyes fell on him while he danced the *Pentozali*, the young man was troubled. Her gaze was intense, her black eyes he fancied were shooting sparks at him, which disturbed him, so much so that a couple of times he missed his step. She looked different, he thought as she stood next to her mother, she had suddenly grown and blossomed; she was not a child anymore. Froso, for her part, couldn't tear her eyes away from the youth. She was sure she had never seen such a *palikari* (young warrior) before, or a more limber and more heroic figure than him. When it was her turn to dance with the other girls, it was Kosmas's chance to feast his eyes on the graceful young maid who had stolen his heart.

When the dance was over, and the men were invited

into the circle to join the women in a mixed dance, Kosmas leapt to his feet and took his place by her side. Once they linked arms and felt each other's physical proximity, they both knew there could never be another for either of them.

Froso, now hopelessly in love, had no one to confide in. She worried in case her father found out, fearful that he would disapprove of Kosmas due to his humble background. She knew that her mother too would be hesitant as both parents were looking for a wealthier match for their daughter. Calliope also had a small child to take care of and relied heavily on her daughter to run the house with her. Besides, everything had its proper time in sequence in those parts: if a young man was sweet on a girl he was obliged to ask the girl's father for her hand. If the girl was too young but he agreed to the match, the boy would have to wait. And Froso was still too young as far as her family was concerned. As the young couple's love flourished, they both knew that they had no option but to keep it hidden. It had to remain a secret.

2

Crete, 2018

After Froso had been talking for some time, she came to a
halt, sat back in her chair, took a deep breath and fell silent.
Calli, transfixed by this tale of clandestine love instead of
the account of her aunt's ailments that she had expected to
hear, hesitated to interrupt although a host of questions
were competing in her mind. The older woman sat mute
for a long while, her eyes fixed in the darkness as if staring
at something, causing Calli to turn expectantly and look in
the same direction.

'He was such a good boy, my Kosmas,' Froso said in a
small voice, 'a hero!'

Calli leaned forward and gazed at her aunt as if seeing
her for the first time. She had assumed in her arrogance
that she had settled for an uneventful home life as a single
woman in the village.

'All we ever wanted was to marry each other . . .' Froso's
voice trailed off.

'Why didn't you?' Calli burst out.

'We had to wait until I was older before he could come and speak to my parents. My mother might have been more tolerant, but my father was fierce, we were both scared of him; we knew he would never have agreed, so until then we had to keep our love secret.' Froso reached for the jug of water on the table and filled her glass. 'You can imagine how hard that was. This is a very small village and in those days it was even smaller.' She took a sip and continued. 'But we managed it . . . you know what they say, if the heart is willing you find a way . . . We continued to see each other secretly for quite a few months until Kosmas finally decided he would go to see my father.'

'How did *Bappou* react? Was he angry? Surely *Yiayia* Calliope was happy that you had found a suitor?' Calli shot out one question after another without waiting for a reply. 'What happened, *Thia*, tell me . . . ?' Calli asked, eager to know more.

'I will, my girl, I will, but not tonight. Tonight, I would like to go to bed thinking of Kosmas as we were when life was filled with love.'

That night Calli lay in bed, her head swirling with all she had learned that evening. Earlier in the day she had expected to be lying awake thinking about Michalis, as he had made quite an impact on her. But the revelations of the evening had overridden the events of the day. *It goes to show*, she thought, *you can never judge by appearances*. All her life until then she had dismissed her aunt as of little interest and unworthy of her attention, while for ten years she had believed that James was highly interesting and her life's partner, only to discover the reverse. The story her aunt had left unfinished had equally surprised her. Froso had apparently been quite a rebel, led by love and passion, contradicting all Calli's preconceptions. She had always considered her aunt to be a quiet, conventional, rather meek and mild sort of person, yet apparently there was a far more dramatic hidden side to her character that her niece had never met. Why had nobody ever mentioned her early history before? Surely her mother must have known about her sister's fated love . . . Calli eventually fell asleep that night eagerly anticipating the next instalment of her aunt's story. The following morning she woke early and ran downstairs to the kitchen in her bare feet, hoping to find Froso ready and waiting to continue with her story. Instead she found a note on the kitchen table.

Gone to Heraklion with Eleftheria for a hospital visit. There are eggs and freshly baked bread on the table for breakfast and plenty of everything else in the fridge for your lunch. See you this evening.

Alarm bells started ringing in Calli's ears. Was her aunt suddenly taken ill, had there been an emergency? She had been so caught up with her new friendships, her attraction to Michalis, and the intriguing love story that Froso was relating to her, she feared she had neglected her poor aunt and her health. She should have asked more questions, she should have gone to the hospital with her, she scolded herself. But Froso had been so dismissive and evasive on the subject of her illness, and Calli, out of respect, hadn't insisted on more information. Guilt washed over her as she stood in the kitchen holding the note.

At a loss of what else to do and reassuring herself that the hospital visit was perhaps a routine check-up, Calli returned to her room, changed into her bikini and made her way to the beach for her early morning swim and to wait for her aunt's return.

Monday mornings were glorious down by the shore with not a soul in sight and the water as warm as a tepid bath. She swam for a long while, before stretching out in the sun and lying on her towel, mulling over what she had heard the night before. She tried to imagine Froso as a love-struck girl, and young Kosmas, the amorous 'heroic' lover as she had described him; and her thoughts turned to those British boys she had interviewed the year before whose teenage love had ended in pregnancy and parenthood, prompting her to reassess her own life. Young love, she thought, had always existed, it wasn't only a modern social phenomenon, and apparently it was always beset by problems.

*

The sound of her mobile in her beach bag made her start, interrupting her thoughts. She only carried her phone with her these days for taking pictures, to save having to take her camera to the beach; she never expected anyone to call.

'*Yiasou*, Calli,' she heard the deep brown voice of Michalis greeting her. 'Where are you, hope I'm not disturbing you?'

'No!' she replied, delighted. 'I'm just on the beach.'

'Would you like to meet up for lunch? I finish work early and I'm free for the rest of the day.'

If she hesitated before saying yes, that was only while she speculated when her aunt might be back and if she might need her; Froso's sudden departure had played on her mind in the course of the day. Returning her mobile to her bag, she realized with surprise and a little guilt that the prospect of meeting Michalis made her pulse quicken. *What is wrong with you?* she scolded herself, smiling broadly. *Behaving like a teenager!* Only a week or so ago she had been romancing a man she had just met on the shores of Ikaria, yet now here she was distracted by the prospect of spending time with another man she had only recently met. 'Clearly I'm making up for lost time.' She spoke the words out loud as she skipped her way along the surf towards her aunt's house. 'But I don't care!' she answered herself out loud again, throwing her arms up in the air in joyous abandon as she began to run. She hadn't felt this free, this jubilant in years and it felt good.

*

The little taverna that Michalis had mentioned the day before was half hidden in an orchard of orange, fig and silvery olive trees, shaded by vines all laden with grapes. As he had promised, they did indeed serve an even better *briam* than her aunt Froso, along with a dozen other dishes. Tucked away off the road which led to his village, it was almost empty when they arrived apart from a noisy table of local farmers, most of them sporting lavish moustaches and sun-baked skin, who were well into their meal and in high spirits, shouting across the table as if bawling to each other over the fields. Calli smiled to herself, recognizing this familiar Cretan characteristic. Once again James came to mind; he would always enquire with alarm what people were arguing about, and she would have to explain that there was no argument, just friendly banter.

'I can't carry on eating like this,' she protested to Michalis, even as she tucked into chunky fried potatoes sprinkled with oregano.

'Food is to be enjoyed,' he said. 'It's a sensual pleasure of life,' and leaned across to put another couple of *pagithakia* on her plate. These succulent yet crisp lamb chops cooked over charcoal were finger-licking tasty and Calli couldn't resist them whenever they were put in front of her. The meat was always tender and any surrounding fat deliciously blackened and deliciously crisp. Every taverna seemed to compete with the others in perfecting this technique.

'Is there anywhere you'd like to visit?' Michalis asked after they had finished their meal.

'I haven't been to Knossos for many years,' she replied. 'Not since I was a girl.'

'Then Knossos it is,' he said and signalled to the proprietor for the bill.

Her experience in Ikaria had aroused her interest in archaeological sites and she had promised herself to pay this ancient place a visit while on Crete.

The mythical home of King Minos was as splendid and as improbable as the myth itself. Calli stood in the ancient ruins, gazing at the landscape that surrounded the site, acres of undulating land, hills and mountains, olive groves and vineyards, with the sea beyond glinting in the summer sun.

Suddenly, as they walked on, Calli was abruptly brought to a halt, her way blocked by a fully grown peacock standing bold and tall in front of her as he displayed his gorgeous plumage in a show of brazen confidence. She stood as if in a trance, gazing at the magnificent bird while he glared back at her.

'Well, well . . . you *have* been honoured!' she heard Michalis exclaim a few feet away. She turned to look at him and as she did so, the bird lowered its fan of iridescent blue feathers and stalked away nonchalantly as if the spell had been broken. 'No matter how many times I have been here I have never had the pleasure of seeing this spectacle,' Michalis said as he came to her side.

'Why is it here?' Calli asked with confusion.

'He's not alone – there are many more of them roaming the grounds, male and female,' he explained. 'I think in Greek mythology peacocks symbolize protection and watchfulness because of their many eyes . . . On their feathers, I mean,' Michalis added. 'I suppose the eyes are meant to be watching over King Minos and his kingdom.' He laughed again and took Calli's arm.

'They are such strange creatures,' she said, still affected by the unexpected spectacle.

'I know, they *are* bizarre,' Michalis replied. 'I've been fascinated by them since I was a boy. They used to bring us here from school on day trips – I remember many of the girls were scared of them.'

'They are disconcerting,' she said, 'but I wouldn't say scary.'

'I looked them up a few years ago to find out a bit more about them,' Michalis continued. 'And I discovered there are all sorts of myths and mystical stories attached to them.'

'Really, what did you find out?' Calli countered, noting to herself that, recently, mysticism seemed to follow her wherever she went.

'Apparently they represent an awakening, they're a metaphor for transformation or something . . . which is hardly surprising, is it? Just look at them!' Michalis laughed, and ushered Calli into what was believed to be King Minos's throne room.

Michalis's words, though spoken lightly, struck Calli as oddly profound. Wasn't that similar to what Maya had said to her? Time for change, time for new beginnings? Hadn't she told Calli something like this before they parted? So, was this bird a sign? A symbol of her new awakening, for her own transformation? *Who knows?* she thought, turning to look at Michalis who was cheerfully expounding all he knew about the site, about the Labyrinth and the Minotaur and the splendour of the Minoan civilization. As he spoke, Calli's mind started to wander off again towards that poor duo, father and son, who millennia ago had tried to escape by turning themselves into birds.

According to Greek mythology, Icarus's father Daedalus was a brilliant artist and a clever craftsman, who along with his son was kept prisoner by King Minos until he had constructed a labyrinth in which to retain his wife's monster son, the Minotaur. As the myth goes, Zeus had sent a bull to seduce Queen Pasiphae, and the child she gave birth to was a creature, half-man half-bull, who had to be constrained.

Their only way of escape, Daedalus decided, was by air so he used his ingenuity and artistry to construct the wings which so nearly took them to safety. Daedalus had warned Icarus to avoid flying too close to the sun as their wings were glued together with wax and would melt, but the boy in his haste and excitement forgot his father's wise words and the inevitable happened, thus plunging him into the sea and to his death.

Calli as a child had visited the site of Knossos with her parents and had been told this story several times, but in those days she considered it as just a fanciful fairy tale. Now, standing among those ancient ruins, she reflected on her Ikaria experience and the story resonated quite differently from those childhood days. Calli's Ikarian story, as Maya had said before she left the island, had followed her. Everything she heard, everything she saw these days, seemed to offer a kind of symbolism: her encounter with Maya had opened her mind to concepts she had never considered or cared about before.

Visiting Ikaria, meeting Maya, Paolo and all those others who had welcomed her with such ease and acceptance into their circle, had revealed a new side of herself that Calli hadn't known she possessed. Until then she had lived a life full of preconceptions, full of self-defined rules and assumptions. To be creative, she believed, meant you had to be an artist, a writer, a painter, a photographer and so on; to be an intellectual, you must have a formal education with a degree or a PhD, be an academic, a scholar. To be successful, you had to be professional. Calli took a deep breath and looked around her. None of these rules applied anymore, and none of it mattered. What mattered was an open heart and an open mind.

'Shall we have a cup of coffee somewhere?' she heard Michalis say, snapping her out of her reverie. 'I know a great little *kafenio* on the way back to the village that makes the perfect *baklava*!'

'Now you're talking!' she said cheerfully and linked her arm through his as they made their way back to the car.

'I really like your company, Calli,' Michalis said rather unexpectedly, turning around to look at her. 'I am so glad you came to Crete.'

'Me too, Michalis,' she replied and meant it. She found his comment touching and honest; they had only known each other for a short time yet she felt a warm affinity towards him as if he was an old friend. She leaned into him and squeezed his arm.

'I've been waiting for someone like you for a long time,' he told her with a beaming smile.

'I've never *known* anyone like you,' she said and smiled back.

During the course of the day, thoughts of her aunt Froso and young Kosmas kept intruding into her mind. If at any point she felt an urge to discuss with Michalis what she had learned, she dismissed it; this was her aunt's business and no one else's. If anyone was familiar with Froso's story, she concluded, it would probably be her cousin

Costis; she made a mental note to ask him about it the next time they met.

By the time Michalis stopped the car at the house the sun had long gone, the mountain behind the village had turned into shades of purple and the sky into an indigo blue, while the first star was already hanging low and bright above the horizon. Michalis escorted Calli into the garden in order to greet Froso, who was sitting with her needlework at the wooden table.

'*Kalispera*, *Kyria* Froso,' Michalis called out cheerfully as she got up to welcome them. 'How was your hospital visit?'

'*Kalispera* to you both,' she replied, smiling broadly, her pleasure at seeing them evident all over her face. 'It was fine,' she said dismissively. 'Come, sit, what can I fetch you both?' she added, already making towards the kitchen.

'Nothing, *Kyria* Froso, I must be going,' Michalis replied. 'I start work early tomorrow. I will come and see you soon,' he promised.

While wishing to spend more time with Michalis, Calli needed to be with her aunt this evening; it was time for her to continue with her story. Besides, Michalis had arranged to meet her again very soon.

3

Crete, 1950

Finding time to be together and alone proved to be extremely challenging for the two young lovers. Kosmas had to go to sea every day, fishing with his brothers and father, and Froso had her domestic duties. Other than the one or two mornings a month when the young girl ventured to the upper village for her books, she was never alone. For the most part they had to make do with seeing each other on Sundays at church. Their imposed segregation served to inflame their passion and each time they met, either standing in close proximity to each other during the Sunday service, if her mother didn't insist she joined her upstairs in the women's gallery, or accidentally touching when they met outside the church, their love and determination to find time to steal away increased.

Once in a while Kosmas faked sickness at the quayside on a morning when he knew Froso was taking the bus to the school and would sneak off, having arranged to meet her in a remote place away from prying eyes. Those

Sunday mornings in church were the perfect opportunities for making arrangements. A discreet note passed between them, always making sure her father was nowhere near, or a furtive whisper were enough to keep them going for days with the heady anticipation of meeting. Kosmas knew of a small ravine in the outskirts of the village with caves and hollows in the rocks, where they could be safe and private, and when he could get away, they would plan to meet there. Froso would first visit her teacher, collect her book, then instead of returning to the square to board the bus back home as she always did, she would walk in the opposite direction, hoping no one had seen her. She would then scramble down the hill and rush to meet Kosmas, who, as arranged, would already be there waiting for her. He would always make the journey on his bicycle, avoiding riding on the bus, thus ensuring that no one had seen him arrive.

Their time together was short and precious; they could not afford to raise suspicion, because then Nikiforos would insist that Calliope must put a stop to Froso's visits to the school. If, God forbid, they were caught together in the cave they would be punished and, worse, be barred from even speaking to one another, hence destroying any chances they had of her family accepting him as a marriage match. Froso also knew that such behaviour from a decent girl would mean ruin for her and disgrace to her family.

'We could run away together,' Kosmas told her one day

as they held each other close in the cave. 'We could go to Heraklio, or Chania which is even further away. No one would ask any questions there, no one would know how old we are.'

'We must wait just a little longer, at least till my next birthday,' Froso replied, 'and then you can come to my father and ask for me.'

'That's not till the winter, it's months away . . . and besides, I don't think your father will accept me,' he protested. The young lad was amorous, his love and passion overwhelming, but Froso was strong and determined to do things the right way. She would not bring shame to her family.

'We can only ask him. We at least have to try. It will be worth waiting for,' she appeased him and kissed him full on the lips.

The two lovers were determined that soon no one could stop them from being together.

During late summer, while the weather permitted, their hideout served them well, but as soon as autumn approached, and the rains began pouring down the ravine, reaching it became hazardous.

'We must find another place to hide,' he told her, his arm wrapped around her waist, holding her against him as they lay on the soft earth.

'We will see each other at the church on Sundays,' she

said with a mischievous smile, knowing well enough what Kosmas would say.

'I'll go crazy if I can't touch you.'

'You will go even more crazy if they stop us from seeing each other altogether,' she told him. 'Besides, just think how it will be when we are finally engaged, and we can be together whenever we want.' Although sex would not be permitted before marriage, once the youngsters were engaged, they would be allowed to spend time together freely.

That autumn the snow started to fall earlier than usual on the high peaks of the mountains and the road to the upper village became increasingly difficult to reach. Froso's visits to the school became less frequent and scrambling to their hideaway hazardous. One day after rain had fallen hard in the night, making the ground sodden and slippery, Froso hurried to meet Kosmas for what they had agreed to be their last time in the cave. She had just left him, the boy still in the cave, and she was making her way surreptitiously towards the village square to catch the bus home, when she sensed someone behind her.

'*Kalimera*, Froso,' a male voice greeted her, causing her to catch her breath. She turned round to see Mitros standing several paces behind her. She knew who he was, she had seen him once in a while in the village; he always made a point of greeting her. 'Where have you come from in such a hurry,' he asked, 'in such weather?' A mocking smile spreading across his face.

'Nowhere . . .' the girl mumbled, the colour draining from her face and her knees trembling as she hastened her steps towards the bus.

Kosmas as usual waited a while after Froso left him before clambering up the hill. Black clouds had gathered, casting their gloom and threatening a downpour. He was making his way towards the field where he had left his bicycle hidden in some bushes when he heard footsteps behind him.

'Leave the girl alone!' a voice hissed. 'She is not for the likes of you.' Kosmas turned to face his follower, but before he could respond he saw Mitros disappearing into the shadows.

What neither Froso nor Kosmas knew was that the young man harboured a secret obsession with the girl and having already made his offer of marriage the year before, Mitros believed he had some unspoken ownership over her. Froso had come to his notice long before he sent word via his mother that he was interested in her. He had picked her out in the village during her last year at school, then observed her later during her subsequent visits to her teacher, and he kept a tally of her movements. He fancied that the girl was as good as his.

A few years older than Kosmas, Mitros was running his

late father's butcher's shop in the village and considered himself as something of a catch. If he wanted a girl for his wife, he would have her, and no girl would make a fool of him. The reply to his marriage proposal from her family had been that the girl was too young and if he was interested, he would have to wait. Well, if she was too young for him then she was too young for anyone else too. As far as he was concerned he had first refusal, and if anyone was going to have her it would be him.

It was a wonder that Froso's clandestine meetings before that fated evening had escaped Mitros's notice, given how he made it his business to keep an eye on her. The incident terrified the girl, who would have liked to tell her mother about it, but dared not without betraying her secret.

'I've seen him around, but I have never spoken to him.' Froso tried to appease Kosmas when he questioned her about Mitros the next time they met at the churchyard after the service. The liturgy that Sunday morning had seemed unbearably long to her as she stood with her mother upstairs in the women's sector of the church, looking down at the male congregation. She could see the back of Kosmas's head and she was willing him with her persistent gaze to turn around and look at her. She loved playing that game whenever she wanted to attract his attention as she was ushered up to the gallery by her mother. As she stared, she saw him bring his hand to the back of his head as if he felt a touch, only to realize it was Froso's eyes upon him urging him to turn to her. As the liturgy came to a close, she gestured with the faintest of movements that she needed to go outside, then, faking a dizzy spell, she hurried to meet him. There was to be a *mnimosino* that day and she knew there would be a delay before the congregation poured into the yard with their parcels of *koliva* from the priest, thus preventing any private exchange they might manage to snatch.

'What business does he have with you?' Kosmas muttered, his lips tightly set.

'I don't know . . . I promise I have never spoken to him,' she pleaded, on the verge of tears. 'I don't know what he wants with me,' she said again.

'He wants *you*! That's what he wants,' he murmured as the congregation began to leave the church.

Froso was at a loss. What should she do? She wanted to talk to her mother, but she dared not; she wanted to meet Kosmas alone, but she dared not. She was frightened to go to the village to see her teacher and collect her book, but she dared not not go, as her mother would want to know the reason.

The only time the two lovers were able to see each other now was either at the churchyard or in the village square after the service, where it was customary for families to stop for a morning coffee before going their separate ways home on a Sunday morning. There was no objection to youngsters being seen talking together if other people were present, though for the two lovers, after having tasted the joys of their private hideout, it was less than perfect.

'You can't go alone to the school again,' Kosmas told her.

'If I suddenly stopped going after making such a fuss before, my mother would interrogate me.'

'What if that creep starts bothering you?'

'I'll collect my book and then I'll get on the bus and hurry home,' she promised.

'I don't know . . . I have a bad feeling about this,' he said, and a shiver went through his spine.

4

With trepidation in her heart yet determined that she would not let Mitros deter or frighten her, Froso braved the bus ride to the upper village once again, hoping to avoid an unpleasant encounter. Trying to recall all the previous visits to the library, she remembered seeing Mitros no more than half a dozen times and then only once or twice had he actually greeted her. Froso had paid no special attention to the young man nor had he made an impression on her. But for Mitros, Froso had become something of an obsession; an obsession that no one knew about apart from his mother, who had been his envoy to convey the marriage proposal to the girl's family on behalf of her son as was the custom of the times.

'She is not the only girl in the world, my son,' his mother would tell him. 'Look around at all the other good girls in our own village of marriageable age. Why her?' But Mitros was consumed by an unhealthy fixation for the dusky young beauty from the lower village who treated him as if he didn't exist. The fact that Froso had barely noticed his presence and been entirely unaware of his infatuation with her was irrelevant to him; he had simply been waiting for her to come of age so that he could take possession of her. Yet now it looked as if she might be slipping through his fingers. The consideration that the girl had no say in the matter, was of no importance to Mitros's plan. Her first visit to the village after their encounter, which Froso made hurriedly with her heart beating fast, went smoothly with no unwelcome chance meetings. She caught the very first bus and arrived just as her teacher was opening the schoolhouse.

'Why so early and in such a hurry, Froso?' *Kyria* Demitra asked, surprised that the girl didn't stay on a little while for their customary chat about the book she was returning.

'I need to get home to help mother,' she lied, wishing that she could have confided in her. *Kyria* Demitra was a good person, a young woman not long married herself, and Froso fancied her former teacher might have some advice for her, if only she could summon the courage to speak to her.

The deciding factor to speak to her own mother arose when on her second visit to the village Mitros blatantly approached her as she waited in the square to board the bus. He stood in front of her, a smile more like a grimace on his lips, hands in his pockets, a cigarette dangling from his lips, and stared at her.

'If I see you again with that hobo,' he hissed at last,

grinding his cigarette under his shoe, 'I'll go straight to your mother and father . . . or worse.'

That night in bed, frightened and disturbed, Froso tossed and turned, dark scenarios playing in her mind. Eventually she decided that if anyone was going to speak to her mother it must be herself. She had to take matters into her own hands: she would not be blackmailed or allow this stranger to terrorize her. She had always been able to talk with Calliope; they had been so close, more like sisters than mother and daughter, she tried to reassure herself. But even if her mother had always been fair, this was different, telling her that she was in love with a boy who she had been secretly meeting in deserted places was not going to be easy. Froso prayed that Calliope would be able to see that no crime was committed and that Kosmas was a decent boy from a good family even if they didn't have much money. She would omit the part about the furtive kisses and embraces in the caves, which she knew would not be well received. She would tell her mother that she and Kosmas were in love and that he wanted to come with his father to ask for her hand. They didn't have to marry just yet, but at least get engaged, make it legal, make it known, and deter this older man who was frightening her. Calliope sat silently listening to Froso speak. When the girl finally finished, she got up, picked up the *bricky* and started to make coffee.

'Why didn't you come and tell me about Kosmas earlier?' was her first question to her daughter. 'If the boy loves you, he should have asked for you. He should have done the decent thing.'

'Because I knew you and father would say I was too young and . . .' Froso's voice trailed off. She knew that was not a good enough reason. She knew that the *only* reason she had not told her mother was because the young lovers' lust for each other was not something that could have been expressed; she couldn't risk her father's wrath – it had to be kept secret. She also knew well enough how decent girls were expected to behave, and she had misbehaved. *Love* was one thing, it could be tolerated; *lust* was another.

'He . . . Mitros . . .' Calliope paused for a moment and looked at her daughter, a furrow appearing between her brows. 'When he asked for you, we told him he had to wait. How could we have known then that he was not honourable, that he was not decent,' she sighed. 'Kosmas should have done the same, he should have come for you. We would have told him that he had to wait too instead of going behind our backs and getting yourselves into trouble.'

'He wanted to . . . it's not his fault,' Froso replied, her eyes brimming with tears. 'Kosmas is a good boy, Mama, he thought Papa would refuse him, that he would think he was just a poor fisherman, not good enough for me, and that he'd put a stop to it.'

Calliope stood silently by the stove, her back turned away from Froso, stirring sugar into the hot water. 'Well . . . there is only one thing to do,' she said eventually, turning to face her daughter. 'The sooner we see you two engaged, the better. It will keep you both out of trouble.'

'What about Father?' the girl asked anxiously. 'What will he say?'

'Leave him to me,' Calliope replied.

It took Calliope several heated conversations with Nikiforos before she convinced him that this was the best course of action to deal with the situation.

'Don't you want your girl to marry for love like you and I did?' she said to him, trying to appeal to his better nature when he started shouting that a fisherman's son was not what he had in mind for his daughter. 'You were a poor farmer's son when you asked for me and my father didn't object,' Calliope shot back at him. 'Money doesn't bring happiness, *you* know that, husband. Sometimes it brings misery,' she continued, putting an end to the conversation. Nikiforos might have been strict and fierce with his children, especially his girl, but when it came to his wife it was a different story: she knew how to handle him.

Once their love was declared and a date for their formal engagement was set, Froso and Kosmas breathed a sigh of relief and were more relaxed about being seen together in public. Christmas was looming and as it was close to the festivities the two families decided to meet together and to pledge that their two children would soon be united in matrimony.

A few days before Christmas, Calliope and Nikiforos invited the boy with his parents and siblings to a celebratory meal to discuss and agree on the union of their two families. Kosmas arrived with his mother, father and his two older brothers, Pavlis and Yiannis, all dressed in their Sunday best, the men, including Nikiforos, wearing traditional Cretan clothes, the fringed handkerchiefs around their heads adding a further air of gravity to the occasion. Pavlis, the eldest, was particularly fond of his little brother as Kosmas had taken him into his confidence about his love for Froso and their predicament. The girl too looked up to the young man and welcomed his support. 'I say make your intentions known to the family,' was Pavlis's advice to young Kosmas when he first told him of the clandestine relationship. 'I'm afraid her father would reject me,' the boy worried. 'What do I have to offer a girl like her?' 'Our good name, that's what,' Pavlis insisted. 'We are a decent family, it's not all about the money, my brother.' But the boy was nervous and agreed with Froso, who was confident that if they waited until she was a little older, he might have a better chance of being accepted.

So on that day Pavlis was particularly happy and joyful that the young couple were finally going to be united.

Calliope had killed her best and fattest hen and made an extra load of sweet festive cookies. Everyone loved her famed *melomakarouna* that were made from either semolina or wheat, dipped in honey and covered in walnuts, and her equally delicious almond biscuits, flavoured with rose water and dusted with icing sugar, both usually reserved for Christmas Day and the New Year. But this was a special occasion: this year they would be holding a double celebration, she told Kosmas's family. They would herald the birth of Christ and celebrate the betrothal of their two children. Nikiforos brought out his biggest bottle of *raki*, as well as his best red wine, made by his brother in the village, while Froso darted about with young Androulios making the house look festive. The little boy, filled with eager anticipation, helped his sister with the decorations, paying special attention to the small wooden ship, which in place of a Christmas tree was the festive centrepiece in every home at that season. The model ship, splendidly displayed, was a custom prevalent in most Greek islands, where the perilous chief occupation of its men was fishing, thus serving as both a symbol of gratitude and an offering for the men's safety. Froso and her brother cheerfully busied themselves, making everything around the house sparkle: colourful balloons from every light fitting, tinsel and ribbons on all the door handles and windows.

On Christmas Day after early morning mass, in front of the entire congregation huddled together in their tiny village church, Father Nicholas blessed the rings and performed the betrothal ceremony, announcing to all present that the two youngsters were now betrothed. After the service the two families gathered in Kosmas's home for the festive meal. The day before, Manolios, the boy's father, had slaughtered his pig, which he had been fattening for months, and Kosmas's mother, Vangelio, spent all her waking hours cooking. She cooked one part of the animal in the oven and another part Manolios roasted over an open spit. Both meats were accompanied with *spanakopita*, a spinach and cheese pie, and several types of salads and vegetables. For dessert, apart from the traditional *melomakarouna* and *kourabiedes*, Vangelio made her famed *baklava*, filled with chopped nuts, flavoured with cinnamon and cloves and served warm and dripping in syrup and honey. That Christmas was the most enjoyable and memorable they had ever celebrated, and the festivities lasted for several days, as did the dishes that Vangelio had carried on making from other parts of the pig that had not been used for the main roasts.

Christmas and New Year came and went and Froso's birthday was celebrated by naming the day for their marriage.

'I always dreamed of getting married on the first day of May,' she told Kosmas as they sat in his mother's kitchen one Sunday after church.

'That's too far away,' he complained, shifting a little closer. 'I don't care which day we marry, so long as I marry you,' he said and leaned over to give her a kiss – but thought better of it as his mother pushed open the kitchen door.

'There will be plenty of time for all that,' Vangelio said as she walked into the room, guessing what was in her son's mind. 'Be patient, you'll be married soon.' She smiled at them both again. She was protective of the girl, she knew what men were like, and nuptials were strictly for the wedding night, although she also knew that if a boy had his chance it was very likely to happen before. But Vangelio was oblivious to the fact that Froso's passion was as fervent as her son's.

'Ever since we told everyone about us, I can't even kiss you,' Kosmas whispered in her ear once his mother left the room again. 'We are always surrounded by people.'

'The rains will stop before long,' she returned, flashing him a dazzling smile. 'In the caves,' she added cryptically with mischief in her eyes, 'the earth will dry soon.'

Ever since the incident with Mitros, Kosmas had kept well away from the village, and Froso had reduced her trips to collect her books; as the festive season meant that the school was closed for some weeks she had had no reason to go there until now.

Froso's first few visits were swift and uneventful; she arrived in the village with the first bus, she made her way to the school just as her teacher was opening up, and then hurried home. At first the skies were still ominous and uncertain with clouds hanging dark and low, but by March the weather had broken, the days grew longer, the temperature milder. The swallows were starting to arrive and were busy making nests, and the air was perfumed with lemon and orange blossom.

It was on a glorious day such as this, when the early spring sun had burned through the winter's gloom, that the two young lovers agreed to meet once more in their hideout and steal some sensuous moments alone, even if it was for the briefest time; though they would soon be married, they were also young and impatient.

Froso didn't go to the school to collect her book that day. Instead, to save time, she made her way directly to the cave. The scent of blossom mingled with the aroma of wild thyme was intoxicating; she clambered down the hill through the low bushes and thorny shrubs to the cave. Kosmas was already there waiting for her, having hidden his bicycle in the undergrowth among the yellow gorse and mimosa trees. They held each other tight for the first time in months, their hearts thumping in their ears, filling them with both excitement and fear. They knew it was risky, they knew after what had happened last time it was madness – *what if they had been seen?* But their love was stronger than their fear and, finally alone for the first time since their engagement was announced, they gave in to their passion.

They were lying in each other's arms, knowing that they must soon set off on their way back home, when they heard rustling in the bushes outside. Froso let out a small cry and brought her hand to her mouth. Kosmas, holding her hand, stood up, then releasing her hand and taking a deep breath stepped towards the entrance of the cave. There, his figure silhouetted dark and menacing against the light, stood Mitros, brandishing a knife.

'*No!*' A single cry was forced from Froso's mouth before she saw Kosmas fall to the ground. She scrambled to her feet and dashed towards him as blood poured from his chest, and placed her palm over the wound. '*Murderer!*' she howled, hurling herself over the body. Mitros tossed the knife behind him and stepped towards her. With one strong hand he peeled her away from Kosmas and pulled her up.

'You are mine!' he hissed. '*He* had it coming.' He spat the words out, and pushing her to the ground, pinned her arms over her head with one arm and covered her mouth to silence her screams with the other as he forced himself on her.

5

Crete, 2018

The night suddenly felt stifling. The breeze from the sea, which had been constant all evening, seemed to stop abruptly, along with Calli's breath. She sat motionless, the perspiration which had broken out on her face now spreading all over her body. She had been listening intently to Froso without interrupting or noticing the passing of time. Now, to her horror, the story of young love and passion which had started so movingly the night before had turned into a Greek tragedy, a Cretan nightmare. She looked at her aunt, her ashen face streaked with tears; with trembling lips Calli tried to speak but could find no words. How could this be true? She had always heard stories and anecdotes about war and bravery, of the unforgiving Cretan temperament, of the hardness of the men mirroring the harshness of the landscape, their history of thrashing the Turks and defeating the Germans. She remembered the elders talking in hushed tones about mysterious events that had occurred in the caves and the ravines up in the wild mountains. But murder and rape, in their own family? The tales and yarns she had heard up until now were set in times of oppression and war, times of survival and slavery, historic times long past, or so she thought. What her aunt had just told her had nothing in common with those stories of long ago. This act of violence had taken place in the twentieth century, a few miles from where they now sat, and the realization took her breath away.

Froso, voiceless now, was sitting upright in her chair, fatigue and sorrow etched on her pale face. She reached for her niece's hand, squeezed it, then got up and went inside.

Calli remained rooted to her chair in the garden, unable to move until the first star appeared in the pale sky. Only then did she take herself upstairs to lie on her bed. But sleep would not come. Nothing had prepared her for what she had heard in the course of the night. How could her mother not have known about her sister's tragic early life? Or perhaps she did know but had not told Calli; perhaps the subject was a family taboo that could not be mentioned. Eleni discussed most things with Calli, they shared so much; surely if her mother knew she would have told her once she was old enough to understand.

Her aunt had said that she wanted to speak to them both before she died, therefore Eleni must be ignorant of her sister's secret past. But how was it possible for her aunt and her grandparents to keep silent all these years? Did *anyone* at all know anything? Questions swirled in her head, giving her a headache. She had to talk to her cousin Costis, to find out if anyone in the family, his mother perhaps, knew any of the story.

As soon as the first rays crept through the shutters and across her bed, Calli gave up on sleep, got up and made her way to the beach. She knew that the only course of action to soothe her and put some order in her mind was a dip in the early morning sea and a walk on the shore.

She was grateful for the coolness of the water, which made her body tingle, reviving her senses, bringing them, and her, back to the present, helping her to leave the terrible past behind. She swam a long way out to sea and then round the rocky promontory that divided the main beach from her own little private cove and lay out on the warm sand in precious solitude. She wanted to be alone, to think of nothing. She closed her eyes and for a few minutes surrendered herself to a kind of sleep, blocking any thoughts of murder and violation.

She came round to the sound of birds' wings fluttering above her. '*Raphael . . .*' she whispered in her state of semi-wakefulness as, opening her eyes, she saw two swallows flying overhead, darting in and out among the rocks and over the surface of the sea. The soft whirring of their wings carried her back to another shore on another island some weeks before, when the same sound had disturbed and moved her so. She lay motionless, watching their playful flight through half-closed lids, as a faint memory started to take hold, of conversations she had picked up from her grandmother and some of the elders around the village when she was a girl, about subjects she had been unable to understand at her tender age.

'It's a blessed house when a swallow chooses to make its nest there,' *Yiayia* Calliope used to say. 'The energy in our village is strong and positive, that's why they come back every year.'

In her grandmother's house a family of swallows would appear each spring to make their nest in the beams of the balcony below Calli's room. She remembered how as a child she would watch with delight the parent birds feeding their young, flying in and out of the nest with morsels of food in their beaks, dropping them into the gaping mouths of their chicks. The spectacle filled the little girl with awe and later, when she was older, she would always try to capture the scene with her camera.

Lying on the hot sand now, her limbs heavy, watching their flight, nimble and black in outline as they wheeled and dived against the blue sky, her mind wandered off again to Ikaria. She thought of the people she had met there and about her own spiritual awakening, prompted by Maya. Before meeting that extraordinary woman, she realized, her mind had been closed, dismissive of so much that she didn't understand; but the older woman had helped her to open her thoughts to new ways of looking at the world and beyond. Once more she felt grateful for their encounter.

The early morning swimmer who Calli had spotted in the distance with some irritation appeared to be swimming towards her, threatening to ruin her solitary contemplation. She made to get up and leave until she realized with pleasure that the person who had neared the shore and was now waving to her, was none other than Michalis.

'Apologies if I am disturbing you,' he said as he emerged from the water and crossed the sandy beach towards her. 'You did tell me you were an early morning swimmer, but I didn't believe you'd be this early.'

'Not normally,' she replied, shielding her eyes from the sun as she looked up at him. 'Had a difficult night and here is better than lying in bed trying to sleep.' She shifted sideways to make room for him.

'Oh?' He looked at her quizzically and sat down. 'What happened?' he asked with genuine concern.

'I'll tell you next time we meet . . .' she replied, not sure that she would. 'I've been watching a couple of swallows for the past half-hour . . .' she added, eager to change the subject. 'Don't you just love them? My grandmother used to say it's a blessing if they come back every year!'

'It's true,' Michalis replied, 'they do say that around here. They say that swallows have a sixth sense and always choose a place with positive energy to stop and rest during their migration. Have you ever noticed how many of them pass through the village? They all line up on the telegraph wires, it's quite a sight!'

Calli was struck by the irony of his words. *Surely*, she thought, *if the energy is so good, then murder and rape should have no place near here* . . . Then again, she decided, the land can be positive and blessed but there is no accounting for those who walk on it; the earth is not responsible for the people who inhabit it.

'There has always been talk of unexplained things in these parts,' Michalis continued. 'Some people say that millennia ago aliens landed here, others that it's the presence of the Holy Virgin that creates this feeling of serenity.'

Or maybe it's the angels, Calli thought, remembering her mentor Maya once again; who knows, she thought again, maybe she had really sensed Raphael's presence earlier on. In fact, what actually made this island so special to Calli was hardly important to her; even despite last night's revelations, it had been the place she had liked best since childhood, and she would be hard pushed now to have to leave it.

'Anyhow,' Michalis said as he started to get up, 'I must go now, time for work.' He reached for her hand, not to shake it in a formal gesture; he took it and held on to it in an act of physical bonding, flesh on flesh: two people who liked each other connecting, in much the same way that people here hugged each other when they met. He held on to her hand all the while he spoke, his big rough palm comforting, almost protective, and she liked it. 'Would you like to meet later . . . this evening?' He smiled as he spoke, and his eyes smiled at her too.

'Yes, I would.' Her reply came quickly before her thoughts turned to Froso. 'Can I call you when I know what my aunt is doing?'

When Calli returned to the house her aunt was not there, but she hadn't left a note this time. She bathed and dressed, hoping that by then Froso would have returned, but as there was no sign of her she made her way to Costis's house to see Chrysanthi. She knew her cousin would be at work, but she hoped his wife might be there and perhaps she might have an inkling about past family dramas; if Costis knew anything it was certain that Chrysanthi would know too. She found the young woman cooking in the kitchen and delighted to see her.

'Honestly,' Chrysanthi told Calli, placing two cups of coffee, bread, honey, and some cheese on the table for them, 'if I'm not at the school teaching, I'm here working in the house. It never stops for us women, does it?' Even when complaining, Calli thought, her cousin's wife did it with good humour. She found talking with Chrysanthi as easy as chatting with her friend Josie back home; she was funny and open, and in the course of their conversation

Calli tried subtly to establish if the young woman had any knowledge of what had happened years ago in her husband's family. But it soon became obvious that she knew nothing.

What Chrysanthi did want to discuss more than anything and with intense interest was how Calli was getting on with Michalis.

'As soon as I met you, I knew you two would be a good match.' She smiled broadly.

'I didn't realize people are still into matchmaking around here,' Calli laughed.

'Of course!' Chrysanthi laughed in return. 'It has never stopped! How else are people going to meet if their friends don't give them a helping hand?'

'Perhaps you're right,' Calli replied wistfully. 'In England we all rely too much on internet dating these days.'

'So, tell me! How did you both get on with each other? Did you like him?'

'Yes, I did . . . I *do* like him . . .' Calli smiled at Chrysanthi's persistence. 'But I can't answer for him.'

Michalis and Costis had known each other for many years and Chrysanthi was always keeping an eye out for a suitable match for her husband's favourite friend and her son's godfather.

He was a very thoughtful person, she told Calli; if she ever needed advice, it was to Michalis that she would turn.

He was well read and had more books than anyone she knew, being a teacher she respected that.

'And he is a good musician, and good-looking,' Chrysanthi enthused. 'He plays the Cretan harp like an angel, and the violin like the devil!' she laughed. Although he had had several love affairs in the past that she knew of from Costis, she continued, there was only one girl, an Athenian, who had come to live with him in the village for a year or so.

'She was nice enough,' Chrysanthi went on, 'we all thought they'd get married – you know, in these parts people eventually marry, especially if they want to have children. But apparently she didn't like living in Crete. She missed the big city, so she left.'

Calli sat absorbing this information about Michalis, which she hadn't asked for but was pleased to receive. Neither of them had as yet spoken much about their past and this spared her from the need to delve with inquisitive questions.

'He is the only one of Costis's friends who is still single, and as far as I'm concerned, he is the best of them all,' Chrysanthi concluded. 'Time he found a wife . . .'

'You'd better start looking harder for him then,' Calli giggled, reflecting that nothing changed in these parts, whichever generation you belonged to. Hadn't it been just the same when, before she met James, all the women in the village were for ever trying to marry her off, and then afterwards urging the two of them to have a baby? In those days their persistence had seemed tiresome and irritating; now she found the warmth and sense of community comforting and touching. Hadn't she learned the same in Ikaria too, that this sense of belonging, this taking care of one another, even if intrusive at times, was the very factor that kept the people of that island contented and living for so long into old age? This close-knit village community might seem a contradiction of the life she had led in London, but she was beginning to wonder if this could be a preferable way to live.

Calli and Chrysanthi sat in the kitchen chatting cheerfully for some time, comfortable in each other's company, until thoughts of her aunt began to trouble her. Where could she have gone so early in the morning? There had been no mention of a visit to the doctor or any other appointment, and given the state they had both been in when they left each other the night before, she was concerned. But her worries were needless, for on her return Calli found Froso sitting at the table under the two olive trees with her embroidery as before, a cup of coffee and a glass of water by her side.

'Ah, there you are,' she said, looking up from her needlework as if it was Calli who had gone missing. 'I was concerned . . . you disappeared so early.'

'And I was worried for you, you disappeared even earlier,' the young woman retorted. 'I couldn't find you anywhere.'

'No matter!' Froso replied. 'We're both here now.' She hesitated. 'I couldn't sleep. Too many memories . . . I went to see old Pavlis, I haven't visited him since you arrived.'

Calli pulled up a chair and sat next to her aunt. 'Kosmas's brother?' she exclaimed, surprise rising in her voice. 'Where does he live?' she asked again, examining her aunt for signs of distress, and reached for her hand.

'At the edge of the village. I must take you to him some time . . .'

'How is he? Is he all right?'

'He is very old and almost blind now, but yes . . . he is all right.' Froso took in a deep breath and patted the back of Calli's hand.

'It's so terribly sad and painful for you . . .' Calli stopped and looked at her aunt. 'I don't know how you managed all these years, I couldn't sleep last night with all you told me.'

'I know, my darling girl,' she let out a mournful sigh, 'why do you think I never spoke of these things before? They are too . . .' her voice trailed off, she looked at her niece and started to say something, then stopped.

'What, Auntie? What?' Calli asked.

'They are too hard to even think about,' the older woman said sadly.

6

'Oh, my dear *Thia* Froso,' Calli said. She stood up to wrap her arms around her aunt's shoulders and kissed the top of her head. 'I have thought of little else since our talk last night.' She observed her aunt, trying to gauge her emotional state and how she might respond to Calli's questions. There was so much she wanted to know but she didn't know how to begin or what to ask first. 'Could you *bear* to talk some more?' the young woman finally said.

'I have started, and I shall continue,' she replied. 'You must know everything, but it will take time. I need to pace myself because the memories are too painful.'

Froso had buried it all so deep and for so long that revisiting the past and bringing everything to the surface was reawakening her trauma after all these years. 'I will tell you more, my girl, but only after I have had time to gather myself. Perhaps later . . . tomorrow, or in a few days . . . then we might talk some more, I don't know, but now I need a break from the memories.'

'Just tell me this, Auntie,' the young woman enquired

hesitantly. 'Does *anyone* else know about what happened? Does my mother know any of this? Was she ever told?'

'No, my girl.' Froso's eyes clouded over. 'No . . . she was never told, why would we tell such terrible things to a child? How can such unspeakable things be spoken to someone so young . . . But yes, some of the village elders knew.' She took in a deep breath. 'Most are gone now apart from Pavlis . . . He's been a comfort to me over the years, we've supported each other.' She fell silent and looked away. Calli sat mutely holding her aunt's hand, not knowing what to say next. 'Kosmas was mourned by old and young alike . . .' she finally whispered and closed her eyes.

Nothing more was said for a long time; the two women sat silently holding each other's hands in the shade of the olive trees, both lost in their own thoughts: Froso in her mournful memories and Calli in confused speculation about what would come next.

The late morning heat was becoming uncomfortable and Calli's sleepless night and early morning start were beginning to take their toll on her. Finally, her aunt stood up and announced she was going to have a rest.

'I imagine you must feel the same.' She looked back at her niece as she made her way wearily towards the kitchen door. Calli followed suit, relieved that Froso had not suggested a lavish lunch as usual. The bread, honey and *mizithra* that Chrysanthi had given her earlier was enough for both breakfast and lunch.

Once again Calli found herself lying on her bed reflecting on what might happen in her aunt's next instalment. She had meant to switch her mobile to silent while asleep but was glad that she had forgotten, for otherwise she would have missed Michalis's call.

'I'm coming your way for some work,' he said. 'I wondered if you'll be free a little later?' He sounded uncertain. 'Have you found out about your *thia* Froso . . . will you be spending the evening with her?'

She was torn between on the one hand wanting to see him and on the other, not wanting to cause a break in her aunt's story if she was ready to continue. She swung her bare legs out of bed and stood on the cool marble floor for a moment, savouring the refreshing sensation before slipping on her sandals to go downstairs and look for her aunt. She found her in the kitchen, brewing some mountain tea.

'I heard your phone ring,' she said, turning round. 'The telephones you young people have these days keep you in touch with everyone, no matter where you are, eh?'

'True, *Thia* – it's good and bad at the same time,' Calli replied. 'Sometimes it's nice to be cut off from everyone but, alas, there is no escape.'

'Was that your mother who called?' She looked at Calli expectantly. 'Do you know when she is coming?'

'As soon as they're back from the Lake District. She didn't want to leave Dad with his twisted ankle after his fall but she's coming really soon, I promise.'

'I've been thinking . . . there are things I need to tell you both, *together*,' her aunt said, sitting down heavily at the table, her limbs suddenly seeming weightier than before.

Although Froso had told Calli earlier that, now she had started, she would continue her story, she was also anxious about saying more without her sister present. She had never intended to reveal so much without her and now she had clearly decided that Eleni must be there too; she couldn't bear going over everything again, that would be too much for her.

As it became obvious that Froso was no longer in the mood to tell her more, Calli's thoughts turned to the phone call.

'It was Michalis who rang earlier, *Thia*. He is coming this way and wanted to know if I'd like to go for a drive.' She looked at her aunt, waiting for her response.

'And you must go!' Froso replied at once. 'You've heard enough miserable things from me for now; go and enjoy yourself, my girl.'

Her earlier conversation with Chrysanthi had whetted Calli's appetite to find out more about this man who had captured her interest. If he thought she was a mixture of Western sophistication and Mediterranean warmth, she found him straightforward and unpretentious. His evident love of the land, his passion for his olive groves, was touching. Calli's journey towards meeting people who followed paths different from those familiar to her up until then was apparently continuing.

'Since it's still early, I'd like to show you one of my olive groves,' Michalis told her as they made their way once again towards the hills in his four-wheel drive. The higher the climb, the sweeter the scent of the air that blew through the open window. She greedily inhaled it and the oxygen which filled her lungs seemed to revive her. The mountain air had an almost purifying effect; it felt as if she was being purged of the distressing story of her aunt's past which during the course of the day had been returning to haunt her.

'This particular olive grove,' Michalis explained after he had parked the car on a steep hill by the side of the road, 'has some of my oldest trees, because it was the one that my great-grandfather had started. He owned a little patch of earth, and at first he planted twenty olive trees, then my grandfather planted another twenty and after him my father extended it further. And now it's up to me and my brother!' He made a sweeping gesture across the plantation.

As they walked and talked between the rows of trees Calli could see through their silvery branches the blue sea shimmering in the distance. 'My grandfather always said that the winds that blow from north Africa make the Cretan soil rich and fertile,' Michalis went on, his voice wistful and proud. 'That's why our olive trees grow so well and healthily. We have been cultivating and producing olive oil in Crete since the Minoan times and that's why our oil is the best in the world,' he boasted again. His enthusiasm was as evident as his undisguised love for his island and his pride in his trees; she really liked that about him. How endearing, she thought, was this passion of his for the earth and all that it sustained, and how much more human, more real his attitude now seemed than the acquisitive ambitions she had known in her city life.

'By late October, November, we will start the harvesting of the olives,' Michalis started to explain, pointing out the budding fruit on the trees. 'For the bigger groves we do have some relatively high-tech equipment but for this one we all get together, young and old, and enjoy harvesting the old-fashioned way.'

Calli remembered as a child hearing her mother and grandmother recalling the olive harvest. They would describe to her and her brother how it was when everyone gathered in the autumn to turn the harvest event into a celebration. Their accounts of hitting the trees with sticks to shake down the berries, and the stories of donkeys and mules being loaded with sacks of olives to be carried down to the coast on their backs, sounded more exciting than anything the two children could imagine, so that they begged to be allowed to take part in it.

'You'll have to wait till you are both older and don't

have to go to school any longer before you can come and help your grandfather,' Eleni would tell them when they pestered her to bring them to Crete for the harvest. But inevitably, as is always the way, once they were old enough to participate, they both lost interest; there was always some other activity far more pressing to do with their time which took priority in their teenage years and later in their adult lives.

'My whole family and all our friends take part in the harvesting – you should join us some time,' Michalis said as they stood under one of the oldest trees. 'Stay till November,' he said softly and moved a little closer. The air smelled of honey and as he talked his olive-black eyes were smiling at her again.

'I will,' she said and thought of nothing that she would like to do more.

While he spoke, he reached and placed his palm on the trunk of the old tree; his hand lingered there for a moment and then patted the gnarled wood with such tenderness that Calli fancied it was a person he was touching so lovingly. She found this simple gesture of his so moving that a lump rose to her throat. She looked at Michalis's kind face and was seized by an almost overwhelming urge to talk to him, to unburden herself of the revelations she had learned over the last few days, and even to tell him about her own life, about the sadness of her own recent experience. But it was clear that what she had been told by her aunt was a private matter, a secret, which for whatever reason had been guarded for decades. Even if she was brimming with her new knowledge, ready to burst with the need to divulge it to a sympathetic ear, she couldn't bring herself to do it.

'Thirsty?' he asked suddenly, breaking into her thoughts and reaching for her hand. She gave it willingly and followed him out of the grove towards the car. 'I know of a nice little *kafenio* in the village up the hill,' he said, putting the car into gear. 'It's not far, an old relative of my mother's lives there.'

As always in those parts the narrow road snaked tortuously up the hill, and with every hairpin bend the car teetered alarmingly close to the edge, giving Calli a clear view of gullies, ravines, gorges and hollowed-out rocks below. She was familiar with these mountainous landscapes which had never made her nervous, yet for the first time they seemed to her to take on a sinister character.

'The terrain looks so menacing down there.' She turned to Michalis.

'They say that thieves and bandits would often take refuge in those caves, and during wartime it was a place to hide from the enemy . . .'

As she peered down through the open window a sense of dread engulfed her, and she fancied that any one of those caves she now saw could have been the doomed lovers' hiding place. 'These caves had many uses in the past,' Michalis continued without taking his eyes off the road. 'Not so long ago, when lovers eloped, it was down in those caves that they ran to hide,' he added, causing her to catch her breath.

As he parked in the village square, again, just as earlier in the car, Calli was filled with a sense of foreboding. This place reminded her too much of that other village that figured in her aunt's story, the one they called the *upper village*. She had heard so much about it; now apparently here it was, complete with bus stop and schoolhouse. Although seventy-odd years had passed she thought she recognized it from Froso's descriptions. How could she be sure that she was not mistaken? Her suspicion could have easily been the result of her over-active imagination and the effect the drive had had on her. Yet as they walked down the street and approached the *kafenio*, Calli felt a gloom descending.

'Do you mind if we don't stay here?' she asked Michalis, feeling foolish for asking the question.

'Of course not . . .' he said, his surprise evident in his voice, 'not if you don't like it.'

'It's not that . . .' she tried to explain. 'I don't know . . . it's something about the aura of the place that makes me feel uneasy,' she said, at the same time incredulous to hear the words coming out of her mouth: she sounded more like Maya than herself.

7

In the time that followed, despite the urge to confide in him and despite having plenty of opportunities, Calli decided she couldn't talk to Michalis about her aunt's secret; she had to honour her privacy. At the same time, Froso too had made a decision to refrain from continuing further with her story; the prospect of having to re-live the upsetting history she had buried once her sister arrived was sending her into a state of high anxiety.

'I now realize I should have waited for your mother to come before starting to talk to you,' Froso told a disappointed Calli. 'Bringing back the terrible events of the past is not doing me any good,' she tried to explain. 'I need all my strength when our Eleni comes, I need to be well for her.' As much as Calli's curiosity and dismay nagged at her, she also understood and respected her aunt's wishes. Eleni would soon be here and the story would continue. Then at least she would be able to discuss the revelations with her mother instead of being left to ponder and speculate on her own; she must just have patience and wait.

'Besides, Calli dear,' Froso told her, 'you too need a rest.

You have been through a good deal yourself. You need a holiday, you need to enjoy yourself – I've burdened you enough for now.'

The time preceding Eleni's arrival turned out to be more enjoyable than Calli could remember for a long time. If the weeks she had spent in Ikaria had revealed things about herself she had no idea she possessed, then her days spent on Crete were to recover aspects of her persona that she had apparently forgotten. She found joy in simply living for the moment instead of pushing herself into producing, planning and working towards the next project. A return to simpler pleasures, those she remembered as a child and then as a young single woman at her grandmother's house before her career took off and before she allowed James's needs to take up most of her free time. She should have listened more closely to Josie, she told herself, who seemed to be the only one to point out James's failings. Everybody else, including her mother and father, took the discreet stance that it was her own life to do as she saw fit, but Josie pulled no punches. Besides, the two women had known each other since childhood and better than anyone, they were each other's best friend; they were soul sisters and Josie had no inhibitions about speaking her mind. 'What happened to you?' she would protest to Calli if she witnessed a particularly petulant incident with James. 'You never used to put up with shit from anyone, why are you putting up with *his* nonsense?' Josie came from a long line of women who told it as it was, and she wasn't going to tolerate any man's bad behaviour when she saw it. But Calli, swimming in a sea of denial, had put Josie's intolerance down to the fact that her friend wasn't in a relationship and failed to understand compromise and negotiating life with another person . . . or so she told herself, ignoring the warnings and her inner voice.

Evenings in her aunt's garden were now filled not with confessions of disturbing events which had taken place long ago, but by visits from friends and relatives all determined that she should enjoy her stay with them in the Cretan way. There were still times when she toyed with the idea of calling her mother to have a discussion about what Froso had told her, but she suppressed the urge – it wouldn't be long now until she arrived. If her decision not to discuss her aunt's story with Michalis had been the right one, then her decision to be candid and open with him about her own life was even better and brought a more intimate connection between them. The better she came to know him, the more fond of him she became.

'It's hard to imagine how you managed to cope after losing everything you held dear and then losing your baby . . .' Michalis said to her one evening as they walked barefoot on the beach.

'It was unbearable, and I thought I would never recover,'

Calli told him. 'But sometimes we surprise ourselves, don't we? Perhaps we are all much stronger than we think.'

'In my opinion, having someone you love who loves you back, and a family by your side, is all a person can want in life,' Michalis replied. 'Not everyone is lucky to have that . . . And then to throw it all away!'

They had been to one of the tavernas along the seafront with some friends when Michalis suggested that the two of them take a stroll on the beach. The night was balmy, the moon was full and the evening breeze warm on their skin. Calli felt that if at that moment Michalis took her in his arms and kissed her, she would have gladly kissed him back.

He looked down at her with an intensity she had never seen before, but as she turned her face up to him and their eyes locked, she was consumed by an unexpected and surprising wave of shyness. He smiled gently then took her hand in his and held it tight as they walked on.

Earlier in the summer she had been involved with another man, and it was hard for her not to draw comparisons between the two, even without intending to do so. When she met Paolo, his appeal to Calli lay in his unfamiliarity, his *otherness*; his smooth lean yoga body and eastern philosophies excited and intrigued her. Michalis, on the other hand, with his sturdy earthiness firmly grounded in the Cretan soil, soothed and comforted her and touched her heart. When she was on Ikaria she had sought a care-free adventure and Paolo had wholeheartedly obliged; their attraction to each other had been sexual, full of curiosity. He was exotic, sexy and spiritual while Michalis, she was discovering, was staunch, solid and straightforward. What she saw in Paolo was new, while her response to Michalis was one of recognition: he was reminiscent of other good men she had met over the years on this island. Perhaps he was even a little like Keith, she thought, a man who could be trusted, relied on – real.

'You are lucky to have had the opportunities to travel so much,' Michalis told her one day, producing a world atlas he kept in his car so that she could point out all the places she had been for her assignments. Chrysanthi had been right when she told her that Michalis had more books than anyone she knew; he was always bringing something or other to show her. Travel journals seemed to be his favourite.

He was admittedly much less travelled than herself, yet he possessed a curiosity for the world and a simple philosophy of life that appealed to her.

'You're right, I'm very lucky,' she replied. 'But no matter how many places I've visited for work I have always longed to share the experience with someone. When you're alone it's never the same.' It was true that much as Calli loved her job and revelled in the privileges and richness of her experiences, she always felt a pang of loneliness when she found herself in a place that touched her but had no one to share it with.

'Of all the countries you have visited, which one did you love the most?' Michalis asked eagerly.

'Africa!' Her reply came without hesitation. 'The little I saw of the continent moved me to tears at times.'

Michalis looked down at the map and pointed to Crete. 'Look how close to Africa Crete is. I've often thought that this island could almost have been a small piece of land that drifted away from there.'

'Strange you should say that' – Calli turned to look at him with surprise – 'because when I went to north Africa and beyond, I had a strong feeling of familiarity. The earth in the parts of Africa I've seen is like the earth in Crete, copper red as if the same blood runs through the veins of both lands.'

'I don't know about African soil, perhaps it's rich in copper,' Michalis replied, 'but in Crete it's probably because of all the blood that has been spilt on it over the centuries. This island has had more than its share of bloodshed,' he said, sending a shiver through Calli's spine.

Evidently Froso was very much liked in the village, and Michalis along with her cousin and friends would often join them with their musical instruments to sit under the olive trees and play, sing and drink *raki*. Invariably Froso would have prepared some *mezethakia* – little dishes of food to accompany their drinking – and was more grateful and happy than ever to have her girl there and see her enjoy herself. For her part, Calli, now that she had seen her aunt with fresh eyes, was delighted to spend time with her remarkable *thia* and to help her in any way she could.

For Froso's next hospital appointment, Calli borrowed Chrysanthi's car and insisted on driving her to Heraklion.

'This is a lot more comfortable than *Bappou*'s car ever was,' she told her aunt as they both recalled with amusement those airport pick-ups of long ago, squashed into her grandfather's Morris Minor. In the past, when Calli had visited Crete with James, the only people they came into contact with were her relatives; other than her young cousins there had been no opportunities to meet and get to know anybody of her own generation. So these new friends she was meeting now through Costis and Chrysanthi were making her feel at home. Her friendship with her cousin's wife was also blossoming, and spending time with her and their family was providing Calli with the warmth and home comforts she always encountered with her own family in London. Their children too, little Katerina and Giorgos, took a great liking to the auntie from London; and although at times she felt a pang of regret that she had no family of her own, the pleasure she received from them was greater than the melancholy it sometimes induced.

'You're still young and there is plenty of time to start a

family,' Chrysanthi told Calli, contrary to what her older relatives had repeatedly told her, to her irritation, a decade ago. Although she knew this was so, time was passing; it was one thing for Chrysanthi to insist there was plenty of time when she already had her family around her, and another for Calli who knew that her childbearing years were flying past all too quickly.

'We'll see . . .' Calli replied, feeling a pang of regret in her heart. Although, when she had found herself unexpectedly pregnant, she had been prepared and willing to raise her child alone, she now knew that if there were to be a next time for her it would have to be with a man who loved her and wanted the same things as she did.

Things always happen for a reason – she kept hearing Maya's words – *and perhaps being a mother was never meant to happen to me.*

8

August was by far the hottest month on the island; Eleni believed July was worse, but Calli disagreed and maintained that August was when the thermometer rose highest and stayed highest, day and night. The advantage of this, in her view, was that by then the sea temperature was even balmier than in midsummer. Calli continued her daily early morning swim and walk on the beach, which she would often share with Michalis; although normally he would start his day even earlier than she did hers, he tried to orchestrate it so they would meet and spend a little time together before he drove to work. She was glad that she hadn't rushed into anything physical with him yet. Their relationship was blossoming into a warm friendship and she couldn't wait to spend time with him; his presence made her feel happy and secure. She found him thoughtful and receptive in talking openly on all manner of subjects, including her own personal worries and concerns.

'I sometimes feel that I think too much about everything, which stops me from being spontaneous,' she confessed.

'Overthinking can stop us acting from our heart,' he replied. 'I should know, once or twice when I followed my head instead, it didn't end well.'

'I'm learning . . .' she said and let out a sigh. 'It takes time to shake off old habits.'

Michalis's spontaneous expression of his love for Crete was infectious and seductive, and Calli needed nothing more than his encouragement to explore with him and, always taking her camera along, drive out to places where she had never ventured before. On past visits she had stayed well within range of her family's village but as Michalis was willing to show her around, she accepted his offer with pleasure.

'There is a little convent dedicated to the Holy Virgin, some way to the east from here, by the sea,' he told her one evening while stopping for a drink with some friends in her aunt's garden. 'You might like to see it. It's very small – just a handful of nuns live there. We can go on Sunday. They say that once or twice a year on certain dates, real tears run from the *Panagia*'s eyes, and whoever kisses the icon during that time will be cured of any ailments of the body or soul. When I was a boy my mother used to take me with her when she visited.'

'It's a really beautiful spot,' Chrysanthi said, overhearing Michalis's suggestion. 'I'm not from these parts but I've heard of this phenomenon.'

'I too used to go there with my grandmother,' their

friend Katerina added. 'In fact, I remember going with her on pilgrimages to visit the icon of the Archangel Raphael as well as the weeping *Panagia*, because he too performs miracles.' At the mention of Raphael, Calli sat bolt upright to hear more.

'Some generations ago,' Katerina continued, 'my great-grandmother believed she had witnessed a miracle and afterwards she pledged to light a candle every year on this anniversary. So all the women in my family would make the journey to the convent and take me with them.'

'What sort of miracle was that?' Chrysanthi asked, intrigued by this new information.

'Something about saving a baby's life a long time ago. It was one of my ancestors . . . I think it was my grand-mother's sister, I'm not so sure . . . but what I do know is that my mother and aunts still make the pilgrimage every year.'

'But of course!' Michalis exclaimed. 'How could I forget that? The women in my family also prayed to him as much as to the *Panagia*. What's more, my mother gave the arch-angel's name to my brother after he was cured from some baby illness or other – I can't remember what.'

'You have a brother named Raphael?' A wide-eyed Calli turned to look at Michalis.

'Well, yes, kind of . . . His name is Nicos, Raphael was added as a second name; you know, a sign of thanks and respect, but no one ever calls him that.'

'Where is he? Does he live in Crete?' she asked again.

'He lives in Athens, he moved there a few years ago. But he visits quite regularly and a couple of times a year I go and spend some time with him too.'

'What's he doing there?' Calli's surprise and curiosity ignited further. She couldn't imagine why anyone would choose to leave the Cretan paradise for the mainland, especially the noisy capital, unless they had to.

'He sells our olive oil there,' Michalis replied, 'and he wants me to join him – but I would never go!' He laughed. 'I've tried living in the big city and it didn't suit me. I make do with visits once in a while, that's plenty for me. I'm trying to convince him to come back, we need him here.'

'I like your brother, he definitely should come back,' Chrysanthi agreed with her wide friendly smile, before turning to Calli. 'You'll love the trip to the convent,' she added. 'I only wish I could come with you.'

The convent, perched at the far end of a small peninsula, gleamed white as a dove against the blue of the sky and sea. From a distance it looked as if it was floating above the water. Michalis parked the car in a field and they made their way up the rocky hill.

Inside the wall surrounding the nunnery they found a small, well-tended garden; as they entered the gate, they were greeted by the cheerful ringing of bells and the aroma from a pair of jasmine bushes that stood on each side of an arched entrance leading into a cobbled court-yard. Following the sound, they walked through another archway towards a chapel where they could hear chanting voices. Was this Sunday morning mass, Calli wondered, or another form of service? Her religious knowledge was limited, neither of her parents having been particularly pious; whichever it was, she found it beautiful. They walked further into the courtyard, around which the nuns' cells were situated. A young novice was watering pots containing basil, scented geraniums and rosemary, all lined up in neat rows outside each door.

'*Kalimera!*' she greeted them and looked up with a sweet smile. 'Have you come to pay your respects to our Lady of Sorrow?' she asked cheerfully. 'The chapel will be empty shortly . . . or, if you like, you can go in now and hear the hymns.'

By the time they made their way to the chapel the service had ended and the nuns were leaving, making their way across the courtyard. As they glided past, cloaked in their black habits, Calli fancied they resembled a flock of black swans.

The little chapel was dark and fragrant and the smell, a mixture of wax and incense, was calming and comforting. The icon of the Holy Virgin stood out among the others on the iconostasis partly because of its central location and also because it was covered by a white lace curtain which the faithful had to move to one side in order to kiss it. Calli reached out and pulled gently at the cloth to reveal the image of the Holy Mother holding her baby boy in her arms. Unlike the other icons, her tunic and headdress as well as the baby's garments were clad and intricately carved in silver, only allowing painterly visibility, in the Byzantine iconic fashion, of their two faces. Both mother and child looked serene and sublime.

Calli made the sign of the cross and brought her lips to the cold silver as she looked up into the *Panagia*'s eyes. For a moment she thought she saw them glistening with moisture; she pulled back, made the sign of the cross again, and smiled. 'I want to believe in miracles,' she whispered and kissed the icon once more. She stepped back and looked around her, this time her eyes searching for Raphael.

She located the archangel's icon in a position of prominence, propped on its own on a wooden stand at the edge of the iconostasis beside the candle holders. She made her way towards him and stood for a while, gazing at the image of her guardian angel. On the right-hand corner of the icon the angel's name was written in the Greek script, ΡΑΦΑΗΛ; his wings were a fiery orange and his garments a combination of red and green. His halo framed a tranquil and benevolent face; with his right hand he held an open box and with his left a spoon; perhaps a medicinal offering, she thought, or the holy communion. After all, didn't Maya tell her that Raphael was the angel of healing?

She stood looking for some moments longer, then crossing herself three times she leaned forward and kissed it. Seized by a sense of awe, she picked up a candle, lit it and plunged it into the sand with others which had been placed there before hers. Staring at the dozen or so candles as their flames rose towards the ceiling, she silently repeated the same plea she had made earlier that summer under a glowing blood moon.

'Isn't it beautiful?' Michalis's voice shook her out of her meditation. He was standing close to her, holding a candle, ready to light it and no doubt to make his own prayer and wish.

'This icon is very ancient,' he explained in a whisper, moving closer. 'Some of the nuns here still paint. They are famed for their work and have a little gallery of icons that we could go and look at if you wish.'

'Do you want to have children, Michalis?' Calli heard herself ask, seemingly oblivious to what he had just said.

'Er . . . yes . . . perhaps, some day,' he replied in confusion. He stood awkwardly, waiting for a moment, unsure if she would continue, before turning to light his candle and place it next to hers.

After leaving the chapel, Michalis and Calli made their way towards the cloisters in search of directions to the painting workshop and gallery and towards some shelter from the now unforgiving late morning sun. The nun they came across in the courtyard, who so graciously invited them to join her for a glass of water and a cup of coffee under the shade of a mulberry tree, turned out to be none other than the elderly Mother Superior. Calli looked up at the canopy of rich green leaves from the tree that spread over them like an organic umbrella and wondered if the nuns kept silkworms. She remembered her grandmother explaining to her that mulberry leaves are essentially what silk is made of, since that is what the silkworms feed on.

They sat talking with the nun for a while, her voice and wise words as welcome and gentle as the cool sea air that blew from the shore. She spoke of life in the convent and of the miraculous performing icons that they were blessed to house in their modest chapel, while the young novice they had encountered earlier brought them slices of orange *glyko*, coffee and ice-cold water.

The visit to the convent had a significant impact on Calli. She had visited monasteries as a child with her parents, she had encountered monks and nuns over the years, yet this occasion had been a different experience for her. The simplicity and serenity of the nuns' lives, the dedication to their faith and work emphasized how little anyone needs to achieve contentment; her own city life felt tainted and superficial.

As they left the convent, Calli entered the chapel once more to light another candle below Raphael's icon. This time her prayer was for her aunt Froso.

9

At last the phone call she had been waiting for arrived – though it woke her out of a deep and delicious siesta. Her mother was finally coming.

'And about time too!' Calli exclaimed in mock annoyance when Eleni told her she would be on the morning's flight to Crete. She knew that her mother's delay was due to Keith's little accident but nevertheless she was glad she was now on her way.

'I know, *agabi mou*, I missed you too,' she replied, oblivious to what Calli might have alluded to, 'but I had to stay with your father. I'm sure you've had a great time so far and we'll soon be together. How's my sister?'

'She's fine, Mum, she misses you, too,' Calli replied. 'We'll pick you up from the airport tomorrow.'

Costis offered to take the day off and drive them to Heraklion but Calli declined, preferring to borrow Chrysanthi's car again. She thought perhaps Froso might be willing to chat to her on the way there if they were alone.

'How would you like to do this, *Thia*?' she asked on

their way to the airport, gripping the steering wheel a little harder than usual. 'Do you want to go through everything again with Mum, and would you like to be alone with her when you do?'

'No! No, my girl, I don't.' Her aunt's reply was emphatic. 'I have neither the energy nor the heart to start all over again . . . Perhaps you can speak to her – would you do that?' She gave Calli a pleading look. 'I still have so much more to tell you both,' she murmured and then fell silent. 'But, please, my girl, please,' she said after a while, 'do me a favour. Don't start on that just yet, not as soon as she arrives. Let's have some time together to enjoy each other before we return to all that sadness again.' Neither of them said anything else for the rest of the journey, each lost in their own particular thoughts.

How was it possible, Calli asked herself again, that nobody seemed to know anything about Froso's story, and how could such momentous events have been kept secret from the family? Calli longed to talk to her mother but for now she had given her word to her aunt to stay silent for a while longer.

Searching the crowd for her sister and daughter, Eleni could feel her anxiety mounting. On the plane she had tried to distract herself from worries tinged with guilt about how she might find Froso. *Calli said it wasn't urgent, but I should have come earlier, cut the Lake District holiday short*, she berated herself. Then she saw them both standing at the Arrivals gate, her sister looking much better than she'd feared, and Calli tanned, golden and more beautiful than ever.

With a huge sigh of relief, Eleni hugged them both and reverted back to her usual cheerful self.

'How are you, my dear sister?' she said, taking Froso in her arms and kissing her noisily on both cheeks. 'Who said you weren't well? You look as perky as a daisy!'

'Looks can be deceptive,' Froso smiled and hugged her back extra hard, 'but you are right, I am fine, especially now you are here with us!'

'So, how have you two been getting on without me?' Eleni joked, settling into the back seat of the car. 'This is the longest the two of you have ever spent alone together.' She leaned into the front seat to take a look at them both: 'How did it go?'

'It has been a joy and a pleasure having your daughter with me,' Froso replied, turning round to look at her sister. 'I have always longed to have her to myself, she is such a good girl, she is just like you!'

'*Good* women run in the family,' Eleni pronounced. 'Just look at the two of us, not to mention our mother. It's in our DNA!'

The return journey to the village was as alive with chat and cheerful banter as it had been silent earlier on. Eleni wanted to know about all they had been doing and she in turn told them about news from home.

'Alex wanted to come with me too, but I told him this was strictly a girls' trip!' Eleni laughed again. 'I told him next time it will be his turn to come with Keith but right now he had to stay home and look after his dad.'

'How is Dad?' Calli asked, remembering her poor father.

'He's fine, it was just a sprain, but you know your dad – he's such a baby when it comes to pain,' Eleni jested.

Mother and daughter woke early next morning but didn't venture down to the beach until later. Breakfast was a generous spread: Froso produced all of her sister's favourite foods, starting with eggs from the hens, chunky village bread and black olives. The three of them sat chatting in the garden until Calli suggested a swim. For the first time since she had been staying with her aunt, Froso came along with them.

'My swimming days are over,' she told them, settling down on a beach lounger shaded by an umbrella. 'I shall sit here and enjoy watching you two having fun.' It had been a long time since she had had the pleasure of being with Eleni and Calli together without any of the menfolk around. She wanted to make the most of their company before she turned to the hidden history which she felt compelled to share with them. Over the years she had considered confessing to her sister the secret of her past, but the whole family had kept silent for so long that it had become a way of life for them all and she couldn't bear to upset those she loved. But now, with the knowledge of her illness and time galloping faster than ever, Froso burned with a desire to make the two most important people in her life understand who she really was. The image by which they knew her – Froso, the woman who had lived a sheltered life, no marriage, no love, no children, no drama – was true, yet not true. She did not want to end her days carrying the burden of the past.

'I think we should get you into the water one of these days,' Eleni said, walking towards Froso and reaching for her beach towel on the chair next to her. 'The salt and iodine will do you good, Sister.'

'I did my share of swimming when I could. Now I'll just stick to *breathing* the iodine,' she chuckled. 'I leave the rest to you, if you don't mind.'

The arrival of Eleni brought all the relatives together again in a fresh round of visits and parties. Calli was eager to introduce her mother to her new friends and above all to Michalis.

'Honestly, Mum, he is one of the nicest, most genuine people I have met – you'll see,' she told Eleni one afternoon when everyone was invited to spend the evening in Froso's garden for their usual get-together. 'He grows olives and plays the *lyra* . . . How much better can it get?'

'I'm glad to hear it,' Eleni replied. 'The Cretan men of

your generation are different from mine: more open-minded, more relaxed, more well-travelled.'

'Michalis hasn't travelled much but he is certainly open-minded and relaxed,' she replied, eager for her mother to meet him.

'I suppose the internet has made a big difference to young people these days. All we had for information about the world was the TV, magazines and newspapers,' Eleni said, as she sliced chunks of juicy watermelon into bowls to chill in the fridge before the evening's gathering.

'I really love it here, Mum. I can honestly say I'd happily stay forever.'

'And I can honestly say I couldn't get away quickly enough.' Eleni smiled at her daughter. 'That's not to say I wasn't happy – I had a great childhood, but by the time I met your dad I was ready to leave.'

'That's because you hadn't been anywhere else and you were curious to experience the world . . . *and* you were in love, of course,' she added. 'We are all so perverse though . . . Do you think we always want what we can't have?'

She picked up a piece of watermelon with her hand and stuffed it whole into her mouth, the juice trickling down her chin.

'You always liked eating melon the messiest possible way,' Eleni chuckled, handing her a piece of kitchen paper.

'I liked it best when *Yiayia* Calliope used to give me a whole slice with the rind still on and send me out into the yard to eat it where the mess didn't matter . . . and I'd spit out the seeds and watch the ants drag each seed to their nest.'

'You enjoyed your summers in Crete when you were little, didn't you?' Eleni said wistfully as memories came tumbling back. She was always grateful that she had been able to provide for her children some of her own child-hood experiences. Growing up with a loving family in a village beside both sea and mountains, she had been free and unrestrained and was determined her own children would have a taste of what she had had, if only for the duration of their summers.

'Oh yes, Mama,' Calli replied lovingly, addressing her mother as she had when she was a child. 'Our holidays here with *Yiayia*, *Bappou* and the family were great.' Smiling, she reached for another piece of melon. 'And you know something? Having spent all this time with *Thia* Froso, I have seen such a different side to her, she is quite wonderful. I feel sort of guilty now that when I was little I used to ignore her.'

'I know, I always felt bad about that, but you can't make children like someone if they don't . . .' Eleni replied. 'I could never understand why you were so resistant to her.'

'It's not that I didn't like her. I guess it's because she used to try too hard and it irritated me . . .'

'Well, I'm really glad that you found each other now. Better late than never, eh?' Eleni said, giving her daughter a little hug. 'She was such a good, loving sister to me, Calli *mou*, she was my confidante and my best friend even though she was so much older than me. When I met your dad, she was the one who talked to my parents and persuaded them not to stand in my way. My mother was fine but the men in the family were resistant. My sister stood by me all the way.'

That evening's gathering in Froso's garden saw the usual crowd of relatives and friends arrive, including Michalis, bearing gifts of food and drink and the inevitable musical instruments. Eleni had been in the village for almost a week by now, most of it passed in a carefree manner, spending mornings on the beach, resting during the afternoon heat, then socializing in the evenings. Impatient though Calli was to continue with Froso's narrative, she decided she must wait for her aunt's signal to bring her mother up to date with the story. But Froso held back, apparently in no hurry to continue.

That night, aside from Michalis, who Eleni was eager to meet, there was another person present that she was delighted to see again after many years, a man who throughout her childhood had been a constant presence, whom Eleni and her siblings loved dearly and called *Thios*. He was old, almost completely blind and had lived as a recluse for years, yet on learning the news of Eleni's arrival, he made the supreme effort to join the party, wanting to see her again.

'Come, Calli *mou*, I want you to meet someone very dear to our family.' Her mother took her arm and ushered her towards their old guest. 'This is *Thios* Pavlis' – she turned to look at her daughter – 'you might have met him many years ago but you were quite little, so you probably don't remember him.'

On hearing his name, Calli turned to look at her aunt. She instantly knew who the old man was even if she hadn't met him yet. Froso had promised to take her to him but the old man had not been well so they'd postponed their meeting. Finally there he was, Kosmas's eldest brother and his only surviving relative.

Calli beamed with pleasure to finally see him. She reached for his hand and held it for a long moment, her throat tight with emotion, then bowed her head and kissed it.

'This is my daughter,' Eleni said, moved at the sight of such tenderness from her girl, assuming that her gesture was prompted by respectful regard for the old man's advanced age and disability.

Pavlis reached forward and touched the young woman's head. 'I give you my blessings, my girl,' he said, his voice as weak as his touch. 'If I had better sight I'm sure I would see you are as lovely as your mother – she was always beautiful, even as a child. May you live a long and fruitful life and bear many children to carry forth our Cretan blood.'

Calli stood in front of the old man, unable to speak, emotion choking her, and as she turned to look at Froso, she saw her eyes brimming with tears.

'*Thia* Eleni! Over here.' Costis's loud voice from the other side of the garden snapped them out of their emotional reunion. 'Come, I want to introduce you to someone.'

Michalis was standing under the olive tree with a bottle of olive oil as an offering to *Thia* Froso in one hand and his Cretan harp in the other. Eleni found him as charming as her daughter had suggested and even more handsome. In the course of the evening her imagination ran away with her and she had Calli and Michalis already married with a couple of babies living in the old house with Froso.

'What a nice guy! I really like him,' she told Calli in the kitchen, lifting the heavy bowls of watermelon out of the fridge. 'How well have you got to know him? I mean, are you sort of dating or just friends?'

'I don't know, Mum,' Calli laughed. 'We've been spending quite a lot of time together since we met . . . since I got here, actually. We are *kind* of dating, I suppose.'

'And?'

'And *what*?' Calli laughed harder. '*And* nothing – we're taking it slow, we are still sort of getting to know each other, no need to rush.'

'You really are a different generation,' Eleni laughed

back. 'In my day, if a man took you out twice, he'd be making his move . . . make his intentions clear.'

'Mum! I could be making a move too, if I wanted to. It's not just up to him, you know, it's not like that anymore. We get on, and we like each other . . . We'll see. You and Chrysanthi, honestly – what a couple of old matchmakers!'

'I'm just saying . . . that's all . . .' Eleni said as they left the kitchen to join the babble of the throng, carrying trays of fruit and drink.

10

'I like your mother, she's fun,' Michalis said a few days later when they met for their early morning swim. Calli had decided that Eleni and Froso needed to spend a little time together without everyone around them, so that morning she left them on their own. 'We should invite your mum to come with us sometime when we go out,' Michalis continued as they swam towards their private cove for a few minutes before he had to leave for work, 'and *Kyria* Froso too.'

'The feeling is mutual. I'm sure she'd love to,' she replied – then thought that as much as she loved her mother, she could do without having her tug along with her and Michalis. 'Perhaps next time we go out with Chrysanthi and Costis we'll get Mum and my aunt to come too,' she quickly added, with a twinge of guilt for her previous unkind thought.

'Good idea. My brother is arriving soon so we'll all go out together,' he replied and reached for her hand to help her step out of the water, avoiding the rocks lurking at their feet. She loved the touch of his strong hand, making her own feel as small as a sparrow nestling in his palm.

They stretched out on the hot sand, giving up their limbs to the golden rays for a short while. Michalis soon had to swim back to start his day, but during that short time Calli reflected as she watched him through half-closed eyelids that the more she came to know him, the stronger her feelings grew for him. She liked his strong yet quiet demeanour, she liked his simplicity and his love of nature, and above all she liked how comfortable he made her feel when they were together.

She had always been sensual; physical attraction and carnal desire had been the primary component in all her liaisons. But her feelings for Michalis were different: although she found him alluring it was other qualities in him that attracted her most. He didn't make her heart race with sexual tension as Paolo had done earlier that summer, but he made her feel secure; he made her feel that if she curled up in his arms he would shield her from any kind of danger, and that if she had a baby with him no harm could ever come to that child, it would always be safe. A sense of familiarity washed over her and a murmur carried by the wind drifted in her ears: *'Don't be afraid, Calli, I'm holding you. I won't let go . . .'*

She lay there on the hot sand next to him reflecting on this, and not for the first time – regardless of her protests and rebuffs to her mother that nothing very serious was actually going on between her and Michalis, such ideas had often passed through her head.

At some point Michalis reached across without saying a word, took her hand in his and gave it a gentle squeeze as if he had picked up her thoughts, as if he too had heard the murmur in the wind, as if in affirmation to her sentiments; he held on to her until he finally got up to leave, promising to call later. Calli stayed on the beach for a few minutes longer after he had gone, musing over their relationship. Did Michalis feel the same towards her, too, or was she projecting what *she* wanted onto him? She had always been so independent – why this desire for protection, this need to be rescued? Her flow of thoughts swirled with many others, making her head ache, until finally she got up and started to swim back to the house. She knew that seeing her mother and aunt again would soothe her confusion and bring some clarity to her thinking. Besides, she was getting hungry for her breakfast and perhaps food and coffee would help banish her fuzzy head.

The scene that greeted her as she walked through the garden gate took her right back to her childhood. Froso and Eleni were sitting at the wooden table chatting animatedly, coffee cups overturned on their saucers in preparation for the grounds to be read, along with a jug of cold water and a half-empty plate of home-made biscuits.

'I see you two have already had your breakfast,' Calli said cheerfully, as she approached her mother and aunt.

'Come and join us,' Eleni replied with delight at the sight of her daughter. 'There are plenty of biscuits left.'

'I'm famished, I need something more than just biscuits, thank you!' Calli laughed and went straight to the chicken coop to see if there were any eggs waiting for her.

She was in the middle of cooking them when Chrysanthi with both of her children arrived through the kitchen door, carrying the usual culinary offerings.

'I know how much you like the Cretan honey, and my father-in-law's bees are the best in the area,' she said as the children lined up several jars of homegrown orange blossom honey on the table. 'Also, I've come to invite you all to a party on Friday night at our house,' she announced with her usual beaming smile. 'A gathering to welcome Aunt Eleni – not that we need any excuse for a party, you understand,' she laughed.

'If it's anything like the last one, I can't wait,' Calli replied, sitting down at the table, ready to devour her breakfast. She looked around the room at everyone. 'Am I going to be the only one eating here?' Looking at the children, she picked up the tray of cookies her aunt had just baked and put it in front of them.

She woke with a thumping head. She was lying in bed, eyes tightly shut to shield them from the light creeping through the closed shutters, her right palm pressed to her throbbing forehead, wondering what had happened to her. It was no one else's fault but her own: she knew perfectly well what indulging in too many shots of *raki* would do to her, yet the previous night she had ignored all the warning signs and her own experience. She knew better than to do this to herself: she had lived for long enough with a reasonably stable and sound mind; now all of a sudden she feared that she was losing it. The hangover would eventually pass, as it always did, but that wasn't the cause of the turmoil in her head and her heart, leaving her both wretched and elated. Downstairs she could hear her mother and aunt talking in hushed tones, trying not to disturb her, but she was already disturbed – not by them, but by the images that filled her mind as she recapped the previous night's events.

Chrysanthi's party was as delightful as ever. Eleni was in her element, enjoying being the focus of attention as the guest of honour, and the evening was passing all too quickly until Michalis arrived. He came through the garden gate, pausing to greet *Thia* Froso with a kiss on the forehead before calling out to Calli who was standing chatting with a group of people. She ran to welcome him but stopped in her tracks when she saw another man following close behind him.

'*Kalispera*, Calli,' Michalis greeted her, smiling broadly, and reached for her hands with both of his to pull her towards him. 'Come, I want you to meet my brother.' He turned to face him. 'This is Nicos, he's just arrived from Athens.'

The two brothers stood looking at her, their identical smiles flashing even white teeth.

'Raphael!' Calli heard herself say softly as she held out her hand to shake his.

'How did you know about that?' Nicos asked with obvious amusement and turned to look at Michalis.

At first glance the two brothers could have been mistaken for twins, but once Calli began to talk to Nicos and had observed him for a while, she established that the only identical aspect in their appearance was their smile. There was no doubt that their likeness was strong: they shared the same intense olive-black eyes and similar solid earthy stature. Yet something in Nicos's manner, something in his look when his eyes were upon her, set them apart – or at least *she* thought so; no one else seemed to share this view.

'The brothers are so alike and not just in appearance,' her aunt said in the kitchen later that evening, 'and they are both such good boys.'

'They are like clones of each other,' Chrysanthi added, seizing another bottle of cold *raki* from the fridge to take outside. 'Don't you think?' She looked at Calli.

'Well . . . I'm not so sure, yes and no,' she replied, wondering what she meant by yes *and* no.

Now, as she lay in bed with an aching head, her mind kept returning to those words; the answer came to her when she recalled her first physical contact with Nicos. *That*, she realized, was where the difference between Michalis and Nicos lay.

It was a mere handshake – which admittedly did linger a little longer than she was accustomed to, as so often in Crete. That was all there was to it, yet the effect on her was profound. She had once read that communication between the brain and the skin is like the dialogue between the brain and the gut in conveying emotions. This made perfect sense to her, since she had experienced a version of this, usually when she heard a piece of music. If it moved her to tears or to joy, she would automatically feel goose-bumps on the back of her neck, sometimes down her arm or even legs. This, the theory went, was triggered directly by the brain, so the emotional stimulus was transmitted into a physical manifestation on the skin; the same applied to touch. That night in Chrysanthi's garden, when Nicos took her hand Calli experienced the thrill of this sensation spreading from the back of her neck down to her spine. The touch of his skin electrified her like no other skin-to-skin contact had ever done before, and during the course of the evening, whenever he touched her the sensation returned.

Throughout the party, Nicos and Calli seemed to gravitate towards each other to the exclusion of everyone else. She was reminded of the scene from *West Side Story*, when Maria meets Tony and the rest of the world fades away. She kept pushing the image away, berating herself that she was being ridiculous, but she couldn't help it. She tried to stay by Michalis's side. She made a point of returning to him each time she found herself spending too long with his brother, but each time it didn't last. Somehow soon they would find themselves together again, as if a magnet was pulling them towards each other. At some point Nicos guided her towards two chairs under a tree away from the hubbub and they sat together, apart from the crowd. He made her laugh, perhaps too much and too loud, but by then she didn't care. They talked and danced and sang and talked some more, as if they were two old friends.

When she first met Michalis, he had made her feel comfortable and calm and curious to get to know him. Nicos made her feel animated and excited and as though they already knew everything about each other.

11

So there she lay that morning, holding her head in confusion and trying to make sense of the night before. Michalis had been her constant companion for weeks; they were good together – had he not said so? Or at least he had implied it, and she agreed. Hadn't she even allowed herself to fantasize about a life and a child shared with Michalis and his olive farm in Crete? Naturally such fancies were hers alone – not to be shared with him or anyone – though she was almost certain Michalis felt the same way.

Yet why was she now suddenly tormented by these perverse pangs of attraction towards another man, when she should be content with her new friendship with Michalis? She needed no more fleeting adventures, she told herself sternly: Paolo had already helped her to regain what James had knocked out of her. What was needed now was stability. Her feelings for Michalis went deep: she could see a future with him, or so she had thought until now . . .

The cheerful voices of Eleni and Froso, who had evidently now moved to the garden, floated through the open window, interrupting her anxious self-questioning and prompting her to go downstairs to join them. As she swung her legs out of bed, she hesitated for a moment, apprehensive that her mother and aunt would almost certainly want to discuss last night's party and her behaviour might well be the subject they would dwell on.

She was halfway down the stairs when her mobile rang. 'I hope I didn't wake you,' Michalis said. 'Nicos and I were just talking about you. We are going up to the olive estate soon and we wondered if you'd like to come with us?'

She felt a churning in her insides, between a guilt-induced queasiness and excitement. 'When?' was all she managed to ask before going out into the garden.

'*Kalimera*, Calliope *mou*!' Froso was the first to greet her, as she walked barefoot towards them in her night shorts and T-shirt. The two sisters were drinking their coffee and interrupted their flow of talk. 'You look flustered,' her aunt said with concern as the young woman pulled up a chair next to hers. 'Is your room too hot? Did you sleep all right?'

'No . . . I mean yes, *Thia*, I'm fine, no problem with my room,' Calli blurted, aware that her face must look flushed after the phone call.

'It was unusually hot last night,' her aunt continued. 'I was worried about you. Maybe today the heat will subside a little.'

'Enough about the weather!' Eleni burst out, interrupting her sister. She gave Calli a long lingering look. 'So . . . last night was an *interesting* evening?' she said, right on cue, and raised an eyebrow.

'Er . . . well . . . yes,' Calli mumbled. She turned to her aunt, ignoring her mother. 'Unless you have anything else planned for me this morning,' she announced, addressing them both, 'I've been invited by Michalis and his brother to go out for a drive.'

'Let's take Calli for a coffee and a bite before we head to the estate,' Nicos suggested when they picked her up soon after their phone call, giving her just enough time to dress and get ready.

'They are both such good boys,' Froso had said to her sister as they left. 'I am glad Calli is having a good time.'

The *kafenio* they chose that morning was nothing more than a shack on the beach owned by an old man and his wife.

'It doesn't look like much,' Michalis said, 'but I promise we will eat like kings here.'

They feasted on a breakfast of freshly picked grapes and figs, crusty village bread, olives, cheese, hard-boiled eggs and honey from local hives. No sooner had they finished eating one dish than another was set before them. Calli, battling with her nervous digestion, did her best; each course tasted as good as the last.

'This is what I miss, away from home,' Nicos sighed. 'Finding a simple place like this on the beach.' He picked up a green fig. 'I never understood why anyone would want to peel a fig,' he said and popped it whole into his mouth as he reached for another; this time he took care to choose the finest one, large and deep purple. 'Try this,' he said, offering it delicately to Calli: 'for me it's the skin that has most of the flavour.'

'The darker they are, the better the flavour.' Michalis nodded in agreement.

Calli leaned back on her chair and bit into the honey-scented fruit. She savoured both texture and taste, pungent and sweetened by the sun, relishing each mouthful. How marvellous it was to be sitting on a sandy beach a few metres from the water's edge, her bare feet plunged into the warm sand, discussing the best way to eat figs. Nothing could have been more perfect at that moment. She closed her eyes and wished it could last for ever.

The two brothers were equally attentive towards her, but the irresistible pull she had felt towards Nicos had not diminished. She had wondered if, in the clear light of day and with Michalis present, the visceral attraction that had drawn her to Nicos the previous night might feel less powerful. But the pull was still there and just as strong. She felt it on her skin and in her pulse and in the pit of her stomach.

She tried to maintain her distance from him, unwilling to cause offence to Michalis. If she stood too close she felt an overwhelming desire to touch Nicos, to feel the current from his skin as she did the night before. Nicos, on the other hand, took every opportunity to take her hand or slip an arm around her waist and guide her towards something or other he wanted to show her.

'Did you know that the first cultivation of olive oil was in Greece and more specifically in Crete?' he told her, pointing at an incredibly gnarled old olive tree. 'We've been producing olive oil here since the Minoan civilization, so no wonder our olive oil is the best in the world.' He beamed with pride.

'As a matter of fact, yes, I did know,' Calli replied, smiling. 'Your brother has already told me something about that.' Nicos's enthusiasm was no less than Michalis's.

'They might say that Kalamata olives are the best in the world, but have you tried Cretan olives? Did my brother tell you that they are even better?' he chuckled as he continued his eulogizing.

Calli spent the entire morning in a perpetual state of euphoric confusion and anxiety. She would steal furtive glances at Michalis as they visited the processing plant, trying to gauge his reaction and mood, but she sensed no change to his usual mild and good-natured humour.

'You see how knowledgeable my brother is about olive oil?' he told her, interrupting Nicos's explanation. He gave him a playful slap on the back. 'Come back, Brother, we can get reps to sell our oil for us in Athens.'

By noon the sun was blazing and too hot for them to be wandering among the trees; besides, the men were complaining of feeling hungry again.

'Let's head to the little taverna up the hill for lunch,' Michalis said, adding to Calli, 'Remember the place? The one with the perfect *briam*?'

She remembered it well; he had taken her there for lunch the first time they went for a drive together. Tucked away from the road in an orchard, shaded by the cluster of trees that surrounded it, the taverna provided them with a welcome release from the midday heat. As they entered the cool dining room, Calli was amused to find that the same group of high-spirited local farmers who had been lunching there that first time had gathered again for their midday meal. On seeing the three friends they all raised their glasses and greeted them noisily.

'I love this place,' Nicos said, leaning back on his chair. The proprietor was already approaching their table carrying a bottle of ice-cold *raki* and three glasses. They ordered the restaurant's speciality, knowing that it was Calli's favourite, and whatever else was on offer that day.

'My wife has been cooking since five o'clock this morning,' the proprietor told them. 'You are in luck because she has made *dolmathakia* with succulent vine leaves picked by yours truly.' He gave a hearty laugh and filled their glasses.

'No one makes *briam* like us Cretans,' Nicos said,

spooning a generous helping onto Calli's plate as soon as the dish arrived steaming from the kitchen.

'I'll drink to that! *Stin yiamas!* To our health,' Michalis said, raising his glass, then turning to look at his brother: 'It's one thing selling oil, and another making it.'

'It's true, I miss walking among the trees,' Nicos replied.

'Then perhaps you *should* come back,' Calli added. 'Perhaps that's what I should do,' she laughed and lifted her glass to her lips.

They delivered Calli back to the house in good time for the customary siesta, which she felt she needed more than ever before. Alcohol during the day really didn't suit her, she would tell people; even a glass of wine could put her out of sorts. She had managed to shake off her previous night's heavy head, but on *this* day she knew the only remedy that would keep her calm and steady her nerves was a drink. The glasses of *raki* the men encouraged her to share with them did the trick, but it also had a soporific effect, so by the time they dropped her off at her aunt's house she was more than ready for an afternoon sleep. Her mother and *Thia* Froso were both well into their own siestas and their gentle snoring could be heard as she tiptoed upstairs to her bedroom, where she promptly fell into a deep sleep.

She woke with a start as the light outside was beginning to fade. Opening her eyes, she realized she had woken herself up singing. She had dreamed that she was flying. She was lying on the span of an angel's wings as if on a magic carpet, singing her heart out and soaring above the blue waters of the Aegean, the warm wind blowing through her hair and ruffling the angel's snow-white feathers against her skin. The angel had Nicos's face. She closed her eyes again, summoning up her dream, when she realized that the song on her lips was one and the same as the song playing on the radio downstairs, an old island folk melody that she had known all her life.

> *Over the blue waters of the Aegean sea,*
> *Where the dove-white islands lie*
> *Rose petals fall from the sky*
> *With each flutter of their wings*
> *As the Angels fly by.*

She lay in bed for a little longer, softly singing along with the music that drifted through the window as her mother's and aunt's voices had done earlier that morning. This time, though, she didn't hesitate to go downstairs to join them; on the contrary, she looked forward to being in their company.

'*Yiasou*, Calliope *mou!*' Froso called, the first to greet her again as she came through the kitchen door to join them in the garden. As before, the two sisters were sitting over their coffee, refreshed and cheerful after their afternoon sleep.

'Sorry if we woke you with the radio, but if you slept any longer you wouldn't be able to sleep tonight,' her mother told her.

'I think I woke myself up,' Calli smiled. 'I was singing in my sleep, would you believe!' She gave a little chuckle and bent to give her mother and aunt a kiss. 'I do believe the angels are circling above us in more ways than in the song,' she said and pulled up a chair next to Eleni.

'How was your day, Calli *mou*?' her mother asked eagerly. 'Did the guys give you a nice time?'

'Yes, Mum . . . they did . . .' she replied with a certain hesitation. Giving a long sigh, she leaned back on her chair.

'Want to talk about it?' Eleni asked and reached for her daughter's hand. She had been concerned about her since that morning. She knew her girl well: Calli wasn't usually one to avoid talking about whatever preoccupied her and her earlier evasive behaviour was uncharacteristic.

Calli sat in silence for a while. Then she reached for the jug of water on the table, poured herself a glass and took a sip. She looked in turn at her mother and aunt.

'Do you believe in love at first sight?' she asked them.

Froso's reply came back immediately, a little too loud and with no hesitation or pause. '*Yes!*' she said, causing Eleni to turn to her in surprise.

'What about you, Mum?' Calli asked.

'I do too!' she replied, her eyes still fixed on her sister.

'I believe it's real.' She turned to look at her daughter. 'The minute I saw your father, I knew he was the one. In fact, I knew before I saw him,' she said, alluding to her psychic qualities.

'So, my girl . . .' Froso said leaning forward to reach for Calli's hand. 'Are *you* in love?'

'I think so, *Thia* . . . I've never felt this way before, it's so unexpected.'

'But evidently not with Michalis?' Eleni added. 'Am I right?'

'Was it that obvious?' Calli asked, leaning her elbows on the table and her chin in her hands.

'Yes!' the two women replied in unison. 'I thought you were so taken with Michalis,' Eleni said, 'and he with you . . .'

'I was and I am, but not in that way . . . Oh God, I don't know . . . it's so confusing.' Calli sat back and lifted her arms in the air in a gesture of exasperation. 'I honestly thought I was falling in love with Michalis . . . Oh, why are we so complicated? Why, why can't things be simple?'

'Things are never simple, my girl,' Froso replied, 'because we are human and because our heart tells us the truth, and because when *Eros* strikes we are done for!'

'Does Nicos feel the same?' her mother asked.

'I don't know . . . I only really know what *I* feel . . . but I believe so.'

12

Once Calli had spoken the words out loud, and acknowledged the true emotions that had led her in this startling
new direction, she decided she had to find out if Nicos felt
the same. As she told her mother, she was of the generation
of women that didn't have to wait for a man to declare
their intentions, it was as much her right and responsibility as his.

However, the next few times when they met it was, as
always, in the company of Michalis too. What she longed
for was time alone with Nicos, to be given the opportunity
to assess and find out how he felt towards her. She found
that being with both brothers at the same time was making
her feel awkward, tongue-tied, confused, even disloyal
towards Michalis. A niggling feeling was quietly nagging
at her, telling her she had to talk to Michalis, that she owed
him an explanation.

The longer she spent in Nicos's company the more her
emotions towards him intensified, making her all the more
anxious to know how *he* felt. She tried to judge what the
main component of her attraction towards him was and

why he was having such a strong impact on her in comparison to his brother. Michalis was just as attractive, she mused, just as charming and intelligent, yet it was Nicos who had got under her skin, or *on* her skin, she thought with amusement, remembering the way his touch was making her feel each time he reached for her. Her sexual attraction towards him, she acknowledged, was indisputable, but it wasn't just desire that propelled her towards Nicos – she had fallen in love.

'I've always thought I'd have a family,' he told her one afternoon, finding themselves alone at last after Michalis had left to attend to some urgent business. 'My brother and I, we were so happy growing up in the village, so much freedom to roam around the hills and countryside; I'm sure that's when our love for cultivating olives began – we learned from our grandfather when we were quite small. I always imagined I would return home some day and have a family of my own here.' He paused to look at her. 'What about you, Calli, how was it growing up in London?'

'It was happy,' she replied. 'My mother is a true Cretan, she brought us up with a strong sense of her culture. London is a multicultural city, at school we had friends from all over the world, and we still do,' she replied. 'My best friend is Caribbean, her family, especially her grandmother, always reminded me of my *yiayia* Calliope.'

'Is London where you want to live and raise your family?' he asked hesitantly, pausing before continuing. 'Do you *want* to have children, Calli?'

His question made her catch her breath. 'Oh yes, Nicos, I do,' she replied. 'More than anything.' She barely finished completing her sentence than her thoughts turned to Michalis; hadn't she asked him that very same question not long ago?

The time, she decided, had come to speak to him, she couldn't put it off any longer. She had to explain to Michalis how she felt. But what to say? It wasn't as if either had at any point made a declaration of love or a pledge of commitment to one another, yet she felt that an unspoken bond had grown between them and breaking it seemed like a betrayal. Her feelings towards him were tender and warm; since she suspected they were reciprocal and she had no intention of hurting him, she was duty bound to talk to him. Yet what would she tell him? Announcing that she had fallen in love at first sight with his brother would sound ridiculously fickle and immature. But she couldn't help how she felt, she was following the laws of her heart, the laws of nature and of love, and it was important that she try to explain to Michalis, out of respect, that whatever her earlier fantasies, the affection she felt for him was a sisterly, platonic love, while it was his brother who had stirred earth-shaking emotions in her.

All the while she was pondering about what to do, a sentence hovered in her mind: *When my body thinks . . . all my flesh has a soul.* The quotation came from Colette, the French writer she loved and admired. She had often questioned its meaning and now at last she understood: her own body, her own flesh, was *showing* her the way.

Speaking Greek as she did, she was familiar with the observation that in the Greek language there are many ways to differentiate love, from the platonic to the parental, to friendship and the erotic. When she was on the brink of adulthood and starting to be interested in matters of the flesh it was the erotic love that caught her interest. It was Aphrodite's love child with his love arrows that captured her imagination and intrigued her. Later, when she was older, Eros did strike her a few times but there had been nothing to equal the way Nicos made her feel. All she now needed was to find out if Eros had targeted him in the same way too.

She had been sitting alone under the olive trees, eyes closed, lost in thought, deliberating what to do about Michalis when Nicos arrived at the garden gate. He softly whispered her name, reluctant to disturb her in case she was asleep, but the sawing song of the cicadas masked his voice. He stood silently gazing at her as she reclined on the faded deckchair, eyes closed, her arms folded behind her head, her skirt slightly raised above her knees, and his heart swelled with desire. This unusual woman, neither

Greek nor English but a child of the world, knowledgeable and bright, wise yet innocent and fun-loving, had got
under his skin. He had been unable to put her out of his
mind since he first laid eyes on her and he too had a great
need to know if she felt the same way about him.

He stood motionless for a while, still gazing at her,
when suddenly, as if she sensed his presence, her eyes
snapped open. She saw a troubled look on his face: his
brow was furrowed, his cheeks faintly flushed, yet his eyes
were smiling down at her.

'Oh! Nicos,' she murmured, 'where did you appear
from?'

'I fell out of the sky,' he joked, ignorant of the significance of his words.

'Were you circling above?' she said and gave a little
laugh. He gave her a perplexed look.

'I was circling the village on my motorcycle,' he said
and moved a few steps closer. 'I've come to take you for a
ride if you are free.' He moved still closer and took her
hands in his, flooding her with delicious shivers.

He parked his motorbike under the shade of a stand of
eucalyptus trees and mimosa bushes and they made their
way towards a deserted beach, so white and so blue they
were blinded by its glare. Throwing their clothes off, they
ran holding hands into the surf and plunged into the cool
waters. She had no idea how long they swam, diving in

and out of rocks, coming up for air, chasing fish with bright shimmering scales that she had never seen since she was a little girl, when Keith would take her into the open sea with him. Finally, exhausted and exhilarated, they waded out of the water and collapsed under the shade of the eucalyptus trees. She lay on her back, limbs heavy on the sand, and looked through the branches at the flawless blue sky, holding her breath in anticipation of his touch. Nicos turned on his side, one arm folded under his head for support, and looked at her. His eyes held hers for a long while before he spoke.

'Calli,' his voice was low and throaty, 'do you feel it too?' He didn't need to say more; she knew what he meant.

'Yes, Nicos, I do,' she said and felt her heartbeat throbbing in her ears as he pulled her to him. She reached for him and her touch made him catch his breath, and when she ran her palm over his forearm, she felt the goosebumps rise on his skin.

'Stop thinking so much, and listen to your heart,' her friend Josie often used to say to her when she judged that Calli was trying to be too accommodating, too compromising. Michalis, too, had said something similar not long ago.

Unable to ignore the clear voice of her heart and her friend's advice, Calli was doing just that, listening, and not only to her own heart, but to Nicos's too – apparently, he told her as they lay under the eucalyptus tree, their hearts were now beating as one.

From that day on the two of them were inseparable; she had all the proof she needed that Nicos felt as she did – having that conversation with Michalis was now starting to be constantly on her mind. The intimacy that had developed between herself and Nicos in such a short time was obvious and she was sure Michalis must have picked up on it. She felt disloyal, she couldn't imagine what he must think of her. If it was the other way round, if she had a sister and suddenly Michalis transferred his attentions to her, Calli was certain she would feel pangs of jealousy.

The three would often meet up as before, although now Michalis seemed to only join them in the evenings leaving Nicos and Calli to spend most days together. What countryside and beaches she hadn't seen in the weeks she had been on Crete, Nicos was showing her now by driving around on his motorbike. He left no secluded beach or hillside unexplored and the proprietors of most of the local tavernas had become their good friends.

Nicos had not intended to stay for very long – he had come for a short break to visit family and friends – but after meeting Calli he postponed his return for a couple of weeks; soon he would have to leave, time now was of the essence, for both of them.

'I wish I didn't have to return to Athens,' he said to her one day while having a coffee at a beach cafe. 'I need to go and deal with our business, but I will return.' He looked anxiously at her. 'I wish I could stop the clocks and turn back the time to when we first met that night, at the party . . .' His voice faded and he shifted closer to put his arm around her. 'When do you plan to leave for London, Calli?'

'I haven't decided yet,' she replied with a sinking feeling. 'I have no reason to go back at the moment.' She couldn't bear to think that their idyll might be coming to an end so prematurely.

'Will you stay, Calli? Will you wait for me?' he asked, his eyes turning serious, and leaned in to kiss her on the lips.

13

The very next day she called Michalis and arranged to meet him at the little beachside cafe on the outskirts of the village. This way, she thought, after having a drink, they could take a walk and talk alone together, away from curious ears, as August was the month that the village saw some action from holidaymakers.

She found him already there, chatting to a couple of elderly local men who were playing backgammon.

'*Yiasou*, Calli,' he called and jumped up to greet her. She looked at him with fresh eyes and registered once again how physically similar he and his brother were. She was nervous. All the way down the hill from her aunt's house she had rehearsed what she would say to him, scolding herself for being so anxious. She had done nothing wrong, she insisted to herself, she must be herself, open and honest; yet her palms were moist and her face was flushed.

They ordered coffee and ice-cold lemonade. Michalis was insistent that she try the delicious *baklava* that was freshly baked that afternoon, but she had no appetite to eat, thinking only of what she must say to him. They sat talking about nothing in particular, while the two old men at the next table joined in their conversation for what seemed like an excruciatingly long time. At last, unable to bear the suspense any longer, Calli stood up and suggested they take a stroll.

They walked barefoot along the shore, their footsteps washed away by little waves as they sauntered towards the end of the long beach to some rocks. Along the way she started to tell him all she needed to say. She spoke in a small breathless voice, her eyes fixed on the horizon, avoiding his gaze. She told him that in the short time they had known one another she had grown very fond of him and that at first she had imagined, hoped even, that their relationship would develop into romance, but it wasn't to be. She told him that she loved him like a brother and that he had become very dear to her, and that he had awakened her love for the island and the Cretan landscape, which she realized she had neglected and which now she couldn't bear to leave. She told him that she wanted to stay until November and beyond, to help him and his family with the olive harvest.

All the while she spoke, Michalis remained silent and thoughtful, listening to her. Then, when she had said most of what she had wished to say, she stopped and began searching for the right words to finally speak of the love she had for his brother. By then they were sitting on the rocks and the sun had started to travel west, the waning rays bleeding into the milky blue of the sky, swathing it in red. Her eyes resting on the straight line of the horizon, she took a deep breath, held it for a moment, then, exhaling, she began to explain about the thunderbolt that had struck her so unexpectedly and the effect Nicos was having on her. When she finished speaking, they both sat mutely gazing out to sea. After a long pause, Michalis looked at Calli, cupped her face in his hands and gently turned it towards him; she avoided his gaze.

'Look at me, Calli *mou*.' His voice was quiet and tender. She raised her eyes to meet his. 'I want you to know,' he began, his hands still framing her face, 'that your friendship, and you, have been the best thing that has happened to me in years.' He leaned towards her and gave her a gentle kiss on the cheek before continuing. 'My brother,' he went on seriously, 'is a lucky man to have won your love.'

The expression that appeared on her face at that moment caused Michalis to lose his grave tone of voice and smile. She had not expected this response from him; she had anticipated at the very least some disappointment or regret, and his apparent approval caught her by surprise.

Releasing her face, he gently stroked her cheek with the back of his hand. 'What I'm trying to say is that I don't blame you, and that I am not surprised.' He smiled again. 'What I am, is happy for you and for my brother. I only wish I was in Nicos's shoes . . .'

Michalis's eyes suddenly clouded over, and it was his

turn to turn away towards the horizon. When he looked back at her again, his expression was serious, his voice trembling a little. 'You see, Calli *mou*, I am not like Nicos . . . my brother and I might look alike, but our natures are totally different.'

He left the words to hang around them before saying more.

'I would like nothing more than to be able to love you like he does,' he said quietly, with a long sigh, 'but I have never been able to love any woman like my brother does.'

Later, back in her room, she wondered how it was possible that she had failed to pick up the signs that Michalis was gay. She had enough friends back in London, both men and women, personal and work associates, who were gay. But then again that was London, one of the most sophisticated places in the world: no one had to hide their true nature there.

He had tried, he told her, he had tried to date girls; in fact, he said, when he was a youth he was much in demand. The two brothers were considered prime boyfriend material by girls of their own age; less than two years apart, they were both equally good-looking, athletic and clever, always at the top of their class at school.

'If anything,' Michalis told Calli as they sat side by side on the rocks looking out to sea, 'when we were young I used to be even more popular with girls than Nicos, much to his irritation. But later on, when I was older, I realized that my popularity was due to the fact that I bore no threat to them, unlike my amorous younger brother. A girl's honour was always safe with me.' A wry smile played on his lips as he spoke. 'One of the reasons I left the village for the big city was to get away from the small community,' he continued. 'I felt so ashamed. How could my mother and father comprehend what I was if I didn't understand or accept it myself?'

Michalis told no one, not even Nicos, for a long time, not until years later. Living in Heraklion in the hub of the big city made it easier to come to terms with himself, and although some opportunities for relationships with both men and women presented themselves, he felt awkward, inhibited, uncertain. 'Then I met a girl, an Athenian, and I decided to try and make a go of it with her,' he told Calli. 'We came back to the village, thinking we could set up home here and get married . . . I thought it would please my mother, you see,' he sighed, regret sounding in his voice. 'I thought I could win, I thought I could fight against it, but fighting the waves of the sea is pointless . . . I realized that I had to give in, I had to accept the power of nature . . . my nature. That was a low time in my life. I felt bad, not only for the girl but for myself, too . . . that was the first time I decided I needed to talk to someone.'

Michalis had thought that perhaps he could talk to his friend Costis: 'He was my oldest friend, we knew each other since primary school. But I couldn't do it. I thought of taking Chrysanthi into my confidence: she too had become a good friend over the years. But I just couldn't bring myself to talk to her either.' Her insistence on finding him a wife, Michalis told Calli, amused and saddened him at the same time. Instead he learned to be evasive and threw himself into his work. His love for the land must be solace enough for him.

'My trees and my olive oil, all that went a long way, and still does, to keep me content and stable,' he continued, 'and I learned to accept my life. If I wanted to live here, I had to accept that this was how it had to be. So I locked it all inside and pretended it didn't exist until I finally spoke to Nicos.'

It was after Nicos had moved to Athens and Michalis went to visit him that at last, away from the village and the family, he summoned the courage and was able to speak about it. 'I knew that my brother would be the only person I could truly trust not to judge me, I was certain that our bond was stronger than any prejudice, and I was right. He has been my rock ever since.'

Calli, grateful and touched that he cared enough to take her into his confidence, sat silently, letting him speak. 'When I first met you,' he said, looking at her, 'I honestly wished I could have been the man for you.' He reached for her hand and brought it to his lips. 'Meeting you has been one of the best things that has ever happened to me, you've brought me courage . . . you brought me hope.' He took in a deep breath before continuing. 'That day in the chapel when you asked me if I wanted children . . . I thought about it endlessly. I couldn't imagine anything more wonderful than having a child with you.'

He picked up a stone and threw it as far as he could into the sea, then turned to her. 'But I am not the man for you, Calli *mou* . . . my brother *is*.'

14

By the time the two friends had finished talking and started to make their way back to the village, the mountains loomed indigo against the darkening sky and the flickering stars above them were beginning to multiply with each step they took.

Michalis walked her all the way back to *Thia* Froso's house but declined an invitation to join the ladies for a drink.

'I've never known him to refuse a coffee or a drink with me,' Froso commented, sensing a difference in the young man's usual jovial manner.

'We stayed by the sea longer than we intended,' Calli excused him. 'I expect they are waiting for him at his mother's house for dinner.'

'And Nicos? Where is he? Are you going to see him?' her mother asked.

'Not tonight, Mum,' Calli replied, pulling up a chair to join them. 'Tonight I'd like to be with you two, and I would like to cook for you for a change.'

The idea of cooking for her mother and aunt had occurred to her while she and Michalis were walking back from the beach and the tantalizing aromas from the little tavernas were wafting in the air.

'So, what do you two feel like eating tonight?' Calli said as she stood up, ready for action. 'Actually,' she added, laughing, 'don't answer that. I'll go and see what there is . . . and I'll surprise you.'

Froso, as always, had been to the market and her larder was well stocked with produce; so Calli, rummaging through her aunt's kitchen, found more than enough ingredients to make a meal. She was no stranger to cooking, having done enough of it for James and herself over the years; although, she mused to herself with a chuckle, it was a pleasure never to have to make a crème caramel or to see another ramekin again.

The tomatoes, green bell peppers and courgettes she found in the fridge offered inspiration enough for Calli to delve among the stock of recipes she had memorized over the years and come up with a plan. The vegetables would be perfect, she decided, stuffed with rice, pine nuts and raisins mixed with herbs and spices from her aunt's cupboard – no Greek kitchen, she knew, would be without oregano or cinnamon or fresh mint. Once the stuffing was mixed and the vegetables prepared, she would bake them in the oven; by the time she had washed, chopped and dressed the salad and had a glass of wine or two with Froso and Eleni in the garden, the dish would be almost done. She gathered her ingredients together and, humming the song that she had woken singing earlier, set about making a feast for her beloved mother and aunt.

This is what life is all about, she thought as she busied herself with peeling, chopping and frying. *It's about the family and people who take care of one another, people who look out for each other, no matter what.*

She recalled all that she had been through during the past year, including her conversation with Michalis that afternoon, and once again thought of the importance of family. She was learning more of this way of life every day, and had been ever since she arrived on Crete. Perhaps, she thought, it was this love and protective care for one's own that had prevented Calli's grandparents from divulging their gruesome family history.

It had been an extraordinary life-changing journey for her so far, and beyond that, she knew that there was more to come, not least from Froso whose story was apparently still incomplete.

That night after they had finished eating and were heading for bed, Froso came to Calli's room.

'It is time for me to continue. It is time now to tell you everything,' she told her niece. 'Please talk to your mother, Calli *mou.*'

Once again Calli had a sleepless night, this time worrying about what to say to her mother and where to begin. Her aunt's story had been disturbing enough for her and she dreaded to think how Eleni would receive the revelations of her sister's past. But there was something else too keeping her awake: Michalis's confession had saddened her and she worried that her friend had opted for a life without love, conforming to some kind of prejudice which in their twenty-first-century world had no place. She had grown so fond of this man, her instincts about him had been right, he was all she thought him to be, sensitive, gentle, loving and tolerant. The idea that he had resolved to live a life of loneliness broke her heart.

Usually she liked to wait until a sunbeam slipped through the wooden shutters before jumping out of bed, but that morning, as soon as she heard the cockerel in the henhouse announce the break of day she was up, dressed for the beach and sitting waiting in the garden for her mother to come downstairs.

'You're up bright and early,' Eleni said as she padded through the kitchen doorway in her nightdress with a cup of coffee in her hand. 'What's the rush this morning?' She pulled out a chair next to Calli.

'I thought we'd go down to the beach before it gets too hot.'

'I don't think your aunt is even up yet,' Eleni replied.

'Just you and me today, Mum, what do you say?'

Froso was glad to see the two of them go out on their

own together, so they left her at home with her embroidery and mother and daughter set off for the shore.

As Calli had hoped, the beach was deserted, the cafes were just starting to set up their tables and chairs on their terraces and the day smelled fresh and cool. They swam around to the little bay where they could talk in privacy in the shade of the rocks.

'It's a great place to sit and think and sunbathe in peace,' Calli told Eleni. 'I've been coming here a lot since I arrived. It's very private – we could even go topless if we wanted to, no one swims this far . . . only Michalis, but he's at work now,' she laughed.

All the while they were in the water Calli was rehearsing how to begin what she had to tell her mother. It was less than twenty-four hours since her difficult conversation with Michalis and now she was about to do it all over again.

Before Eleni arrived in Crete, her great concern had been how she would find her sister's health, but since her arrival, to her great relief Froso seemed well enough or at least that was how she presented herself – calm and stoic. 'I am not the first or last woman with breast cancer. Many recover. But if not, no one lives forever,' she had said when Eleni anxiously enquired about her condition.

Now the story she was hearing from her daughter threw her into a turmoil of emotion greater than any she had anticipated. While she was in England Calli had led her to believe that Froso's health, if not good, was stable; there was no medical crisis and her visit to Crete would be a pleasant reunion and support for her sister. What she now heard was far from the pleasant restorative get-together she had anticipated, and from what she was being told it seemed there was more to come. Eleni sat listening with overflowing eyes until Calli finished talking. Then she buried her head in her hands and wept.

'Oh! My poor, poor, sister,' she repeated, wiping a tear-streaked face with her hand. 'How could this have been kept hidden for so many years, why wasn't I told?' Eleni whispered.

'All I can think of is that there are some things that carry shame in this community,' Calli replied. 'Rightly or wrongly, the family decided you should be spared that knowledge and be protected from it.'

'I can understand that they couldn't talk of such things when I was young, but later . . . when I was growing up, when I met your dad . . .' Eleni's words faded; she wiped her eyes again with the back of her hand. 'We were so close,' she began again, 'she could have told me then.'

'I know, Mum.' Calli reached for her mother's hand. 'I kept asking myself the same thing . . . We go through life assuming we know all there is to know about the people we love, and then, wham! We find all our assumptions were wrong . . .'

*

They found her as they had left her, sitting under the olive trees, a glass of water on the scrubbed wooden table by her side and her needlework in her hands – although Calli, looking closer, noticed that the work hadn't progressed since they had left her there.

15

Crete, 1951

Froso had no idea how long she had been lying semi-conscious on the ground before her sight and faculties returned. Dragging herself to her feet, she stumbled towards Kosmas's bloodstained body sprawled across the mouth of the cave. Howling, she threw herself upon him and hugged and kissed the lifeless boy. Then in a state of confused frenzy and terror, not knowing what to do next, she stumbled from the cave to the place where she knew he always hid his bicycle and hurried to her village to raise the alarm. She didn't go home to her mother; instead she made straight for Kosmas's house in the hope that his brothers were there, and beat on the door with all the strength that was left in her. At the wretched sight of Froso, Vangelio let out a piercing scream and collapsed on the cold tiles, causing Manolios and their two sons to rush to the door.

Soon a crowd gathered; angry voices and shrill laments echoed throughout the village. A group of men climbed into Manolios's truck and headed for the ravine.

Froso had the strongest sensation that she was sleep-walking; her vision was blurred, and her hearing muffled. Her mother was found and came to take her home. She removed Froso's torn, soiled clothes and threw them onto a bonfire that Nikiforos had started in the yard, bathed her and put her to bed. Calliope asked nothing more of her daughter; the girl had suffered enough.

The magnitude of the double crime that had been committed must be avenged. But first Kosmas's brothers, Yiannis and Pavlis, together with their father and more men from the village, clambered down the ravine to the cave and carried the dead boy to the truck. They laid him in the back, covered him with a blanket as if he was asleep and drove back to the village.

When they arrived in the square the church bell started to toll mournfully while half a dozen men along with his father and his two brothers carried the boy on their shoulders, as if in a funeral procession, and delivered him to his bereft mother. Her own wailings and lamentations, and those of the other women, could be heard all over the village and reverberated across the hills and valleys and into young Froso's ears as she lay in bed in a state of feverish delirium. She wanted to run to him, but her limbs would not move. Her mother, by her side, soothed her, stroking her brow and hands to make sure she lay still.

The funeral took place on the following day. Once Kosmas was buried, it was time for the men of the village to take action. Mitros was a condemned man.

After his brutal attacks committed in a frenzy of jealousy, Mitros vanished. His mother had been going out of her mind since his disappearance, fearing that perhaps he had done something terrible. Too frightened to raise the alarm or tell anyone, she locked herself in her house and waited for him to reappear. She knew of her son's obsessions and feared what he was capable of; his preoccupation with knives had caused her much anguish.

'He is a butcher's son, killing is in his blood,' her husband would tell her when he was alive, but she fretted about the disappearance of stray dogs and cats that roamed the neighbourhood. 'It's one thing to butcher a farm animal, a goat or a pig – another to harm dogs or cats when they've done nothing to hurt him . . .' she would protest under her breath. But the father was proud of his son's butchering work, proving that he was a real man. Now that her husband was gone, she was left alone with Mitros and had no way of controlling him, even if he was her only beloved child. There were times when his behaviour alarmed her so much that she blamed herself for spoiling him with her excessive love.

Mitros had been gone for two days and two nights, yet the mother said nothing to anyone. Rumours of the killing of a young man from one of the villages by the coast reached her ears and she feared the worst: if Mitros did not return soon, she suspected he might be implicated, although as yet nothing had been said about a girl being involved. His obsession with Froso had worried her, fearing he might turn to violence if he didn't get his way. Then again, her son was unpredictable: anything could have provoked him to act in a lawless manner. She prayed day and night that he had run away to the city or to the other side of the island; otherwise, she knew the inevitable would happen – in those parts nothing went unpunished. Only one thing was clear to her – she could not mention her concerns to anyone. If her son had killed a man and it became known, there would be no mercy; for the mother of a murderer there were no guarantees, not even for her own safety. Silence was her only option.

Throughout the night after the funeral, the black-clothed women kept vigil in Vangelio's house, mourning the dead boy, their laments echoing throughout the village. The men sat huddled together in another room with the windows shuttered and barred, planning the revenge. They sat red-eyed and sombre and, solemnly taking an oath of secrecy, swore to each other that they would hunt Mitros down and kill him. The secret would remain in their village forever; they would carry it to their own graves.

They went looking for him in his village and eventually

found him hiding in one of the caves, biding his time while he planned his escape. He guessed that his pursuers would come out to look for him soon after they buried the boy, but he miscalculated by a day. Many men of all ages from the village joined the search and they pooled their knowledge of the places in the mountains where an outlaw might hide; he was not the first. They killed him by the knife, as he had killed Kosmas, then, under the black shroud of night, Manolios and his two sons dumped his body in their fishing boat and sailed into the night. The sea roared like a wild beast as if Poseidon himself was in as much of a rage as theirs. They sailed out as far as they dared to where the seabed shelved steeply, then pushed the lifeless body, weighted with an anchor, overboard into the deep to rot beneath the waves, never to be mentioned again.

In the upper village, Mitros's mother waited for his return but as time passed his fate became obvious to her; now, alone in the world she had to consider her own safety and future. The explanation she gave to her neighbours and inquisitive villagers about her son's absence was that he had gone abroad, emigrated to America, as so many young men did in those days. Staying in the village, she had no other course of action.

Froso spent several weeks in bed while her mother and father along with all the female members of her family

nursed her back to health. At first the girl was so traumatized by her ordeal, she seemed to be struck completely
mute, she found no voice to express her sorrow. Gradually,
as she started to regain some of her senses, she began to
cry and wail at the loss of everything she held dear and
clung to her mother for support.

The rape, though acknowledged, was never spoken of
again. Calliope, though distraught herself, maintained a
calm exterior and threw herself into aiding her daughter
towards recovery.

Almost three months later, the young girl at last started
to eat and to regain her physical strength. Froso's emotional
state was still fragile; she suffered from nightmares and
night sweats and her body felt alien to her. For long weeks
it was beyond her capacity to accept that Kosmas had been
snatched away from her and had gone forever, all happiness and the future she had dreamed of destroyed in a few
moments.

The realization that Froso was pregnant hit both mother
and daughter like an earthquake. Calliope remained reso-
lute, all the while praying to the *Panagia* for her guidance.
Froso, on the other hand, after her initial state of shock at
the discovery that she was with child, was certain, as she
told her mother, that the baby in her belly belonged to
Kosmas. She was convinced beyond doubt this was the
fruit of their union on that fateful day when they consum-
mated their love for the first time. The baby she was

carrying was the gift that her beloved had bestowed on her. If she couldn't have Kosmas, she would have his flesh and blood. She was sure that this was the truth, no less, because the Virgin Mother came to her in a dream and told her so – the child would be the living manifestation of their love; she had no doubts.

But Calliope had her misgivings. She feared the worst. She tossed and turned in bed, prayed to God and to all the saints and angels. She made her pilgrimage to the Archangel Raphael and begged him to guide her actions. At last she concluded that the baby must be loved and cherished as any blessed child that came into the world and the circumstances of its conception were immaterial. The baby would be innocent at birth and he or she should grow up bearing no stigma of shame or doubt. A precious life had been granted to them and, since it was God's will, they would love and cherish it.

Still Calliope spent more nights and days pondering and assessing their predicament. Eventually, in the course of her visits to the church during which she devoted much time entreating guidance from the Holy Mother, she reached a profound decision. She resolved that the wisest course of action, in the best interests of the child and of them all, would be for her, Calliope, to assume the role of the mother while fifteen-year-old Froso became the big sister. A young unmarried girl with a child would certainly arouse disapproval and suspicion in the neighbouring area. That secret must be guarded at all costs. The two of them, with the help of Nikiforos, would raise the baby in the loving context of the family fold, protecting the child from the stain of illegitimacy and more pain that the special circumstances of its birth might cause. The pledge of silence that the village had taken on the night of Kosmas's burial applied to Calliope's decision too. The secret of one family would be the secret of the entire community; everyone was implicated in the crime, they would all make sure that the girl was kept out of sight during pregnancy from nearby villages and the truth would remain hidden always.

At first the girl rebelled against her mother's plan. 'You will always be the child's mother, Froso *mou*, no one can take *that* away from you,' Calliope counselled her daughter. 'Look how your little brother feels about you: he loves you more than if you were his mother, you are his friend too. We have to think what's best for the child, my girl. This is no time to think only of yourself.' Froso had to agree with her mother; besides, no one would be taking her baby away from her. They would all live under the same roof as a family. But when the time came and especially when baby Eleni began to talk and would call Calliope 'Mama', Froso felt the sting in her heart.

16

The silence which descended upon the three women after Froso finished speaking engulfed them like a fog. It rendered them and, it seemed, the world around them, mute: not a leaf stirred, cicada song ceased, even the waves of the sea were hushed.

At first all Eleni was aware of was her pulse pounding in her temple and neck, until a small faint sound became audible: Froso's muffled sobs. Eleni blinked as if trying to clear her vision and looked at the older woman.

'You . . . my *mother*?' she whispered in a voice alien to her, as if someone else had spoken.

Froso took in a gulp of air, held it for a moment and closed her eyes. 'Yes . . .' she finally murmured, 'my life has been one long secret.'

Calli, who had been sitting motionless between her mother and Froso, became aware that she had stopped breathing. She took several deep breaths and stood up abruptly as if she had been stung; then, sinking back into her chair again, she opened her arms to hold the shoulders of the women on either side of her, silently pulling them towards her. No sound was uttered. None of them was aware how much time passed while they remained huddled together in this embrace. At last Calli dropped her arms, stood up and went into the house, returning with a bottle of *raki* and three glasses. She placed these on the table in front of Froso and Eleni as they sat, still holding each other.

'We need help to unlock our tongues and our hearts,' she told them. She looked at Froso and poured out the drink. *'Yiayia?'* she murmured and handed her a glass as tears rolled down her cheeks.

It was still early in the day. During the last few weeks when Froso began telling her story to Calli it had always been after their evening meal and she talked well into the small hours of the night until fatigue and emotion got too much for her, leaving Calli wanting more. This time was different. They had the whole day ahead of them, it had hardly gone past lunchtime when she finished speaking and Calli was grateful that they had time ahead to try and process what they had just heard, even if she knew that this was only the beginning of that journey. Their world had now been altered forever.

At first Eleni was unable to speak: her thoughts were incoherent, and no clear emotion had taken hold; then gradually the tears began to pour, and the weeping followed. Nausea mixed with rage rose in the pit of her stomach. She looked at Froso and demanded to know how could *she* and the entire family keep silent during all those years? What right did they all have to keep this from her?

'Silence hides the pain,' Froso replied wearily. 'Once the decision was made, there was only one thing to do, and that was to abide by it. You cannot imagine how many times I breathed those unspoken words just to myself: "I am your mama, Eleni *mou*. Calliope is your *yiayia*." I would stand alone in front of the mirror in my room and whisper the words so only I could hear them.' Froso's voice broke into a sob again. 'You cannot imagine how my heart ached, especially at the beginning, but eventually we all became used to it. You were a happy child, you were growing well, and I had always to remind myself that it was for the best, for your own good.'

Eleni sat voiceless, struggling to keep under control the trembling that had taken hold of her body. 'Your father was beautiful in every way, body and soul,' Froso said. 'He knew you were here, I felt him near me every day.'

'How can you be so sure!' Eleni suddenly burst out, anger rising in her voice again.

'The same way I knew undoubtedly that you were his.'

The afternoon was slipping past and neither food nor drink had passed the three women's lips since Calli had brought out the *raki*. Like the night before, she realized that it was time for some nourishment and she was best able to put her mind to the task. She left Eleni and Froso in the garden and took herself to the kitchen. Bread, olives, cheese and a salad of tomatoes and cucumber were as much as she could manage to prepare, her mind still full of her aunt's new revelations. She was assembling the plates on a tray when her mobile rang, almost causing her to drop the jug of water she was filling.

'Calli . . .' Nicos's voice echoed hesitantly, 'are you free?'

'No . . . maybe later?' Hearing his voice restored some of Calli's equilibrium. She needed to see him but for now she needed to be with Eleni and Froso more.

Late afternoon found them still sitting under the olive trees. Although more needed to be said, the time had come when the three women had no more strength to continue. Sorrow, anger and regret had shrouded them for hours, talking, demanding, crying, until fatigue overwhelmed them and there was nothing more to do but rest.

Back in her room, Calli began reflecting and sifting through all that had been said. Her mother's existence and knowledge of who she was had been transformed, and the same went for herself too. She remembered what she had told Eleni earlier, without realizing its significance: life is rarely what it appears to be. Her thoughts turned to Froso and once again since her arrival on Crete, she felt pangs of remorse. All through her childhood, Calli's attitude towards this woman had consisted more of rejection than of acceptance; now, the irritating expressions of love the older woman had lavished on her started to make sense. Froso had a love in her heart that was inappropriate for the role of an aunt and had to be kept secret. If silence hides pain, Calli thought, surely secrets fester and create wounds that cannot heal if left unspoken. How ironic, she mused, that she had always longed for a grandmother and missed Calliope when she died, yet all the time she had a *yiayia* who was alive and well and was desperate to love her and be loved in return. At last she fell asleep, images from her childhood jostling in her head. The path ahead was going to be a difficult one for them all, and as long and winding as those Cretan mountain roads.

She woke with a start. She had slept deeply without dreams as if to block out the revelations of the day. As consciousness and memory returned, Calli leapt from her bed and ran to her mother's bedroom, only to find it empty. She found Froso alone in the garden, sitting motionless at the table under the olive tree, her hands on her lap, eyes closed.

'Where's Mum?' Calli asked, alarm in her voice.

'She's gone.' Froso's reply was almost inaudible. 'Hours ago. I heard the garden gate open.' She spoke in staccato breathless sentences. 'I was in bed. I've been sitting waiting for her.' Froso fell silent, closing her eyes again as if shutting out the world. Calli's anxiety rose; she looked fretfully around her, wondering where her mother might have gone in her distressed state.

Lying in bed, utterly drained, Eleni longed to rest, to regain some vestiges of strength to continue. Fatigue had claimed both body and mind, the depletion of physical energy resulting from emotional exhaustion. Although she could barely keep her eyes open, wishing for blessed sleep, her brain would not allow it. Among the troubling thoughts that filled her head, a niggling question kept repeating itself: how could she, a woman who believed she had psychic powers, a gift that she had been so proud of all her life, have failed to sense any of the dramatic events that had just been related to her? How could she have lived this long without some kind of sign? Was her everyday family life, her background and upbringing, all she had ever believed in and accepted without question, based on a lie? Finally she got up, threw on some clothes and crept out of the house; there was no point in lying there unable to breathe. She needed air, to run in the open and to be alone, as she had done when she was a child and felt hemmed in at home. Haunted by a thought which she dared not articulate or bring to the foreground of her mind she fled, taking a path that led towards the hills. She knew of a small grove with a few carob trees that had been spared the fate of others hacked down and replaced by olives: a little plot of land which she had claimed as her own private hideout. She ran most of the way until exhaustion and emotion took hold of her once again, and arrived panting, face streaked with tears. Once she had been able to run there with ease, barely breaking into a sweat; now she was no longer young, and though she was still slim and agile for her age, her heart was heavy. She stood under a gnarled old carob, laden with pods which hung from its dusty branches like black stalactites. Eleni threw her arms around the trunk and stood hugging the tree, sobs wracking her frame. Could she ever have imagined all those years ago, when she had escaped here as a girl seeking solitude and peace, what she now knew? Peaceful was the last thing in the world that she felt as she leaned against the tree, trying to draw breath. She wanted to scream, to release the tension in her throat and in her soul; to push that dark thought further into the recesses of her mind and exterminate it altogether, but she could not. All that she could do was to let her tears flow, until there were none left.

At last she wiped her eyes with the back of her hand and, hardly thinking, reached up to pluck a carob pod hanging above her head. She bit into its leathery outer skin, thankful that her teeth were still strong enough to reach the softer, fleshier part of the fruit that was easier to chew on. Its sweet pungent taste instantly, subliminally, transported her to a happier time, a time of innocence when life was simple, when she knew what all the familiar people who were dear to her stood for, and who *she* was. She lowered herself to the ground; leaning back against the tree trunk, she sat there chewing, spitting pips onto the earth, until the entire pod was gone. As she ate, she let her mind drift randomly, until the pressure she had felt in her chest and throat all day started to lift. What sleep had failed to achieve earlier, the time it took to eat that carob fruit succeeded in bringing to her. She let her mind wander back into the past, the faces of family members and friends superimposing themselves in her thoughts. At last an idea started to take shape, causing her to stand up, brush herself down and hurry towards the village until she arrived in front of old Pavlis's house.

She found him sitting on a wooden chair out in his yard listening to the news from an old transistor radio.

Eleni pulled a chair close to him, hoping that if she was in his direct vision he would be able to see and hear her better as she spoke. Now she waited for his response.

'Yes, it is all true,' the old man finally said.

She had already started to piece together vague images and events from childhood as she sat under the carob tree. Memories of visits to the village cemetery with Calliope, Froso and often Uncle Pavlis started to return to her like faded reels of film. She began to recall being taken along from a very early age on those visits by her mother and big sister, and while she played among the cypress trees and chased butterflies the two women would sombrely busy themselves at the graves. Visiting the dead was a common and regular occurrence for all families, not only in order to pay their respects but also to ensure the graves were maintained, to replace the flowers and light the candles. Although many of their deceased relatives and friends of the family were buried there, one particular tomb – Eleni now remembered – seemed to take more of Froso's time and beside it she would fall into mournful silence. Uncle Pavlis too, when he visited with them, would hold Froso's hand and linger with her beside that grave.

'I never had any doubt that you were my brother's child,' the old man said, finding Eleni's hands and cupping them in his. 'My brother died for nothing. His life was cut short before it began properly. But your existence, my girl, was a comfort to us all. It was as if we had part of him still with us.'

'How could you be so sure?' she said with a sharp intake of breath – then instantly wished her question unsaid. That idea had to be exterminated, it must never surface again; she could not tolerate its existence even as a glimmer of a thought.

'As sure as the sun that rises every day,' the old man replied. 'You have his eyes.'

'Then why was I not told?' she demanded, knowing what his answer would be.

'The oath of silence was sacred. Even if the crime we committed was justified, we still had to keep it hidden from outsiders and from the surrounding villages; no one must know, it was too risky. Your grandmother's decision about the circumstances of your birth had to be respected too. Froso was so young and what happened then was our village secret. It was between us and God and no one else's business.'

As a Cretan herself, Eleni knew and recognized all that Pavlis was saying. Having been brought up on this land, she was familiar with the passions and vendettas that had taken place over the years, and of the hot blood that ran through people's veins. Yet still her brain rebelled and rejected the silence.

The old man let her stay while her questions kept coming, her curiosity and sorrow found the way to express themselves in words and after all these years he was finally able and willing to speak.

'I am probably the only one left from the old folk,' he told her. 'Most of my generation are now gone or too old to be of any use. Froso has lived with this burden all her life . . . I know she wanted to talk to you about it for years, she told me that many times but couldn't summon up the courage. When the end feels near then courage returns, or perhaps it's not courage, perhaps it's the wish to depart with a clear conscience.'

'*She* didn't commit a crime . . .' Eleni's voice trailed off.

'She carried the weight of that secret all her life, she often talked to me about her burden but there was nothing to be done. We all did our best to make sure you had a happy life, Eleni *mou*, a normal life. What's the difference – a mother, a grandmother, a father, a grandfather? It's all the same so long as there is love, and you had love all around you, my girl, from everyone.'

17

At a loss as to what to do or where to look for her mother, Calli reached for her phone and dialled Michalis's number.

'Does your aunt have any idea where she might be?' was his first response, without knowing what could have provoked Eleni's disappearance.

'I don't know . . . I haven't asked,' Calli replied, flustered, and turned to look at Froso. After finishing her call she pulled up a chair next to her aunt.

'Do you know where Mum might have gone?' she asked gently, trying to keep calm.

Froso opened her eyes but her gaze was distant; she looked past Calli.

'She's probably gone to see Pavlis,' she whispered, and closed her eyes again. 'Leave her, she needs to be with him.'

She took Froso's advice and instead of searching for Eleni, Calli asked Nicos and Michalis to collect her and take her somewhere private, where the three of them could be alone to talk. At first she had been reluctant to leave her aunt, but Froso insisted.

'Go, my girl, go with your friends,' she told her. 'Besides, your mother will be back soon and I need to have some time alone with her.'

Calli wondered how much she should reveal to Michalis and Nicos, while feeling certain that the time had come to share with them some of her family's hidden history.

They drove out of the village towards the hills, where Michalis lived. It was the first time Calli had visited his house; when they met he had always chosen to take her to a restaurant or bar or explore the countryside. Only once had she asked about his home, and then he had brushed it off as being something of a building site.

Some years earlier, the two brothers had inherited a small house from their grandfather: just two rooms with an outside lavatory in the middle of an olive orchard, which Michalis had recently set about turning into a home. He had lived there alone since he returned to the village and had virtually rebuilt it himself, adding an extension for more rooms, a modern bathroom, a fitted kitchen. He had made a terrace with a view of the sea in the distance, and had cultivated a fragrant garden. The plot was big enough to accommodate two such houses and Nicos had already started building a second for himself.

'This is where I'm going to live when I come back to Crete,' he said, taking Calli by the hand. She couldn't hide her surprise and pleasure as he showed her around. 'I suppose that's partly what I'm waiting for – to finish the house and then return home for good.' Nicos looked at his brother.

'Not long now . . .' Michalis smiled.

'Looks practically done to me,' Calli added, perching on the terrace wall while Nicos went inside to bring more chairs.

Concerned how the brothers would react to Froso's tragic story, Calli took some moments to summon the courage to start, but once launched, her account flowed. She told them about the young lovers' affair, about Mitros's obsession with Froso, she told them about the rape and the brutal murder of Kosmas, and finally she told them about Calliope's plan to bring up Eleni as her own. The one thing she did not mention was the killing of Mitros: *that*, she decided, was not for her to divulge. She did not have the right to break the silence of an entire village that had lasted for generations.

The two men sat silently, listening without interruptions, until she finished speaking. Only then did they respond.

Michalis was the first to speak. He looked genuinely distressed at what he had been told. 'Poor *Kyria* Froso, what a life!' He gave a deep sigh. 'I've always been very fond of her . . . so different from other women of her own age around here, always considerate and tolerant.' His voice faded away. 'I suppose that's why I was drawn to her – she was a bit of an outsider, like me. Not surprising, after the life she's had.'

'I assume Mitros got what was coming to him.' Nicos spoke up.

'Yes . . . in these parts, at that time, a man would stand no chance of going unpunished after committing such crimes.' Michalis nodded in agreement.

Calli was taken aback by their matter-of-fact reaction and accurate conclusion. Intrigued, she sat quietly waiting for them to continue. These two were Cretan men, born and bred on this island: it was natural that they would know the ways of the people better than she did.

'Passions run high here and the blood boils,' Nicos continued. 'I'm not saying it's right to take the law into your hands, of course not . . . but those were different times. Our grandfather often talked of such goings-on and I'm certain Mitros got what they thought he deserved. They had their own set of rules in those days.'

'It has changed a lot, I'm glad to say,' Michalis added.

'Yes. But even now, I wouldn't like to be around to see what might happen to anyone who did such things . . .'

By the time the brothers dropped Calli back to the house the first stars had started to flicker in the darkening sky. Froso and Eleni were sitting talking together in the garden, a pot of herbal mountain tea and two cups by their side.

She pulled up a chair as they both looked up at her, their eyes red with emotion but otherwise more calm than when she had last seen them.

'Have either of you eaten this evening?' Calli asked. 'I know I haven't . . .' She got up and made for the kitchen; as before, she was right in assuming that neither Eleni nor Froso had thought of food since she last provided nourishment for them all. Once again, bread, olives, cheese and tomatoes were as much as she could put together, but it was enough to revive them a little. Her head was heavy with thoughts and emotions but her heart felt lighter. Speaking with Nicos and Michalis earlier had done her good; they had brought a clarity and an element of pragmatism to the family's fraught emotional predicament. She had been wanting to confide in Michalis ever since her aunt had begun telling her story, but then she had never imagined how events would develop, and what an impact they would have on her own life.

If Eleni had tormented herself with the thought that she might be the offspring of a rapist, Calli too wondered whose blood was running in her own veins.

Can a person change the perception of themselves halfway through their life and beyond? she wondered as she busied herself laying food and crockery on a wooden tray to take outside. Would her mother, having reached the age she was now, ever be able to refer to the woman she thought was her sister as Mama? And could Calli herself now start calling Froso *Yiayia*? Did it even matter what label a person is given, and does the love we have for them change according to that label? A host of questions competed in her mind, none of which she could answer. *Is ignorance bliss*, she continued to muse, *when knowledge brings doubt and expectations?* She thought not.

She picked up the tray and carried it out to the garden, well aware that these were questions without easy answers, needing consideration and discussion. She looked at Froso and her mother, two women with years of life experience behind them, yet they were all still learning. The learning process, she concluded as she stepped out into the garden, never stops; this summer alone was proof of that. Calli set the tray of food on the table and pulled up a chair next to her mother.

'I went to see *Thios* Pavlis today,' Eleni said, turning to her daughter. 'We talked for a long time. He told me he has no doubt that I am his niece.'

'Oh, Mama,' Calli said tenderly and shifted a little closer to hug her mother, 'it must be comforting, he is such a lovely man.'

'I have never doubted *that*, not for one moment,' Froso suddenly burst out, 'but I wish with all my heart that I could wave a magic wand and change what has happened!' She stopped as abruptly as she had begun, unable to fight back her tears. 'If only Kosmas and I had waited until we were married, and never gone to that cave, things would be so different now. But we didn't, and there is nothing I can do to change that.'

She reached for her cup of tea, took a sip and looked over its rim. 'I loved you with all my heart, Eleni *mou*. You have been the joy of my life, and so have your children. You cannot imagine how I longed for Calli to love me as much as she did my mother, but it didn't matter.' Froso turned, her eyes tenderly on Calli. 'These few weeks, this summer, while you have been here with me, my girl, have made up for a lifetime of longing.'

The three women sat together under the night sky, sometimes talking, sometimes lost in thought, until fatigue claimed them and once again they reluctantly went their separate ways upstairs to bed.

Calli fell asleep just as a dream took hold. She dreamed that the three of them, Eleni, Froso and herself, were in a small boat in the middle of a storm; the boat was in danger of capsizing, until a flock of seagulls gathered around them and, shielding them from the wind, guided them to safety.

18

Calli woke to the insistent buzzing of her mobile. The call was from Nicos. She had switched the phone to silent without turning it off, as she had planned to call him before she fell asleep. It was early – the clock on the bedside table showed 5.15 a.m. *The sun must only just be thinking of rising*, she thought.

'Calli, are you awake? Can you hear me?' he said, his voice fast and urgent. Without waiting for her answer he carried on. 'I wanted to tell you that I love you, Calli, and I'm not going back. I'm staying here if you will stay with me . . . I want to finish the house for us, for you and me. I'll even build you a little darkroom if you want . . .' He seemed to be running out of breath but continued, '. . . and we can make a life together, you and me, if you will agree?'

Then he paused to take a breath and waited for her to respond.

'Yes!' she said without hesitation, without even knowing if she meant *yes*, I love you, or *yes*, I want to stay, or *yes*, I want to make a life with you and stay in Crete for ever. It was only after she had said it that she realized her *yes* was to all of those things and more.

'I'm coming now to fetch you. Are you up?' he asked in the same urgent voice as before.

'I am now!' she laughed and leapt out of bed. She pulled on a pair of shorts and a T-shirt and with pounding heart ran to the garden gate. She found him already there by the roadside, leaning on his motorbike, evidently from where he had just made the call, smoking a cigarette.

'I couldn't sleep all night thinking about you,' he said, stubbing out the cigarette, and reached to pull her close. He held her tight and the goosebumps returned. They kissed and she could feel the bristles on his unshaven face.

'I didn't know you smoked!' she exclaimed.

'I don't,' he replied and smiled. 'I was nervous, I thought it might help. I had to see you.' He helped her to climb up behind him on the saddle and she wrapped her arms tightly around his waist. She pressed her face hard against his back and breathed in his scent that smelled of the sea. They sped towards the beach where they had made love under the eucalyptus trees; the light was still dim and without colour as dawn was just breaking. He parked the bike and they made for the beach. The sun was rapidly rising now. Holding hands, they stood spellbound, watching the burning globe climb towards the heavens, setting the dawn sky on fire. Silently they stripped naked and hand in hand waded into the water. They stood in the beam of orange light and in turn cupped seawater in their palms and poured it over each other's head as if in an ancient purifying bathing ritual. Once they were both wet, they immersed themselves in the sea and swam towards the sun: all without words, until at last they emerged from the water to nestle side by side under the trees.

'I couldn't stop thinking about what you told us last night, about your aunt Froso . . .' He turned on his side to look at her. 'I kept thinking how life is so strange . . . so brief, so fleeting . . . what are we all waiting for?'

'I think I have been waiting for you,' she said and reached out to touch his face.

'I know this happens all the time to people, I know it happens the world over, but it has never happened to me.' He turned and kissed her palm as it cupped his face. 'I know that I have been waiting for you, too . . . all my life.' She shifted closer and they held on to each other.

'I want to have a child with you,' he whispered. 'A child that we can love and cherish *together*.' He emphasized the last word, and kissed her.

She felt her heart swell with love and soar to the sky to join those angels that spread their wings above the Aegean sea in the song. 'Thank you, Raphael,' she murmured and her eyes filled with tears.

They stayed on the beach, limbs entwined, making love as the sun rose higher. Feeling its warm rays filtering through the leaves, Calli's thoughts turned with a pang of sadness to Michalis. She felt so lucky and blessed at that moment – she and Nicos were making plans for a life together yet her dear friend had chosen to live without the joys of love.

'Do you think Michalis will ever find someone?' She turned to Nicos. 'It's so sad to think that he will go through life alone, he has so much to offer, so much love in him.'

'Don't imagine that I don't think about that too,' Nicos replied, turning on his back and folding his arms behind his head. 'I discuss it with him from time to time, but in the end it is his choice, he has to do what feels right for him.'

They lay on the beach a while longer, unable to tear themselves away from each other until Calli remembered her mother and aunt. She had to go to them: Eleni would be awake by now and would need her. Mother and daughter shared most things; there had never been secrets between them. If something of importance happened to Calli she would always hasten to tell Eleni, and the latter would drop everything in order to listen to what her daughter had to say. But however eager Calli was to tell her mother her news, she knew that this time she must wait. It was her turn to listen to Eleni. Her own moment would soon come; for now, she had to be there for her mother.

Eleni was at the stove making coffee and Froso at the kitchen table cutting bread. The two women looked up at Calli and smiled. It was a serene scene, relieved of yesterday's drama. The young woman was taken back, she hadn't expected it.

'*Kalimera*,' Eleni said and smiled again. 'Couldn't sleep, or just an early bird today?'

'Both,' she replied as she sat down next to Froso, trying to appraise the situation.

'Did you two sleep all right?' she asked.

'Not really,' Eleni replied, 'but it's fine. Sleep will come in its own time.'

Calli looked at Froso: her eyes were red, but she was smiling and nodding. 'It will take time, my girl,' she said. 'I've lived with this knowledge all my life, but your mother needs time . . .'

'We are going to go to see Pavlis later. We'll take him lunch and eat together.' Eleni turned to Calli. 'Come with us?'

Of course she would go, she thought, and nodded. Apart from being fond of the old man, she knew he was the only member of Kosmas's family still alive, their link to the past.

They sat in the kitchen with the doors and windows opened to the garden as they had done so many times in the past. This time it was Eleni who busied herself with the preparations, insisting that Froso took it easy.

'Will you get the eggs, my girl?' Froso asked Calli. She didn't need to be asked twice. To her delight, she found that the hens had graced them once again with four large brown eggs, still warm, nestling in the pen. She picked up each one in turn and placed it in the basket, a task she had performed so lovingly during her childhood for her *yiayia* Calliope. On her way back she plucked a few ripe red tomatoes and a bell pepper which was hanging down ready for the picking. Returning to the kitchen she handed Froso the basket.

'Here you are, *Yiayia*,' she said and kissed the top of her head, 'your hens have been busy this morning.'

Froso lifted her head, her eyes brimming, and nodded, emotion stifling any words she wanted to say.

They had a peaceful breakfast together, little being exchanged between them. Then it was time to prepare the lunch which they would take to old Pavlis: nothing complicated, something simple and tasty. Froso frequently cooked for him and they would often take lunch together in his house; he lived alone and largely relied on friends and relatives, but Froso had been his most regular provider and visitor. In the summer they would eat in his garden under the shade of the trees with a fresh breeze blowing from the shore, while in winter when the rains came, they would sit in the warmth of his kitchen with a blazing wood fire in the hearth. Froso couldn't say which season she liked best; though life was easier in the summer months – no mudslides, falling trees or heavy downpours – she still enjoyed those winter days with Pavlis. She couldn't explain it, but when she sat at the table in his cosy kitchen, the rain lashing against the windows and the sound of the sea roaring in the distance, she felt Kosmas's presence most strongly. It was as if he were there with them.

'Pavlis has always been fond of my *briam*,' Froso told them. She had already prepared it and was putting it into a pot to take with them. 'But sometimes I try to take him something different, like a joint of chicken or pasta, as well.' Together, in unison, they peacefully busied themselves with the lunch: three women harmoniously putting their minds and skills into preparing this meal for someone dear, someone who they all knew played a pivotal part in their lives.

Once everything was ready Froso neatly parcelled the food in cooking pots, wrapped them in crisp white tea towels, and they set off for their visit. They found the old man waiting for them under a leafy lemon tree in his garden, listening to music from the small transistor radio by his side on the table, a couple of cats lying at his feet in the shade.

'In my youth I used to play the *laouto* and the *lyra* and you should have seen me dance the *Pentozali*,' he told them with a chuckle as Froso started to serve the food.

'I can vouch for that, he was almost as good as Kosmas – but not quite,' she said with a smile as she spooned a helping of *briam* onto his plate.

19

Michalis received the news of Nicos's homecoming with jubilation. Not only would his brother rejoin him, but with him would be a new addition to their family – Calli, who had become as dear to him as any close relative. The prospect of her coming to live in the adjoining house with Nicos was better than he could have ever imagined.

'Time is precious. We need to seize the moment, and this is my moment,' Nicos had said when he announced his intention to propose to Calli. 'I've fallen in love before, as you well know,' he told his brother, 'but never like this . . . I have never before met a woman who made me feel as she does.'

'You're a lucky man and she's very special,' Michalis agreed. 'I believe you will make each other happy. There are so many people in the world who never get the chance to meet their soulmate.'

'That is very true, but *you*, my brother, *did* meet your soulmate yet you let him go . . .' Nicos's expression was serious as he waited for Michalis to respond. The soulmate that he was referring to was the only man that his brother had ever spoken to him about. His name was Alexandros and he lived in Athens. Michalis had met him when he took a holiday break to visit Nicos on the mainland a couple of years ago and in the hub of the big city he felt free at last to let go enough and get romantically involved with a man. He was an artist, a painter, and they had met in the gallery where Alexandros worked to supplement his income. He longed to come and visit him in Crete, proclaiming that he had always believed it was the land of inspiration, but Michalis preferred to keep their meetings clandestine and in Athens. Their relationship continued for a while until he decided he couldn't carry on any longer, thus breaking the young man's heart. It had been the first time that Michalis had allowed himself to fall in love and to even possibly envisage a long-term relationship with a man, but what he couldn't envisage was returning to Crete with Alexandros, despite his brother's encouragement and reassurance that together they would speak to the family. Since Crete was where Michalis wanted to live he had to make a choice.

'Perhaps it's time you got in touch with him again,' Nicos told his brother. 'I see Alexandros from time to time in Athens and I know he still loves you . . .' Nicos said no more, he knew his brother well enough, he didn't do things in a hurry ever.

Calli on the other had accepted Nicos's proposal and plan to set up home together without a second thought.

The voice in her head, which she vowed never to ignore again, told her this was the right thing to do, and her heart was in total agreement. Not only had she fallen in love with Nicos and would gladly make a life and a family with him, but her love for Crete had been reignited too. As an artist she saw beauty everywhere; now her art would blossom here, she was certain of it.

'Will you marry me, Calli?' Nicos had asked the morning they lay under the eucalyptus trees.

'Yes, Nicos, I will,' she replied and couldn't believe her ears. All the years she lived with James, all ten of them, she never once thought about marriage, nor did he. It seemed so unnecessary, so antiquated – who had to have a bit of paper to say you were committed? All that was needed was the pledge of love and friendship. But now, here, on this island under the hot rays of the Cretan sun, she could think of nothing more wonderful than to be joined in marriage with this man who had stolen her heart. As Maya had told her: *Often we don't know what we want until we find it.*

'May!' Nicos called out and sat up to look at her. 'Let's get married in *May*. The house would be totally finished by then and I would be back here for good, long before that.' *A spring wedding!* Calli thought and, throwing her arms around him, covered him with kisses. Maya was right, she mused. The oracle that was that marvellous woman in Ikaria had guessed their reunion. She couldn't wait to tell her her news. A Cretan spring wedding and her friends from that wonderful island to help her celebrate – what more could a girl want from life?

Though Calli felt that the moment had not yet come to share her decision with her mother, she longed to share it with someone. All through lunch at Pavlis's house her thoughts would return to Nicos and their conversation; the memory of his touch still lingered on her skin and her heart beat fast with excitement. She wished she could run along the beach, shouting her news at the top of her voice for all to hear. She wished Maya was there so she could tell her friend that her predictions had been correct: that ever since they met on Ikaria, life had been one long series of surprises and revelations. But Maya wasn't there, so in her absence she decided that Chrysanthi was the perfect substitute. She was sure that her cousin's wife would receive her news with approval, so after lunch she made directly for her house.

'I don't care which one of the brothers has stolen your heart – they're both worth it!' the young woman had exclaimed when Calli stopped talking. Chrysanthi's persistent attempts to pair off Calli with Michalis had appeared successful at first but she soon realized that her plans had gone awry when Nicos arrived on the scene. 'I even spoke to Costis about it,' she said, her infectious laughter taking hold. 'I could tell all was not as it should be by the way you were avoiding me. I wanted to marry you off to someone in the village and keep you here the minute I set eyes on you. I thought Michalis was an ideal match, but Nicos is just as good!' Her joy was evident in her voice, which had risen an octave with excitement. 'He is a *good* man, as *good* as his brother and they are a wonderful family, you will have beautiful children with him,' she said, all in one breath. 'And we will have a beautiful spring wedding!'

After leaving her cousin's house, Calli started to make her way back home. She had left the two women with Pavlis, still talking in his back yard under the lemon tree, and wondered if they had returned by now. She sensed that she must still stay close to her mother. On her return she found that Froso had taken herself to bed while Eleni was sitting in the garden, nursing a cup of coffee and evidently waiting for her.

'Can we go for a walk?' she asked the instant she saw Calli, standing up. Although Eleni appeared to be outwardly calm, especially in the presence of Froso, she was less than relaxed. 'I was talking with your dad just now,' she said, 'I want him to come, I need him here . . .'

'OK, Mum, that's fine. Good idea – let's ask him to join us,' Calli replied, her voice calm and soothing. She put an arm round her mother's shoulders. 'Come, let's go for that walk now.'

Her father's presence there would be a great help, she decided. He had such a clear head and always knew how to handle matters. Keith was good in a crisis.

They didn't go to the beach this time. Eleni wanted the solitude of the hills again, so they made their way to the same spot she had escaped to the day before. This time they walked pensively, taking their time; once in a while, Eleni would look at Calli and ask a question.

'Do you think it's better to remain unaware,' was her first concern, 'to remain ignorant of the truth?'

'I wondered about that, too, Mum. But no, I don't think so . . .'

'What good can it do to *know* at this stage in my life . . . is it not selfish of Froso to drop this on me now?'

'I don't know, Mum. I think knowledge is better than ignorance; better to know than not,' Calli replied, having already come to that conclusion.

'But I still don't really *know*, do I?' she said, her voice rising with frustration. 'I still don't *know* who I am.'

They had reached the carob tree and sat down together at its roots. Eleni picked up a pod that had fallen on the ground, brushed the dust off it and absent-mindedly started to rub it with her thumb as she spoke.

'What I *knew* all through my life was that I was Calliope and Nikiforos's daughter . . .' Her eyes turned to meet Calli's. '. . . that I had Mavrantoni blood running through my veins . . . But now? Now I learn that it was all a lie, that

I am not who I thought I was or . . .' she stopped and averted her gaze, 'or even worse!' The last two words came out in a whisper.

'*Mum!*' Calli protested. 'Mum,' she repeated, her voice softer, more soothing, realizing what her mother was referring to. She reached across and wrapped her in her arms as if she were a small child. 'None of that matters. You are *not* your blood. You are *you!*' she said, gently rocking her.

'That's what your father said,' Eleni replied after a long pause and wiped her eyes with the edge of her skirt. 'You really are your father's daughter,' she said and smiled through her tears. Shifting a little closer, she leaned her head on her daughter's shoulder. They sat together for a while, mother and child lovingly connected. Calli thought of the countless times she had been comforted this way by Eleni, of the many tender moments and all the support this woman, her mother, had given her in order to face the world when she was growing up and beyond.

'I am so lucky to have you, my child . . .' Eleni told her. 'You and your brother are the pride and joy of my life.' Calli turned and kissed the top of her mother's head as Eleni had habitually done to her when she was a little girl. 'I used to pity my sister for not knowing the joys of motherhood,' she continued, 'especially when we used to visit her when you and your brother were small and I saw how loving she was with you and Alex, how she longed for your affection and attention . . .'

'Oh, Mama . . .' Calli murmured, and a lump rose in her throat, 'it's so sad . . .'

'I want you to know that I will always be there for you, Calli *mou*. You can be sure that for as long as I am alive, I am your rock, and so is your dad . . . All I have ever wanted for you is to be happy.' She looked up at her daughter. 'I don't suppose Froso wanted anything less for me either, but life didn't deliver her such a good hand as me, did it?' Eleni let out a sigh. 'I am doing my best to understand, Calli *mou*, and no doubt in time I will, though right now I am struggling. But I am blessed to have you and such a good family by my side.'

If any moment could be the right one to tell her mother about Nicos and her decision to stay with him in Crete, this was surely it. Calli turned, took Eleni's hands in hers, looked her in the eyes and began to explain.

As Calli had hoped, her mother's response was no less approving and even more jubilant than that of Chrysanthi. She had been worried that Eleni might feel abandoned if she was to leave London for Crete, especially at this time, when she might need her daughter's support.

'Your happiness is all I care about, and you deserve to be happy, my darling girl. You've been through enough,' she told her. 'I shall have your father and your brother at home, and you will be at the end of a telephone.' She took her daughter's face in her hands and kissed her tenderly on the forehead. 'Besides,' she smiled, 'from now on I shall be spending as much time in Crete as in London.'

By the time mother and daughter made their way home arm in arm down the hill, the sun had started its descent, tinting the world pink. A distant church bell was trying its best to be heard above the deafening sound of birds settling for the night. On returning to the house, the two women found Froso entertaining Michalis and Nicos in the garden.

'There you are!' she called out when they walked through the garden gate. 'I don't suppose these young men have come to see *me*.' She smiled at Calli.

'You know perfectly well that we came to see you, *Kyria* Froso,' Michalis protested with a smile. 'Don't make out that this is the first time I've come to visit you.'

'It's true,' she replied. 'You are very considerate, you visit me often. And look' – turning to her daughter and granddaughter – 'look, my girls, look what the boys have brought me!' She pointed at three bottles of extra virgin olive oil, a huge jar of black olives and a bottle of *raki* sitting on the table.

Despite having heard tales similar to Froso's while growing up, the brothers had found her story both moving and disturbing. Over the years many such dramas of love, jealousy and crimes of passion had been spoken of, but those were anecdotal stories that had happened many years before to folk who were strangers to them, never involving people they themselves knew and liked.

'We wanted to pay you *all* a visit,' added Nicos, leaping to his feet to embrace Calli who had walked towards him. Ever since their morning on the beach he had been in a state of unsettled excitement; like Calli herself he was eager to share their news, especially with her mother and grandmother. On arriving at the house and in the absence of Eleni and Calli, Nicos couldn't contain himself any longer and confessed to Froso the reason for their visit.

'I love her with all my heart,' he told her excitedly, 'and she's agreed to stay . . . marry me, make a home here with me.' Froso reached out and took the young man's hand in hers. 'I give you my blessing, my boy, and the two of you in return have given me a great gift. I waited a long time to have this girl close to me and finally she has arrived.'

'If Calli loves you then I love you too,' Eleni said with a beaming smile after Nicos tried rather awkwardly to ask for her hand and blessing. 'I'm happy for you both, my boy, and I appreciate your respect,' she said and reached forward to kiss him on both cheeks. 'Calli's grandmother has known you for many years and she already loves you.' Her eyes were welling up as she turned to look at Froso, who was glowing with joy. 'Soon her father will arrive too so you can ask him officially for her hand.' She chuckled with amusement at the young man's old-fashioned gallantry.

'I'm sure he will be as happy as we are' – she turned to Froso again – 'to give his consent.'

'A drink!' Froso called, pushing herself to her feet and reaching for the bottle of *raki* on the table. 'Eleni, fetch the glasses!' she said, beaming. 'It's not every day that I receive such good news about my granddaughter.'

20

Keith arrived on the early morning flight from London, accompanied by Alex, who on hearing the news insisted on coming with his father.

'This is a family matter, Dad. We all need to stick together,' he'd said after Keith had explained the story to him. 'It's a tough one . . . Mum needs us. We managed to pull together with Calli and that idiot James! We'll do it again now.' Alex had inherited his father's reliability and love of the family, and staying together had always been his way; even as a little boy he had considered it his duty to protect his sister and his mother. Calli drove to the airport alone in Chrysanthi's car to collect them, intending to let them know a little more about the situation.

'How are they both?' was Keith's first question, wondering how the two women were reacting to each other now.

'It's hard to tell, exactly,' Calli said. 'I mean . . . Mum is not calling Auntie Froso Mama just yet or anything . . .' she tried to jest before realizing this was probably in bad taste. 'It's difficult, Dad,' she continued more seriously. 'One moment Mum is OK and then she's distraught. Her spirits go up and down.'

'It's going to take time. These things can't be rushed, they have to be processed gradually,' Keith replied. 'In many ways a shock like this is almost like a bereavement.'

'I'm so glad you've come, Dad,' she said and reached out to squeeze her father's hand. 'And you, Alex. It will be good for Mum.'

On arrival they found Eleni and Froso waiting for them in the garden. They had both wanted to drive with Calli to the airport, but she had put them off: 'No space in the car, what with their luggage and all . . . the two of you had better stay here, don't you think?'

Eleni agreed reluctantly, but anticipation got the better of her and she spent most of the time it took Calli to collect them in the kitchen, cooking. Froso sat at the table, looking on while she worked, aware that it was Eleni's way of dealing with her anxiety. In the quietness of the kitchen, with no one else around, Froso started to talk.

'I would have given anything for things to have been different, Eleni *mou*,' she began. 'I knew I should have spoken to you. It was your right to know.' She paused and looked at Eleni, waiting for a response, but none came; Eleni kept her head down and continued with her chopping. 'I knew I owed it to you to speak up . . .' Froso paused again, 'and now . . . now it's almost too late, but it was so hard to find the right time, to find the right words. I knew it would change everything and that you might resent me or worse still, hate me for lying to you.' She sighed. 'I accept that it was cowardly of me. But I couldn't bring myself to speak and I suffered for it all these years. Then once I got sick, I couldn't put it off any longer. I had to absolve myself of this secret which had been eating away at me. It was time I spoke the truth.'

Froso looked up at Eleni again with pleading eyes. 'I thought that at least we could spend what time I have left on this earth being what we truly are to each other . . .'

She stopped talking, leaned forward on her elbows and waited expectantly. Finally Eleni turned round and looked at Froso. She wiped her hands on her apron, dried her eyes with the back of her hand, walked over to the table and put her arms around the older woman's shoulders.

'None of it was your fault, Froso *mou* . . .' she said, her voice cracking with emotion and kissed the top of her head. 'You have carried this burden for long enough . . . now it's time to share it. I might not be able to call you Mama because I have lived all my life loving you as my sister, but the love is *no* less.'

'I have loved you as my child since I was a child myself,' Froso replied, eyes overflowing. 'Now that you know, it is enough for me. I am your mother and I will be that for as long as I live.'

'You have plenty of time yet, Froso *mou*,' Eleni said as

she sat down next to her. 'I've seen your medical notes. Your prognosis is good . . . If need be, we'll take you to London to see our doctors there.'

Mother and daughter sat in the kitchen, holding each other and letting their tears silently fall, until eventually they helped each other to their feet and, arm in arm, stepped out into the garden to sit in the shade of the two olive trees and wait for Calli, Keith and Alex to return.

That afternoon, after the family finished their lunch and before the sun started to wane, Eleni took Keith's arm and led him to her carob tree hideaway; she needed time alone with him. The sun was still warm on their backs and the breeze blew gently from the shore as they slowly wound their way up the hill. Keith was her soulmate, her mentor, her friend, her beloved husband of so many years who had listened and supported her and had loved her ever since they first met. They had been through so much over the years, births and deaths, joys and sorrows, and she knew that together once again, with his support she would be able to cope with whatever lay ahead.

'The trouble is, Keith,' she said, holding his hand tightly as they settled themselves on the ground under the tree, 'however I look at it, I still return to that dark place, to that hateful thought that takes my breath away . . .' She inhaled a gulp of air as if deprived of oxygen. 'What if I'm *his* child . . . ?' The words faded on her lips and the colour drained from her cheeks. 'What if *that* is the case, Keith?' she asked again, her eyes searching for a flicker of reaction in his. 'Tell me, how do I live with that? What if I'm not, as Froso says, the product of love, her love child . . . but created by malice and hate?'

Keith didn't respond immediately. Instead, he sat thoughtfully, holding her hands in both of his.

'Listen, Eleni *mou*,' he replied after a pause. He took a deep breath and lifted her hands to his lips. 'I don't know what you think of this, but if you really are so set on knowing . . .' He faltered again for a moment before he came out with what he was thinking. 'Consider this . . . old Pavlis is Kosmas's brother, he is Kosmas's kin and his only relation. If you really are so desperate to know . . . you can find out if Kosmas is your father through a DNA test. It's easy enough.' Eleni made no sound; she sat staring at Keith, mouth ajar. 'Personally, I wouldn't bother,' he smiled, shrugging his shoulders, 'but it's your choice.'

She remained motionless, holding her husband's hands, unable to respond. *Perhaps I should*, she eventually thought. It would be the logical course of action if she was so troubled by uncertainty. Then she would know once and for all and could stop obsessing. But the thought was not comforting; confusion clouded her mind again. Keith sat with her hands in his, waiting for her to speak. She looked visibly distressed. Suddenly she stood up. 'No, I don't think so!' she burst out. 'It's too risky . . .' She looked shocked. 'I mean, I don't know . . . and what about Froso?'

'You are a woman of intuition and you have always claimed that the women in your family were so gifted, too; am I right?' His voice was low and soothing as he reached up and pushed back a lock of hair that had fallen over her left eye with one hand, and then gently stroked her cheek. '*You*, my love,' he went on softly, '*you* have always claimed that your intuitive powers were strong, remember? You have always told me you knew exactly when Calli and Alex were conceived. You are forever boasting of knowing the moment of conception . . . True?' Eleni nodded as Keith continued. 'Well then, why are you tormenting yourself and doubting Froso, who also has consistently said she too knows of the moment *you* were conceived; shouldn't you perhaps believe her? Everybody else seems to have done so. Didn't you say old Pavlis told you he had never doubted you were his brother's child?'

'He did, and he said I had his eyes,' she murmured. 'He showed me a photograph, but I couldn't tell from that – he was just a boy . . .'

'Well . . . maybe you should just leave it alone and believe what you are told . . .'

Keith pulled himself up to face her and took her in his arms. 'You don't have to decide anything now, my love, and you don't have to do anything that you don't want.'

*

By the time husband and wife started walking back to the house the sun had started to sink; a faint aroma of honey lingered in the warm air, carried by the breeze from the hills. She leaned on his arm and they walked at a leisurely pace, without words. They found Froso, Calli and Alex sitting in the garden with Nicos and Michalis, drinking coffee and eating *baklava*, evidently waiting for them. At the sight of them Nicos leapt to his feet and made towards Keith.

'Welcome,' he said warmly, striding towards him with an outstretched arm. 'I was told you would be here soon.' He looked at Eleni and shook Keith's hand eagerly. 'So glad that we meet at last.'

The small family reunion that gathered in Froso's garden that afternoon soon began to turn into a much larger festive gathering. As always, when family members returned to the village from abroad, they had to be welcomed by family and friends in true Cretan spirit. Costis, Chrysanthi and their children were the first to arrive with food, and then one by one others followed. At some point Michalis was assigned by Froso to go and fetch old Pavlis in his car. 'And while you are at it,' Costis called out to him as he was leaving, 'bring your harp and violin so we can sing and dance tonight. We have much to celebrate.'

As on so many other summer nights over the years, the famous family hospitality surrounded them, much to the relief of Keith and Alex, who had feared that this visit to the village might be less than the cheerful affair that usually greeted their arrival. Once again, they were reminded that even in a crisis on this island, food, song and dance were always the best antidotes to a problem.

The conversation between husband and wife that afternoon was not mentioned again; Eleni knew Keith was right. If she had always trusted her own female intuition, why in God's name wouldn't she trust Froso's?

The *raki* flowed and the dancing and singing continued till late, and Nicos took the opportunity to talk to Keith about Calli, who then in turn told her father of her joy at finally finding happiness and love again with a good man.

Michalis and one of the uncles were in full swing playing a soulful melody, and young and old were dancing. Eleni was sitting close to old Pavlis, holding his hand and talking to him. They had much to catch up on, there was so much she wanted to know; nothing would ever be the same again for any of them. Froso was sitting with Keith and Alex openly enjoying talking with her son-in law and her only grandson. She had much to feel happy about. The heavy weight she had been carrying in her heart all through her life had finally lifted and felt much lighter now, and there was also the news of the spring wedding to add to her joy.

Nicos had his arms tightly wrapped around Calli's

waist when he started to lead her towards the garden gate.

'Look up at the sky, my love,' he said, pointing above them. She turned her head and through the branches of the olive tree a yellow moon was playing hide and seek between the shimmering leaves. 'It's full tonight,' he said and ushered her even closer to the gate. 'Let's head to the beach,' he breathed in her ear, 'no one will miss us for a while.'

They stepped quietly onto the road and ran towards the empty shore, guided by moonlight, its luminosity making the lemons and oranges on the trees and the prickly pears on the cactus bushes glow as if sprinkled with gold dust. They arrived at the sea's edge out of breath, took off their shoes and plunged their naked feet into the cool surf. Turning their faces to the sky, they looked at the source of light above them, looming as huge and red as that other moon Calli had gazed upon with awe at the beginning of her summer.

'It's almost as big and red as the blood moon,' she said and reached for his hand.

'This is the harvest moon,' Nicos said as he pulled her closer. She looked up at the sky again and wondered what this moon might bring. The last one, as she had been promised by Maya, had brought change and joy, and sadness too, but above all it had brought her boundless love.

She turned her eyes to Nicos. He smiled, and his eyes glistened in the moonlight; he bent and softly kissed her lips. She leaned her head on his shoulder and let out a gentle sigh. 'Thank you, Raphael,' she murmured and lifted her arms to the sky.

Acknowledgements

As always, I'd like to thank my agent and dear friend Dorie Simmonds for her constant guidance and support, my editor Caroline Hogg at Pan Macmillan, Samantha Fletcher and Nicole Foster for their incredibly keen eye for detail and Anne Boston for my first draft edit.

I would also like to say a big thanks and express my gratitude to my friends Roberto and Serena Dalfini for their hospitality in their home in Crete and for tirelessly taking me around the island while researching this book. They showed me a Crete that no visitor could ever have discovered unaided. I'm grateful to my friends Andrew Jacovides and Bruce Thomson for alerting me to the wonders of Ikaria and Pam Bertschinger for sharing some of her Ikarian experiences.

Finally, I give thanks to Raphael, and to two marvellous Greek Cypriot women, my friends Maro and Aegli, for sharing some of their inspiring knowledge and wisdom with me.

Read on for an extract of *Between the Orange Groves* by Nadia Marks – an emotional and sweeping historical novel spanning decades in the lives of two families from different religions on the island of Cyprus . . .

Prologue

London, 2008

'There never was a more loving friendship than ours . . .' Lambros said, his eyes filling with the memory. '*Nowhere* on the island could you find such good friends as the two of us, despite our differences. Orhan and I would do anything for each other, we were family . . . we were like brothers. How could we let our friendship perish like that? It's unforgivable!'

Stella sat silently, listening to her father talk. She had heard these stories of love and friendship repeated many times over the years but she never tired of hearing them. She took pleasure in his tales from a far-off country, marvelling at the bond that had so closely tied those two boys and their families together. From a place and a past that was opening up to her through his words. Yet in contrast to the pleasure *she* received from her father's stories, the melancholy of recounting them invariably ended with the old man shedding tears of sadness.

Father and daughter were sitting in the garden among

the roses, basking in the sun on an unusually hot day in early June. Stella had come to visit him. This was her favourite month and even on days when the sun didn't grace them with an appearance, nature always did her best. This peaceful garden in north London was bright with flowers and sweet-smelling herbs, thanks to the hours Lambros spent tending them.

She came to visit her father often now that Athina, her mother, was gone, even though she knew he could cope perfectly well on his own. While her mother was alive her parents had always been busy, forever dashing off to something or other. It had been a constant source of frustration that they were less available for her than she would have liked them to be. She missed the old family house in the leafy London suburb favoured by many Cypriots and where her parents made their home when they first got married. She and her brother had been born there, her own children spent most of their pre-school days there with their *yiayia* when Stella was working. She missed her mother, she missed having little children, she missed the old days. Now that her father was alone she enjoyed recalling some of those times with him. Her visits gave them the chance to talk of the past, to remember. Lambros especially needed more than ever to recapture his youth, his friendships, a time of innocence and love, before he came to England, before he married and had a family . . . before he became someone else.

Stella had grown up with her father's stories from his youth but these days she was hearing them more often.

'We have to do something about it,' she told her brother one day while the two of them had lunch together. 'Honestly, Spiros, all he talks about when I see him now is Orhan. He remembers the old times, their youth, and what happened – and then he cries. What could have happened that was so bad to make an old man cry like that?' Stella looked at her brother.

'I know . . .' Spiros replied, 'I noticed it too and can't imagine. You've got to get him to talk about it; he'd tell you.' He gave Stella a little smile. 'You're good at that.'

'I've been thinking we should try and find him, bring the old men together.'

'You're right,' Spiros mused. 'Since Mum died he talks about Orhan and the past a lot. Do you think he's a bit depressed?'

'No, I don't think he's depressed, I just think he is very sad, and that's why I think we could try and find Orhan. You never know, he might still be alive.'

'He's the same age as Dad, isn't he?' said Spiros, reaching for his glass of wine. 'Eighty-something isn't so old, especially for these old Cypriot boys.'

The next time Stella went to visit her father he had just made himself a Turkish coffee and was about to carry it out to the garden. She let herself in and announced her arrival from the hall, hoping he could hear her – he was getting quite deaf these days, but since his hearing was apparently the only faculty that was failing him so far, no one was too worried. *'I hear what I need to hear,'* he would tell them.

'Yiasou, Papa!' she called out cheerfully. 'Where are you?' she asked, much louder than usual.

'In here . . . in the kitchen,' his reply came immediately. 'And no need to shout, the whole street knows you're here now,' he added with a chuckle.

The French windows leading into the garden were wide open, flooding the room with light, and Stella could see the newspaper spread out on the garden table outside where Lambros had been sitting.

'Come, I'll make you some coffee too,' he said, putting down his cup and picking up the *bricky* to make another. 'You like it *sketo* don't you?' he asked and pulled a face. 'How can you drink it without any sugar at all? Far too bitter for me . . . but then you ladies are always watching your figures . . .' he chatted on, glad to see her.

Once again Stella joined her dad in his fragrant summer garden with a plate of sesame biscuits she had bought from the Cypriot patisserie. Sitting down, she allowed him to transport her back in time to a world of people she could only imagine, yet which over the years had become as real as the world she lived in now.

Cyprus, 1946

The light summer breeze carried the call for evening prayer over the rooftops along the narrow streets of Nicosia to the two young men's ears. Lambros and Orhan had been taking a stroll inside the walled city after studying all day when the *muezzin*'s voice announced that the sun had started to set, so it was time for the faithful to remember Allah once more and make their way to the mosque for prayer.

'Is that the time already?' Orhan turned to his friend, incredulous at how late it was. 'I thought it was much earlier,' he added, as they turned left into a side street towards the mosque.

'It must be something to do with my stimulating conversation,' Lambros said jokingly, 'or maybe because it's high summer.' He looked up at the sky. 'I thought it was much earlier too.'

No matter where he was, or with whom, the Turkish boy, Orhan, always observed the prayer five times a day. More often than not, the two friends were taking their customary stroll together when evening prayer was called. The Greek boy, Lambros, was always glad to accompany his friend to the mosque and wait outside, guarding his shoes while the other prayed. Although one was Christian and the other Muslim, the two young men shared a deep friendship based on mutual respect and love for one another despite their different faiths.

'Don't you ever get mixed up with all of these shoes here?' Lambros pointed at the sea of footwear outside the mosque when Orhan re-emerged. 'I often wonder if anyone ever makes a mistake and walks off with someone else's . . .' He added, 'There are so many of them and they're all so alike.'

'*You*, my friend, might get mixed up but *I* do not,' Orhan retorted while doing up his laces. 'I'm well acquainted with my shoes – maybe you have too many to remember them all?'

'I think you know well enough that's not true . . .' Lambros replied, pretending to be offended, but aware that his friend's remark bore an element of truth. His family's apparent wealth bothered him only if it meant that it might set the two of them apart. Lambros's family was indeed quite well off; his father and uncle were the owners of the local bakery and general store which supplied the neighbourhood and beyond with bread and groceries, while Orhan's family lived less comfortably. But the disparity between the households hadn't always been there.

The two boys, born in the spring of 1928 in a remote village in the Troodos Mountains to the west of the island, had begun life quite differently. Orhan's father, Hassan Terzi, was a master tailor with a thriving business while

Lambros's father, Andreas Constandinou, owned a small and meagre general store in the village.

Hassan was the only decent tailor for miles, continuing in his father's and grandfather's footsteps. His reputation had travelled as far as Paphos, the third largest town on the island, supplying the entire male population of his own and most of the surrounding villages with his hand-made suits, shirts and overcoats. Andreas Constandinou, on the other hand, had to compete for his living with the municipal market and local farmers.

'The only way to make a proper living is to leave this village,' Andreas would often complain to his wife Maroula. 'If we want to prosper and provide for our children we need to go to Nicosia.' His grandfather owned a plot of land outside the city walls of the capital and Savvas, Andreas's older brother, who had been living and working away from the village for years and was now running a successful business in Nicosia, was always asking them to join him there.

'Savvas's business is thriving and I could be part of it,' Andreas would try to convince his wife. 'He has already started to build a house and we can all live together, we can give our children a better future there.' But Maroula was reluctant. She was happy in the village. She had no complaints or ambition for wealth. Her boy Lambros and her daughter Anastasia were growing up nicely out here in the country. The big city alarmed her. The children were still young, though it didn't stop her worrying about their future, especially the girl's. A daughter had to be provided with a dowry if they were to find her a good husband and Maroula was more than happy to help to supplement the family's income.

'God will provide, Andreas, there's no rush. We're managing, aren't we?' she would argue. 'We have enough to eat and I'm not frightened of work.' Maroula was a good seamstress and was able to take in sewing work which Hassan made sure came her way regularly.

'God bless him and all his family,' she would tell her husband when another garment came into the house for alterations. 'We couldn't wish for better friends, Andreas. If we lived in the city would we have such good neighbours?'

'There are good and bad people everywhere, Maroula,' was his reply.

'There is much danger in the city, Andreas. How could we marry our girl off to a good man when we don't know anyone there? *A patched-up shoe from your own village is better than a brand-new one from another.*' She would quote the old and much-used adage alluding to finding a good match from your familiars, close to home. 'I'm happy here with the people I know,' Maroula continued. 'Where would I find a friend as good as Hatiche in the city?'

The two families lived side by side. Lambros and Orhan were the oldest siblings in their families and they were inseparable, like their mothers.

Among the Lemon Trees

By Nadia Marks

Anna thought her marriage to Max would last forever. They had raised two happy children together, and she looked forward to growing old with the man she loved. But when a revelation from her husband just before their wedding anniversary shakes her entire world, she's left uncertain of what the future holds.

Needing time to herself, Anna takes up an offer from her widowed father to spend the summer on the small Aegean island of his birth, unaware that a chance discovery of letters in her aunt's house will unleash a host of family secrets. Kept hidden for sixty years, they reveal a tumultuous family history, beginning in Greece at the start of the twentieth century and ending in Naples at the close of the Second World War.

Confronted by their family's long-buried truths, both father and daughter are shaken by the discovery and Anna begins to realize that if she is to ever heal the present, she must first understand the past . . .

'My book of the year. An utterly gripping
story of love and family secrets'
Vanessa Feltz

Secrets Under the Sun

By Nadia Marks

The truth will surprise you . . .

On the island of Cyprus, in the small seaside town of Larnaka, three childhood friends have reunited for the funeral of Katerina, the much-loved old woman who had a profound effect on their lives.

Eleni, Marianna and Adonis grew up together, as close as siblings. Although from humble beginnings – a house-maid from the age of thirteen – Katerina's love, wisdom and guidance helped shape them all.

Her loss leaves the friends bereft, but the funeral is not just a time to mourn and remember. Adonis's mother decides that with Katerina's death comes the time to share the family's secrets and answer the riddles of their childhood. A story of deception, forbidden love and undying loyalty unravels. What she reveals will change everything . . .